THE BRIDGE BETWEEN FRIENDS

NORMA CURTIS

Boldwood

First published in Great Britain in 2025 by Boldwood Books Ltd.

Copyright © Norma Curtis, 2025

Cover Design by Alice Moore Design

Cover Images: Shutterstock and [Joanna Czogala] Arcangel

A CIP catalogue record for this book is available from the British Library.

Paperback ISBN 978-1-80656-090-5

Large Print ISBN 978-1-80656-089-9

Hardback ISBN 978-1-80656-087-5

Trade Paperback ISBN 978-1-80656-086-8

Ebook ISBN 978-1-80656-085-1

Kindle ISBN 978-1-80656-095-0

Audio CD ISBN 978-1-80656-093-6

MP3 CD ISBN 978-1-80656-094-3

Digital audio download ISBN 978-1-80656-092-9

This book is printed on certified sustainable paper. Boldwood Books is dedicated to putting sustainability at the heart of our business. For more information please visit https://www.boldwoodbooks.com/about-us/sustainability/

Boldwood Books Ltd, 23 Bowerdean Street, London, SW6 3TN

www.boldwoodbooks.com

For Paul

1

SUMMER 1992

Cora had been talking about her big birthday for months and for that reason everyone was either invited or they invited themselves. 'Where will you fit everyone, Cora?' 'Are you going to have a rota system?' 'A second seating?' And more furtively, 'Will there be children?' Inviting children meant that adults had to act like grown-ups, which was the last thing any of them wanted to do at a party.

Cora was very happy about it – she liked a celebration, people, wine, food. Her son Gwyn was planning it. She'd never been one for not making a fuss, didn't understand the concept. Where was the fun in that?

Party day was sunny with a pale blue sky marbled with cloud and Cora sat by the wooden picnic table in the quivering shade of the apple tree, coloured bulbs swaying and bunting waving festively from the branches. With her roots freshly done and her floaty white dress she looked like a healthy ghost. She could hear her son Gwyn and granddaughter Lottie organising things in the kitchen. She was keeping out of the way; it was her birthday, after all.

Gladdie turned up early, unannounced, because she came into the garden through the back gate carrying a bottle bag with a Christmas tree on it. She was wearing beige trousers cut off at her shins, orthopaedic sandals and a Marks and Spencer blue check blouse. Her pink hair was newly cut and asymmetric, touching her earlobe on one side and jaw-length on the other.

'Happy birthday, Cora! Well? What do you think?' She shook her head for full effect.

'It's not level,' Cora said.

'Get with it, Cora! You could do with a touch of style yourself.'

'Style is it now?'

'Remember how your hair went green when we were Budgies? It suited you, that green, truth be told.'

'Budgies.' Cora laughed at the memory. 'I never minded them calling us that, did you, Glad? Dew! Those were the days! We had money and freedom! Good times, weren't they, while they lasted?'

'Apart from the bombing.'

'Yeah.' Cora pursed her lips. 'Apart from the bombing.' The bombing was a different story, packed away in a different part of her memory.

'And the deaths. Owen,' Gladdie added drily.

Her little brother, Owen. What a thing to forget. Although the truth was Cora hadn't forgotten him, she'd just overlooked his place in the pattern of things, like a dropped stitch.

It had been her father's idea to send eight-year-old Owen somewhere safe for the duration of the war, namely Canada, because they lived close to the munitions factory. It was a prime target for the Luftwaffe. When that was hit they'd all be blown to kingdom come.

Her father reasoned that the boy would come back fresh when it was all over, nerves untarnished by bombing and, more importantly, all in one piece. He would need to be. The country would have to be rebuilt, and there was no knowing how many men would survive to come back home, that's what her father said, and they would need every one of them.

It was a powerful argument and a logical one.

What man wouldn't want to save his son if he had the chance?

Gladdie put the Christmas bottle bag on the picnic table with a thud. 'Here's your present: it's Penderyn Welsh Cream liqueur. I haven't tried it yet and I want to see if I like it. I'll have the bottle bag back if you don't mind. I'm recycling.' She glanced at her watch. 'Where's Megan?'

'She won't be long, she's got some horse liniment from the vet's to rub on her knees before she comes. It was expensive, mind, but it's worth a try.'

'You can trust a vet.'

Cora grinned. Megan hadn't been having much luck with her young GP who said that at her age having painful joints was to be expected and was there anything in particular it was stopping her from doing?

Crosswords, Megan had replied.

It was a bad idea to use sarcasm against doctors; they weren't used to it, you see. Or maybe they were, because pasted around the surgery were signs warning that Abuse of Medical Staff Would Not Be Tolerated, which was a mistake in Cora's opinion because it put the idea into your head.

Anyway, she had her own medical story to share. 'I went in to make an appointment and they said I had to phone them, even though I was only a couple of feet away from the receptionist, close enough to shake her hand in fact. I asked if I could use her phone to speak to the doctor and she said I had to go home to do it because that was the rule. Oh, here's Megan now, galloping into the garden like a racehorse.'

'Don't laugh,' Megan said, hobbling over to them, her yellow floral dress billowing in the breeze, her grey hair lively as a storm cloud. 'Once they're straight I can't bend them, and once they're bent I can't straighten them.' She fell into a picnic chair with a grunt, gripping the arms firmly. 'Happy birthday, Cora,' she said, looking her up and down. 'I didn't know it was fancy dress. You look like a negative.' Her gaze drifted, sharpened. 'Lor, Gladdie, what's happened to your hair? It's all lopsided.'

'Very amusing. I could ask you the same thing,' Gladdie said, 'you look like a wild woman. You need product, that's what you need, to sort out the frizz. Seren would have done it for you. They've got pensioners' rates on a Tuesday. What shampoo are you using?'

'Shampoo? Waste of money. What's wrong with Fairy Liquid?'

'Nothing, if you're washing your hair and your pans at the same time.'

'Stop arguing! It's my birthday,' Cora protested cheerfully. 'Look! Here's Gwyn with the champagne. Hurry up, Gwyn, we're parched out here!' She smiled at her son fondly. He was wearing a turquoise linen shirt, and his sunglasses had some kind of turquoise tint to them. Dark blond hair cut short, good-looking man, Cora thought. Takes after his father. It was Gwyn's idea to have this party for her big birthday, once she'd suggested it to him.

He put the three glasses down on the table, peeled the pink foil off the bottle, unscrewed the cage, and twisted the squealing cork until it popped free.

Cora caught the blushing foam in the glass. 'Cheers!'

'Quick,' Gladdie said, 'let's drink it all before anyone else gets here.' The doorbell rang in the distant hall. 'Too late.'

Friends, neighbours and family all arrived at once, on the dot, coming into the garden and wishing Cora a happy birthday, kissing her or hanging back awkwardly, depending on how well they knew her, and moments later they were milling around happily with glasses or bottles in their hands.

Elisavet was there too, the cleaning lady the three of them shared. She wasn't wearing the usual white hairband which made her look like a nun, so for a moment Cora couldn't place her. She was clasping her hands in front of her and wearing a dark trouser suit. Her long black hair was loose and lavish around her face. She looked very smart, very calm, oddly official.

'You came!' Cora said.

'Yes,' Elisavet replied in her usual serious way, and gave a brief nod of acknowledgement to Gladdie and Megan.

Cora, Gladdie and Megan looked up at her with interest, hoping for a smile.

Elisavet stared back at them. Her dark eyes seemed to absorb the light.

'Help yourself to a drink,' Cora said quickly, and started waving wildly to Gwyn. 'Gwyn! Gwyn! Get Elisavet a drink, will you? Anything she wants!'

Good old Gwyn.

He strolled over amiably. 'Hullo, Elisavet! I've heard a lot about you,' he said. 'What are you having?'

They carried on watching the two of them for a few minutes to see if they could catch Elisavet smiling, and then they gave up, distracted by food, wine, conversation, cream liqueur. Cora chewed the edge of her thumbnail and screwed up her nose. 'Did it seem as if I was trying to get rid of her?'

'Yes,' Gladdie said.

'Good-looking girl, isn't she,' Megan said thoughtfully. 'But I think we annoy her.'

'Really?' It was a disturbing thought. 'How could we? We're lovely!' Cora glanced up through the branches, expecting to see dark clouds between the bunting and the coloured bulbs, but the sky was still summer blue.

Mid-afternoon came. The sun had moved around the garden, shifting the shade, darkening the grass, and the opportunistic wasps were darting around stealing crumbs from plates.

Cora had never been happier. She started telling Megan and Gladdie a story about tarmac, didn't know what prompted it, when her son Gwyn clapped his hands and called for attention, sending the magpies clattering out of the bushes. He had a booming, carrying voice, very well suited to his profession of solicitor.

Cora clasped her hands between her knees in the cool of the cotton dress and thought happily: this will be the cake, now. I hope the breeze doesn't blow the candles out before I do.

But it wasn't the cake after all. Her teenaged granddaughter Lottie came over barefoot and handed her a large white envelope adorned with a huge purple stick-on bow.

'Happy birthday!'

Beautiful girl, Lottie was, with long blow-dried brown hair and a smooth, perfect face. She was wearing a red sleeveless dress. She gave Cora a quirky smile and crouched on the warm grass beside her. She tossed her dark hair from her face and looked at Cora with that one inherited ironic eyebrow, like a mirror image. The other eyebrow, on both of them, was perfectly conventional and straight. Who knew you could inherit an eyebrow?

A couple of years ago, Lottie had gone through a phase of shaving both eyebrows off and drawing them on again as a matching pair and it was surprising how anonymous she looked, how disturbingly ordinary. It was people's flaws that made them unique. Neighbours would peer at her closely, trying to work out what on earth was different about her.

'Open your present,' Lottie encouraged her. 'We hope you like it.'

'I'm bound to like it, aren't I,' Cora said warmly, touching the purple bow, and she realised from the expectant hush that had fallen over the garden that she was meant to open the white envelope there and then, in front of everyone.

She felt suddenly reluctant, wondering if it was something gimmicky like a zip wire or a skydive. Lor! You read about that sort of thing all the time, pensioners falling from the sky, mouths agape, loose cheeks flapping, with a man strapped to the back of them. It was one thing to pretend to be 'with it' in her old age, and another to find you were expected to prove it in public.

She opened the envelope slowly and carefully, buying time, and took out two folded sheets of printed paper with tickets clipped to them. 'What's this then?' she appealed, holding the papers at arm's length. 'I haven't got my glasses on me.'

'Tickets to Island Farm Camp,' Lottie explained. 'They're having an open day and we can go there and have a look around.'

'Oh! Island Farm Camp, is it?' Cora marvelled. 'Well, I never!' The words seemed to stretch over the years like an ancient language, reminding her of the thrill of adventure, recounting the passion and the fear of being young.

The camp had been abandoned and overgrown for decades now and they had got so used to it being there that they no longer saw it. But recently the place was being brought to life again, and as proof, here were the tickets. The printed sheets trembled in her hand. Well! Who'd have thought?

She glanced up at her son Gwyn and saw the look on his grown-up face, the look of a boy wanting to please his mother. And she smiled at him, because he *did* please her, he'd always pleased her in every one of his guises: baby, schoolboy, teenager, solicitor, father. Through ever-changing roles, and despite the tumult of life, her son had kept within him the same solid core of soundness and loving decency.

She looked down at the sheets of paper, unclipped the tickets and studied them intently, even though she couldn't read them, lost for words. *I'm going back to Island Farm.*

And when she looked up again, everyone was still crowding around her expectantly, silently, studying her, waiting for her reaction. She realised then that they were in on it, this gift, and had been all along. 'Well!' she said, fanning herself with the papers. 'My word! This is a surprise! Thank you!' She pressed her fingers against her lips to stop them quivering. It was all she could manage to say right then, and it wasn't much of a speech, she knew that.

But looking up at them again, she knew they'd heard the words she didn't say, and from their smiles and satisfied murmurs it turned out that was good enough.

2

Island Farm Camp hadn't always been a prisoner-of-war camp – no, indeed. It had been constructed so close to where they lived that Cora thought of it as an unpredictable neighbour because you never knew who was going to turn up next.

The camp had been built in 1941 with the best of intentions as accommodation for the workers at the Royal Ordnance Factory. Cora had the advert in her scrapbook. Beguiling, it was:

£3 A WEEK
Average pay
OFFERED TO 6,000 WOMEN
in South Wales
SIGNING ON NOW
Light work on munitions
Here in South Wales we are making munitions. Guns and shells. Some for
the Red Army. Some for our men going overseas. Some for this island
which has to be a fortress.
We must help Russia. We must equip our own forces.
We have all this to do and it has to be done fast.
Come and help us. Take one of these jobs.
There are good jobs with decent pay and conditions.

Light work that any woman of 18 to 60 can do.

The first week the hours are seven and a half a day: second week
eight; third week nine and a half a day, then back to seven and so on.

Pay is by the hour and averages three pounds a week. The factories
are in the district served by buses and trains (exact locations cannot be
stated, for obvious reasons). Excess of fares over three shillings a week
is paid. Excellent hostels are available. Time for shopping can be
arranged.

Taking this job may mean a change to your way of living – but it's to
prevent a greater change – it's to save us all and our children from passing
into Nazi slavery. We can defend ourselves only by making the arms to
do it.

Don't wait until it's too late –

APPLY NOW

at any employment exchange.

Cora, Gladdie and Megan did their duty and signed up together to work
in the filling factory where Cora quickly learnt that the advert, like all good
adverts, had put a bit of a gloss on things.

It didn't mention the inescapable din of machinery, and the relentless
monotony of the work, or the way the fine yellow TNT powder that they filled
the shells with coloured everything it touched bright yellow.

First Cora's hands turned yellow, then her face, and despite the protective
cotton overalls and turban, the powder got into her blonde hair and turned it
green.

It wasn't just her, either. Gladdie's lustrous black hair turned bright
orange and Megan's wild, frizzy brown hair became such a startling shade of
yellow that she could have doubled up as a dandelion.

Cora tried bleach on her cheeks and vigorous scrubbing, but it turned her
yellow skin raw, so if they were going dancing or somewhere special, they
disguised their yellow complexions with Miner's pancake make-up and Coty
face powder.

Funny, she thought, how they got used to it.

They got used to the noise, too, and the radio blaring in competition, and
they learned to stay calm if there was a 'blow-up' in their section. Cora sometimes wrote messages on the gleaming shells for servicemen to read. *Good*

luck! she wrote, *Keep safe!* She concentrated on working efficiently, knowing their lives were in her hands.

In the same way that the enrolment poster had put a gloss on the 'light work on munitions', it had exaggerated the 'excellent hostels' as well.

When it first opened, Island Farm Camp housed workers from all over the country; a community of men too old to enlist and lively women who drank in the local with three pounds a week to spend. However, none of them stayed there very long. It was safe to say the Island Farm accommodation was a bit of a rush job, hastily built, function over luxury. The problem was that the camp was designed on the lines of an army barracks. The huts were built on clay overlooking fields and bordered by woods. Beyond them lay the bare and desolate hills in the distance. They were cold, soulless and slightly damp. Cora heard rumours that the camp was haunted, even though no one had lived there for very long, never mind died there.

Gradually the stream of people being ferried to and from the camp dwindled and the war workers opted for travelling on the buses and trains instead.

Much better. The atmosphere inside the buses after a hard day's work was over sounded wonderful, as carefree as a chapel's Whit Monday Mystery Trip. There was singing, a knitting competition, gossiping and a cheerful community feel because they were doing their bit for the war effort, and better still, for the first time in their lives, making good money as well. Better money than the miners were getting, as a matter of fact. Sore point.

The huts gradually fell into disuse. They remained empty until one day the Americans came and made them interesting again.

What a shiny bunch of men those GIs were, wolf-whistling at them as they passed on their way to work! Gladdie fell recklessly in love with a Texan named Charles who courted her with gifts and their romance was straight out of a Hollywood film, a movie, as Charles called it.

Cora smiled when she thought of the GIs. Clean and bright and cocky, they were, with sweet chewing-gum breath – boldly showing off their moves in the Star Ballroom and teaching them to jive on a Saturday night, seducing them with their loud film-star accents. For a while Island Farm was the most glamorous place in Wales – Cora would go as far as to say the most glamorous place in the world outside of America – until the GIs were re-mobilised to fight in the D-Day landings. Whoosh!

They left as quickly as they'd come.

And after the vast and terrible slaughter on the beaches of Normandy, Cora tried not to dwell on what happened to them after that.

After D-Day, Island Farm filled up again. It became a prisoner-of-war camp for captured Italian soldiers.

Lovely they were, Cora thought, with their tanned skin and their smooth hair and eyes dark as Welshmen's, standing behind the railings and barbed wire saying beautiful things in Italian, or at least things that to her sounded beautiful. They were happy to be there, happy to smile at Welsh girls, happy they didn't have to fight.

But lovely as they looked, they were reluctant to work on the farms and when encouraged to put their backs into it, they sabotaged machinery to remind the Welsh exactly whose side they were on. See? The thing about people, even good-looking ones, was that you never really knew. And one evening, as Cora walked past on the way home, she saw the huts were deserted again.

The Italians had left as quickly as the GIs.

A short while later, in November 1944, when the days were short and the nights were bitter cold, the German prisoners of war arrived by special train in Bridgend station, and Island Farm was renamed Camp 198, and everything changed.

3

The garden was almost dark now and, of Cora's party guests, only the three women were left outside. The kitchen glowed with lights like a doll's house, and the garden was lit up with coloured bulbs, like a grotto. Cora, Megan and Gladdie were still sitting under the apple tree, tinted in jewelled tones like figures in a stained-glass window.

'Here she comes,' Megan said out of the side of her mouth.

Walking carefully up the garden, tiptoeing in her heels and neutrals, Gwyn's fiancée Fiona, a sharp-faced blonde, habitually late, said firmly, 'Just to let you know we've tidied up and we're off now, Cora.' Propping her hands on her hips, she added, 'And by the way, Island Farm Camp was Gwyn's idea, not mine. I don't do camps.'

Fatal.

'Don't you, Fiona?' Gladdie asked her in mock surprise. 'We do. We've always done camps, haven't we, Cora?' Under the gentle glow of the coloured lights, Gladdie's pink hair had turned orange.

'Always,' Cora said seriously.

Fiona narrowed her eyes.

Cora smiled at her to show it was a joke because Fiona was almost family now.

Fiona lifted her chin belligerently. 'I told Gwyn you'd like a silk scarf, but he didn't listen.'

'Aww. That would have been nice, too.'

Before leaving, Gwyn came across the lawn with a plate of hot sausage rolls to keep them going. No sooner had he set them down than Fiona grabbed his arm, almost spilling them on the table.

'I've told them we're off,' she said pointedly.

'That's right. We're off.' Still linked to his fiancée, Gwyn kissed Cora's cheek awkwardly, and Megan's and Gladdie's, and then he rested his free hand on his mother's head. 'Your hair is all green.'

Cora caught his hand, and squeezed it.

'Oh, by the way,' he added, 'I had a long chat with your cleaning lady. She was a lawyer, back home, before the war started. Interesting woman.'

'Where's home?' Megan asked.

'Kosovo.'

'Oh, right.'

'Did you get her to smile for you?' Cora asked him curiously. 'She never smiles.'

'Eh?' He looked confused. 'Was I meant to try? Ow!'

'Good night,' Fiona said to them firmly, flapping her free hand. 'Don't stay up too late.'

As their two black silhouettes flattened the silvery grass and went into the house, Megan reached for a sausage roll and said, 'She pinched him, you know. I saw her knuckles go white.'

'"Don't stay up too late"?' Gladdie repeated in a low and scornful tone. 'Cheek!'

'Fiona's all right. Gwyn seems happy at any rate.' Cora could love her forever for that.

'She's no Regina though, is she?'

'No,' Cora agreed, 'she's no Regina.'

Regina had been sweet and kind, and no one had a bad word to say about her, not even Gladdie, who could find a weak spot in a person in a single probe.

When Gwyn was forty and Lottie was fourteen, Regina had died of sepsis. Cora knew from experience that there was no right way to handle grief, no signposts; you just had to battle through it as best you could.

For Gwyn it meant shutting himself off. For Lottie, it meant going with boys. She had gone off the rails for a while, big time. Smoking, boys, cider.

There was gossip, of course, and Cora heard it without comment or defence. Well, if it helped her to cope, that's just the way it was. There was no point in pulling her up on it or threatening her with the worst that could happen. The worst *had* happened.

Sepsis. Cora had never heard of it before, it seemed like some new and dreadful disease, but it turned out it was another word for blood poisoning. Blood poisoning, in this day and age! And her so houseproud! It was the disease of the battlefield, of injuries, bacteria, bad sanitation. But the sepsis had got Regina, very unfairly, as she was a lovely wife, a sweet mother. It was cruel.

During those endless days of sorrow, Lottie came to stay with Cora on and off, when she felt like it. It wasn't an arrangement as such, it was just somewhere to go when she needed to grieve somewhere fresh. Gwyn had his own grief to get through. There was a disconnected look about him. He never blinked. He was unreachable, watchful, resigned – as if he was locked away alone in a cage and there was no escape.

He came round to Cora's too, sometimes, to get away, and those nights when the three of them were in the house, even though or because it was for such a sad reason, Cora would stay up late on the sofa, guarding them. She was fiercely glad to offer them sanctuary. With them asleep upstairs it felt like home again.

And then Gwyn met Fiona, and she was so pretty and carefree that his dimmed spirit grew bright again.

But the truth was, through no fault of Fiona's, Regina was a hard act to follow.

'It's amazing the things you get over,' Cora said now, and she was, truly, genuinely amazed.

'Yes!' Megan said passionately. 'Thank the Lord!'

Gladdie's thoughts had taken a different turn. 'So Elisavet was a lawyer back home. She might have told us. Deceitful, I call it. Which war is it, do you think? It's hard to keep track.'

'All wars are the same in the end. No wonder she doesn't smile,' Cora said. 'Imagine,' she reflected, 'moving somewhere with very little of your own. Leaving everything behind like that, starting afresh in a new land, with a new language, and not easily understanding or being understood. The small details of a life – home, clothes, a china tea service, invitations for parties and weddings, service sheets from funerals, leaving everything that has a part of your history attached to it.' She suddenly remembered Elisavet's question to her, the only question she'd ever asked her, now she thought about it: *Was he a soldier?*

A night breeze rocked the glow of the lights, green, blue, orange and yellow, stroking their faces, their clothes with colours. Cora glanced at her watch. It was still her birthday! She reached for the bottle with a sudden surge of happiness. 'Many happy returns to me!' she said.

4

Cora had found Jelisaveta via a notice in Mr Patel's window and because she'd had her big birthday coming up she'd wanted the place spick and span for the guests.

Cora mispronounced her name. *Just call me Elisavet*, the woman said.

After a month, she still didn't know much about her, only that her house had never been cleaner. Gladdie needed someone to do for her too, and asked Cora what she thought of her.

It was a tricky question.

'She's a good worker. Spotless, my house is. She does it all once a week, from top to bottom.'

'That's no good to me. How can you clean a bungalow from top to bottom?' Gladdie asked.

'From side to side, then,' Cora said mildly. Gladdie was a teacher before she retired and she liked arguing about trivialities. 'But you can't tell her what to do, because she doesn't like it. She takes it as criticism, I think.'

'It's your sceptical eyebrow, Cora. It probably puts her off.'

'I expect that's it,' Cora lied. Age, and her cock-eyed eyebrow, made her seem critical when she really wasn't being. It wasn't fair; Gladdie should have been born with the eyebrow because sarcasm came naturally to her.

No fooling Gladdie. 'Go on. But?' she asked. 'What's wrong with her?'

'But she doesn't smile,' Cora said, summing up Elisavet in a sentence. Best to be honest about it. Her gaze rested on the strip of white on Gladdie's neon-pink centre parting where her roots were growing out.

'As long as she can do housework, I'm not bothered about the smiling,' Gladdie said firmly.

No, Cora thought, *but you will be.*

She knew this from experience. She remembered a time when smiles had been painfully scarce at home. Misery was a wasteland, a sorrowful contagion because you couldn't smile at someone who didn't smile back; it was insensitive, or even insane.

'Megan's having her on Tuesdays and I'll tell her you want her to come to yours on a Friday, shall I?'

'Yes, do that, I like the place to be nice and clean, ready for the weekend,' Gladdie said. 'And you watch, I'll have her cackling with laughter in no time, you know me.'

* * *

The following week, despite Gladdie's optimism, Cora couldn't see any change in Elisavet at all. She was as serious as usual, silent, focused, hardworking. She got to work polishing, sweeping, vacuuming, spraying, taps running, always energetic, always busy. She had a small, bare face and her black hair was held back with the white Alice band that made her look like a nun. It was hard to tell her age. Sometimes she looked quite young and other times she looked middle aged.

Cheer up, it might never happen, Cora wanted to say to her.

Usually she went out shopping when Elisavet came, to save getting in her way, but today it was raining so Cora put the kettle on and offered her a cup of tea. Got an abrupt shake of the head back. Cora persevered. 'Coffee? Bottled water? Coca-Cola?'

'I'm fine,' Elisavet said, frowning.

'Okay. Good.'

She's like a locked box, Cora thought. Makes you wonder what's inside.

She had experience of locked boxes because Frank had left a locked box behind when he died. Black metal, it was, an old cash tin about the size of a shoebox. It had something inside it, something heavy. When you shook it you could hear it knocking around in there.

She had never asked Frank what was in the box. She had stopped seeing it years ago, although it had been at the bottom of the bookcase in the hall all through their long marriage. It was only recently that she'd noticed it again, and that was because Elisavet had dusted it to a gleam. Since then it had started to obsess her. She wanted to know what was in it. At the same time, she was afraid of what she would find. Whatever it was, it must have been important to Frank, because why else would he lock it away?

Discussing it, Megan told her to leave well alone, take the locked box to the dump and forget about it.

Gladdie, on the other hand, told her to hit the lock with a hammer, look inside and set her mind at rest.

There was something to be said for both suggestions.

With nothing to do on this rainy day except to keep out of Elisavet's way and seem busy, Cora went to the oak bookcase to fetch the shiny tin – not a speck of dust on it, she noticed. She set it on the kitchen table and rummaged in the bits and bobs drawer for something to pick the lock with. Amongst paperclips, batteries, pens, Christmas cracker contents, Cora found a selection of keys, a couple of which were bafflingly ornate and possibly for winding up old clocks. Why they'd kept the keys but not the clocks, she wasn't sure.

She pulled up a chair and sat at the pine table, discarding the keys that obviously weren't going to fit, and after a few minutes or so of trying the remainder she found the right one by a process of elimination. It slid into the lock neatly, and she turned it.

Clunk.

Easy as that.

She hesitated before opening it, filled with sudden apprehension.

What was she expecting the box to reveal?

In her heart, her biggest fear was that she would find something that would make her see Frank differently, make her realise that in death she'd never known him at all. Having already lost all of him, she was afraid of losing more of him. It was ridiculous, really.

She stared at the rain-streaked window and listened to the approaching drone of the vacuum cleaner. Before she could get to her feet the vacuum cleaner whined down into silence in the hall and Elisavet came into the kitchen with a yellow duster in her hand, looking surprised to see her.

'I've just found the key to this box,' Cora explained brightly, because for some reason she felt she needed to. 'It belonged to my husband. It's got something inside it,' she said, rapping the lid with her knuckles. 'Wait! Don't go!' she added as Elisavet excused herself.

Elisavet turned back and raised her dark eyebrows a fraction. Paused. Shrugged. 'Okay.'

'Right then,' Cora said, taking a deep breath. She lifted the lid and let it drop open with a clatter. 'Oh!' The thing that had been banging about in there was a dried-out lump of orange clay the size of a lime along with a small leather-bound notebook covered with clay dust. She blew the dust off and opened the notebook. It was filled with Frank's neat writing. It stirred her deeply to look at all these words direct from his pen and from his heart, but it frustrated her too. 'I can't understand a word of it, it's all in German,' she said to Elisavet in frustration. 'Ridiculous, isn't it, that he didn't teach me a few words? But it made sense at the time to put his own language behind him because he wanted to fit in. That's all a person wants, isn't it? To belong?' She wiped her hand over the cover. It was soft with age, and she passed the book to Elisavet.

Elisavet opened the first page, then flicked through it and put it on the table.

'And this!' Cora picked up the lump of clay.

It was the weirdest thing to find locked away in a tin box, the last thing she'd expected.

She weighed it in her hand – for some reason it felt like something she ought to do – and then she handed it to Elisavet.

Elisavet took it from her and gave Cora a quick, puzzled look. 'Mud,' she said.

'Yes.'

Elisavet gave her back the lump of clay and Cora looked at it carefully and rolled it around in her palm in case there was something about it that they'd missed. 'You know,' she concluded, 'I have absolutely no idea why my husband would keep these things locked away in a box all these years.' She added irritably, 'And I can't even ask him!'

No fault of his, of course, but he could at least have left a note to explain. She almost put them back in the box and then she changed her mind. 'They obviously meant something to him, though, didn't they?' she said. 'And now they mean something to me.'

Leaving the notebook on the table, she scraped back the chair and took the clay into the sitting room. She put it on the mantelpiece next to the Royal Doulton figurine of a boy with a suitcase in one hand and a package under the other. *The Evacuee*, the figure was called. The boy was wearing a green cardigan with a label tied on it, blue shorts and grey socks – one of which was slipping authentically round his ankle. His cheeks were faintly flushed, and he looked heartbreakingly baffled due to the skill of the painter's brush.

Elisavet stood next to her, frowning as Cora repositioned the lump of clay.

'It's all right, you don't have to dust it,' Cora reassured her. 'My husband must have kept it since the war.' The war! She heard the possessive way she said it, as if there had only ever been the one. 'World War II,' she added for clarity.

Elisavet looked at her. Her eyes were dark and probing. 'Your husband was a soldier?' she asked.

For the first time since they'd met, Cora felt Elisavet was actually seeing her. It was an unsettling feeling and she almost looked away. 'Yes.' She blushed as if she was lying, although it was the truth.

'A soldier,' Elisavet stated. She pulled her black hair over her shoulder and stroked it once, twice, as slowly and meditatively as one would stroke a dog. 'So.' She nodded, pulled her yellow duster out of her pocket and turned her attention to the mantelpiece.

So? So what? Cora wanted to ask her, staring at the slender shoulders under the blue overall. 'Be careful with that,' she said as Elisavet picked up the evacuee figurine.

Elisavet looked at her sharply, a Mother Superior look. 'Of course.'

'Sorry. I'll leave you to it, then.'

Cora's cleaner before Elisavet was Mrs Roberts. Talk about opposites! Mrs Roberts was a gossip, friendly, gave her all the latest lowdown on the slovenly habits of the other people she cleaned for and never vacuumed under Cora's bed where the dust lay thick as felt.

You couldn't exactly describe her as diligent. In the kitchen, a teaspoon that Cora accidentally dropped lay on the floor untouched through a series of weekly visits as Mrs Roberts respectfully cleaned around it as if it was a holy relic. Cora didn't move it either, not out of stubbornness but more as an experiment, to see how long it would stay there.

Probably it would still be there now if Mrs Roberts hadn't found a packet of ribbed condoms in Gladdie's bedside drawer when she was 'doing' for her, which was nobody's business but Gladdie's (although to be honest, Gladdie had never married and was well past the menopause), and then told her other clients about it.

Well! That was it! Two questions bounced around the town from woman to woman until everyone knew about this intriguing discovery, but only one of the questions was askable: what on earth was Mrs Roberts doing going through Gladdie's drawers in the first place?

Gladdie confronted Mrs Roberts in the Spar shop, and to save face in the ensuing counter-accusations Mrs Roberts handed in her notice on lined paper in purple felt-tip. No, sorry. She didn't actually hand it in, she pushed it through Gladdie's door with the written explanation that she was moving to Spain for her arthritis. They still saw her in Bridgend sometimes.

So there it was, one cleaner would talk too much and the other didn't talk enough.

Sometimes Cora toyed vaguely with the idea of doing her own cleaning, but it was so nice not having to do it. The worst part of living alone was being totally responsible for yourself and she was all for subcontracting things if she could.

From the doorway, she watched Elisavet spray the mantelpiece, polish it vigorously, dust the pieces and replace them carefully one by one. She left the lump of clay until last, almost as if she'd taken Cora's advice to heart not to dust it. But then she picked it up, balanced it in her hand, and turned to look at Cora over her shoulder. She caught her eye for a moment.

What kind of look was that?

A spark of interest, that's what it was, as if something meaningful passed between them, a mutual understanding of some unspoken knowledge shared between friends. Still no smile, of course, but her holy features softened slightly. Elisavet replaced the lump of clay in line with the other treasures, positioning it with such exaggerated care that it almost bordered on mockery.

I'm definitely going shopping next time she comes, Cora vowed, and went for her handbag. She put Elisavet's cash discreetly in a white envelope, left it on the kitchen table and opened the front door to see if the rain had stopped.

It had, so she put her coat on and went to tell Elisavet that she was going out, said it with a smile.

She saw a slight horizontal crease above the bridge of Elisavet's nose, as if she was displeased.

Cora's smile drooped. The woman was a mystery. She wished they could have a decent conversation just once and get to know each other, but really – why did it matter? Why did she have to know anything about Elisavet at all, she wondered. She was there to do a job, and that was it. She didn't have to befriend her or bond with her, she just had to pay her. She could appreciate her hard work without knowing anything about her at all.

On the other hand, she wanted Elisavet to like her. That's what a smile was all about, it was an exchange of good feeling, the shortest distance between two people.

Wanting Elisavet to like her gave Cora a feeling of anxious uncertainty, like the early days of courtship.

Their relationship was wholly unbalanced. She knew nothing whatsoever about Elisavet but Elisavet knew all about her, her house, her possessions, her general character, her discretion in putting the cash payment in an envelope – whether she appreciated that nicety or considered it pointless, Cora didn't know because she took the cash and left the envelope to be reused next time. But she had eradicated the fluff under the bed, and whenever a beam of sunlight came in through the window it shone bright and pure, dust free. Elisavet was a sort of cleansing religious experience, an angel.

Cora buttoned her coat. 'I'm off. I've left your envelope on the table.'

'Okay.'

On the way out, Cora looked at herself in the hall mirror to see herself through Elisavet's eyes. The hall mirror was particularly kind to her wrinkles. She had an inoffensive face and honey-blonde hair from the hairdressers. There was nothing to particularly dislike except for the irregularity of her arched left eyebrow, which made her look sceptical or quizzical at times, through no fault of her own. She stared at herself ironically for a moment, and sighed. 'Well, there we are,' she said aloud.

5

Gwyn's surprising revelation that Elisavet was actually a lawyer really shouldn't have made any difference, but it did, because now Cora felt obliged to tidy up a bit before she came. It was embarrassing for the woman to have to do these menial tasks, and the least Cora could do was make life easier for her.

She put the dishes away and propped up her birthday cards on the kitchen windowsill where the breeze had blown them down.

'Come in, come in,' she said heartily when Elisavet arrived.

No response, as if she had no time for earthly matters.

Face to face, Elisavet still looked like a nun with her unsmiling face framed by the wide white band, preoccupied by suffering.

'I'm sorry we didn't get much time to talk on Saturday,' Cora said. The truth was, she'd had plenty of time, but never mind that now. She followed Elisavet into the sitting room. 'My son said you'd had a nice chat.'

Elisavet frowned at her and tilted her head slightly, as if she was trying to make her out. She took her blue overall out of her bag, unfolded it, put it on and buttoned it up. Said nothing. Then she busied herself retrieving the yellow duster and Mr Sheen.

Cora could hear the ingratiating way she was talking to her, couldn't help herself. She was trying to be friendly! Next thing she'd be wringing her hands obsequiously, and what was the point? It was funny, really, to be so very anxious to please. *But she's a lawyer!* She gave Elisavet a smile and a playful nudge. 'Now it's your turn to say, "Yes, your son's a lovely man, you've brought him up well." Something like that,' she prompted. This was the kind of thing she'd say to Gladdie or Megan.

Elisavet's frown deepened. 'You want me to say those words to you?' she asked seriously.

'No. Never mind.' Cora felt like an idiot. 'It's a joke.'

'A joke,' Elisavet said contemptuously, breathing hard and turning to the mantelpiece. She leant on it for a moment as if she was overcome by despair. 'You think life is a joke.'

It stung like a slap, took Cora's breath away.

Cora knew very well that life wasn't a joke, she only pretended that it was. It was a deliberate choice. And now she was breathing hard, too, feeling the anger rush through her. 'Better to treat it as a joke than a tragedy, don't you think,' she replied sharply.

'Oh, you think that, do you really?' Elisavet said coldly. 'Well now, let me see then, here is a little joke you will enjoy.' She bunched up the yellow duster and in one swift, deliberate movement, she swept the china figurine of the boy evacuee right off the mantelpiece.

The figurine smashed and the pieces went skittering across the hearth and Cora fell heavily to her knees. She cried out in agony and felt herself break too. She reached for the curve of a flushed cheek and picked up the hollow chest in a green cardigan, her grief lodged solid and immovable in her throat. Here now was one pink leg in a drooping grey sock. She cupped the pieces in her hand with a whimper. 'Owen,' she tried to explain in a small, tight voice, and felt the terrible pain of devastation burst free of her.

She let out a hoarse roar of grief. Her tears were steaming hot, and although she was appalled by her noisy, ugly anguish she couldn't stop herself. She had never cried for Owen before, not in fifty years, but now, holding this broken evidence, she howled at the unfairness of his pointless destruction. The hot tears fell freely into her cupped hands, wetting the fragments, soaking them, dripping through her fingers, salty as the sea.

6

AUTUMN 1940

Sitting at the kitchen table with his fists clenched, Cora's father David Owen, known as Dio, was trying to explain to Cora and to Jane, his wife, why he wanted to send his son Owen away. He was making a poor job of it too, which Cora found unsettling because he was known for being a man who was good with his words.

Cora couldn't understand why he felt so strongly about it when Owen had never spent a single night away from home in his life. And she had the feeling that her father didn't truly understand it himself.

But she could see in his black-rimmed eyes his burning sense of urgency, a compulsion to get the boy as far from the dangers of Bridgend as he could.

She glanced at her mother, expecting her to put her foot down at any moment, because Jane was well known for her common sense. She had a temper too, if you pushed her too far, and she never lost an argument because her temper was fuelled by the heat of self-righteousness.

Not this time, though.

Cora saw the way her mother was staring at her father, eyes sharp, looking deep into his soul where the future was laid bare. She saw her mother catching her father's dread as if she could see it as clearly as he did.

Cora felt their fear touch her. Dio was a coal miner, see. He was familiar with danger. He recognised it, smelled its presence; he came face to face with it every day he worked down pit. Coal dust collected in the rims and corners of his eyes like make-up. When he blew his nose, the handkerchief was black, and when he cried, his tears were black. He was a tough man, a man that was made of coal.

Dio unclenched his fists and laid his hands palm upwards on the table helplessly. Protecting his son was an easy decision up here in his head, he told them, but in reality it would not be easy at all, he knew that.

He was frightened for the boy and, like them, he ached at the thought of the separation. Yet the emotional pain was his sacrifice, which he would endure willingly if it meant keeping his son safe. He never doubted it was the right thing to do and Cora was swept along in the current of his certainty.

Dio signed Owen up on the government scheme to send Sea Evacuees on a Children's Ship to the security and safety of Canada. Canada was their ally, a country filled with people with warm hearts and open arms.

His absolute belief wasn't even shaken when three weeks before Owen's ship left, another children's liner, the SS *Volendam*, was torpedoed en route.

Dio didn't see this as a warning. If anything, he told them, it made him feel better about his decision. In the case of SS *Volendam*, all the children had survived, none had been injured, and the only reported casualty was one child struck by seasickness. According to the newspapers, the chairman of the Overseas Reception Board had declared on the record with heartfelt conviction: 'There was a guardian angel watching over them.'

'Amen,' Dio said, and he held onto those words with fervent faith.

That proved to him that the boy would be safe on the SS *Benares*, safer than here in Bridgend at any rate.

The truth was, Cora knew that her father was frightened for Owen in the same dark and visceral way that Owen was frightened for himself.

But Dio kept his dread quiet and hidden, instead using all the eloquent power of his preacher's tongue to influence Jane and Cora into agreeing with his way of thinking. In the face of his unwavering conviction, Cora and her mother's doubts had little say in it.

As evidence of the danger of keeping Owen with them, Dio recited the latest news about the bombing of Hafod, Greenhill, Cradle Common (twelve people killed); no guardian angels for them, were there? And then, adding power to his argument, on 1 September two hundred high-explosive bombs and a thousand incendiaries were dropped over Swansea. As the rescue workers scurried to assist, the planes flew in low and machine-gunned them down, killing thirty-three people and injuring over a hundred.

'When they bomb Bridgend,' Dio said passionately, hammering the words into the kitchen table with his fist, looking into his wife's eyes, 'how are you going to feel, knowing that your own selfishness kept Owen here? How will *he* feel?'

Because Owen was a worrier. He had always been a fearful lad, scared of his own shadow. No wonder.

Owen's shadow hadn't been a normal one stretching like elastic on the ground around his feet but one that hovered over him, shading him from above, keeping him from the warmth of the sun.

It was impossible to console Owen with reassurances. He didn't hear them. He made his own mind up about things. Except for once, when he'd come to Dio in the night.

Dio told them that Owen had woken him up by crawling under the bedclothes at the foot of the bed and lying curled up, cold and trembling.

Jerking awake, 'Bed! Now!' Dio said in swift anger because he had an early shift and he needed his sleep.

The boy crept out of bed again and cowered by the door, round-shouldered with fear.

Dio closed his eyes. When he opened them again and lifted his heavy head, the boy was still there. His heart softened. 'What is it, Owen?'

'One day you and Mam are going to die,' his son said in a small voice, struck for the first time by the tragedy of the knowledge.

Dio sighed at his sorrow, pushed away the warm bedclothes and swung his legs out of bed. 'Oh, come here, lad.'

The boy shuffled over in his pyjamas, too miserable to look at him, staring down at his bare feet. He pressed his hands on his father's knees, giving him his burden to bear. 'It's true, isn't it,' he muttered.

'Aye.' Dio's head was muddled with sleep. 'Don't you worry about that yet,' he said.

Now the boy looked at him, his eyes large and bottomless. 'But I am worried.'

Dio put his large, coal-ingrained hands over his son's small, clean ones. He reached into his memory for the words that he himself found comforting, brought them out in a whisper. Deliberately and softly, to save disturbing his wife, he said, 'Let not your heart be troubled, neither let it be afraid.'

His son was staring at him silently, his eyes a gleam in the dark.

Dio carried on hoarsely, because the words moved him with their promise. 'In my Father's house there are many mansions. If it were not so, I would have told you.' He nodded, reassured by the bare honesty of it. 'I go to prepare a place for you, and if I go and prepare a place for you I will come again and receive you unto myself, that where I am, there you will be also. See? Do you hear that, Owen?' That was enough, it said it all, no need to say any more. 'It's a promise,' he told his son. 'And when *I* go, I'll be going to prepare a place for you. Get it ready, like.'

His boy was quiet for a long, thoughtful moment, sucking his cheeks into hollows. And then he nodded and said, 'Will you write it down for me?'

'Yes. Tell you what, better than that, when I get home tomorrow I'll show you where it is in the Bible. It's about time you had a Bible for yourself.'

Just the New Testament, he thought. There were all sorts of dubious shenanigans going on in the Old Testament one way or another, of a sexual nature. Thrilling, it was, in Sunday school, passing the Bible to Temperance and Idwal in gleeful astonishment. It was why he became a preacher, now he came to think of it. 'Come on, let's get you back to bed.'

The two of them made their cautious way in the dark, arms outstretched against obstacles, back to Owen's tidy room.

His son got into bed and lay on his back, arms stiff by his side, and Dio tucked the bedclothes around him, making a show of it until his son lay there wrapped up tight like an Egyptian mummy, staring up at him. 'Sleep well, my boy.'

'Good night, Dad.'

* * *

Cora helped her mother to pack Owen's suitcase for him, wrapping at the last minute a loving note in his pyjamas. Jane laid the Bible on top in tight-lipped silence. She took Owen to Liverpool on the train to see he got away all right, not being able to bear a second longer of time apart from him than she needed, making the most of her last few hours with him. And Owen, triangular face and thin features, was exhausted from excitement and fell asleep, warm and solid, heavy against her arm.

She came back alone and quiet and got on with pounding the laundry with the washing dolly.

* * *

Four days later, the Canon David John Thomas visited the house with the bad news. No tears, but a stoical aridness came over them that left them cracked and hard.

The confirmation letter was delivered on the morning of Friday, 20 September 1940, blunt and matter of fact:

> *I am very distressed to inform you that in spite of all the precautions taken, the ship carrying your children to Canada was torpedoed on Tuesday night, 17 September.*
>
> *I am afraid your children are not those reported as rescued and I am informed that there is no chance of there being any further lists of survivors from the torpedoed vessel.*

It was the bleakest letter you could imagine, no promises, no hope. Cora's mother's reproach burned off her like a fever.

Cora bore it solidly, her life depended on it, keeping the feel of Owen hugging her legs as if she was solid, a pillar. She wished she hadn't smiled at him as she'd said goodbye. It was the betrayal behind the kiss.

7

1992

Elisavet's face was white, white as her hairband.

Kneeling next to the fireplace, Cora's eyes were blind with tears. She struggled to her feet awkwardly and carried the broken bits of china to the coffee table. At last she looked up at Elisavet.

'My little brother was an evacuee.' The words stuttered on her lips. 'His ship was sunk by a U-boat.'

She heard herself say it.

It was the first time she'd spoken the words aloud and they tasted hideous, like filth in her mouth. They cut open a solid seam of dread in her guts. Oh, Owen bach.

He'd gone through it all by himself, little boy. The torpedo struck late at night, noise, smoke, fire and chaos, the ship listing, the lifeboats swinging, dropping into the tilting sea and scooping up water, splashing and wild screams like joyful children in a paddling pool and then the fading silence as they all went home to bed, floating listlessly over the lifeboat seats in their sea-filled pyjamas.

Owen's last frightened thoughts would have been about his family, how he was sent away from home on a sinkable ship, a paper boat with its precious cargo of children on a journey to an unknown land of strangers with false promises of safety.

The heaviness of it was a rock on Cora's chest. None of the twelve Welsh children survived... No, not one.

Elisavet crouched by the green slate hearth, her face cloaked by her dark hair, picking up the remaining shards of china. 'I can fix it,' she murmured through gritted teeth. She put the bits on the table and sucked her finger.

Cora saw drips of blood on the slate.

She gave a shuddering sigh and looked sorrowfully at the broken pieces. Fix it? No. There was nothing to be done with them. They were recently produced, these commemoration china figures. She could buy herself another.

The thought didn't make her feel any better. 'I'll get you a plaster for your finger,' she said as she went to the bathroom cabinet for an Elastoplast and antiseptic wipes, blowing her nose into toilet paper. Her head was hot and throbbing and she swallowed two ibuprofen with water from the tooth mug, feeling storm-battered and vulnerable.

Back in the sitting room, Elisavet had wrapped her duster around the cut and was cleaning the windowsill.

'Give me your hand.'

Elisavet's fingers were slender and cold and Cora wiped away the blood and yellow fluff that stuck to the wound. She lost herself in the gentle task and when it stopped bleeding she applied the plaster firmly. 'There,' she said. 'I suppose you'd rather stop work for today,' she added hopefully.

'For today? No. It's fine.'

'Well, I'll leave you to it then.' Cora went into the kitchen, picked up her bag and put Elisavet's money in the white envelope. She pressed it flat on the table.

That was it. They couldn't carry on employing her after this, now that she had seen this destructive side of Elisavet. It wasn't something you could turn a blind eye to; after all, it was her fault, she was responsible for answering the advert in the window and introducing her to Megan and Gladdie, even though, as they'd warned her, she knew very little about the sort of person Elisavet was. She'd taken her on trust.

Cora felt again the wind of fury of Elisavet's sweep of the arm, the muscles moving under the skin. Of course she would tell them.

But she still felt the chill of Elisavet's passive fingers in hers.

When she left the house she wasn't ready to talk to Gladdie about it. Her face was puffy and flushed. Once Gladdie knew, the news of Cora's upset would spread, it always did around here, and be made much of. *Did you hear about Cora's cleaner smashing her place up? Broke her heart, it did.*

The tears rolled slowly. She was heavy with grief. *You need a plumber, girl, not a hankie.*

Without making a conscious decision, she headed down the alley which backed on to the open fields behind Island Farm, keeping her head down and her shoulders hunched, hoping she wouldn't meet any friendly neighbours on the way.

Lodged firm in a place of misery, she needed to have space around her, so that she could feel small and pointless and inconsequential again.

She stopped on the path and lifted her face to the fragrant westerly wind blowing across the fields behind the camp, letting it dry her cheeks.

The expanse of yellow blossoms shimmered against the familiar, unknowable hills lying prone and lazy on the horizon. To get that upset about the china boy...

In the past, see, you didn't dwell on things. You moved on. No one spoke about Owen afterwards, and the rip in their hearts was invisibly mended, no one's fault, no, indeed, because no one deliberately puts their son in harm's way.

But it was Dio's fault and everyone knew it.

Dio's hair turned milky white, not overnight but gradually over the next three weeks. And he gave up preaching. It was his fault for playing God, for lacking faith in the Almighty's ability to look after them.

As it happened, the munitions factory, that peach of a target, never did get bombed, and Bridgend was never blown to kingdom come and them with it. Miraculous, it was.

Owen would have been safe at home in their arms, as it turned out.

So they never spoke about him, neither with love nor reproach.

You make sense of things however you can. You decide that Owen was always destined for a bad end. That he knew it in his ancient soul, and the knowledge was the source of his constant fear. He was a homing missile for fate.

He had left them willingly, bravely, a scapegoat, label flapping, small suitcase gripped tight in his small hand, he left them to go on that voyage to a distant land without a fuss so that he could save them, and his sacrifice caused the armaments factory to be miraculously shielded from the enemy's bombs.

Why not? Who was to argue otherwise? And what was the point?

Life was all myths and legends anyway.

8

If Cora told herself it was fresh air and wide spaces she was after, well then, that was true enough.

But she also wanted to see Hut 9.

Hut 9 was the only hut still standing in the former POW camp. It was a single-storey building, and it wasn't sentimental or historical reasons that had saved it from demolition, but the bats that colonised it.

The grass around the hut had been neatly cut recently and the daisies and dandelions had not yet grown back. As far as Cora could tell, the place was deserted.

She stared at it from the path and then made her way towards it carefully, treading down the brambles to reach the green railings. She clutched them till her knuckles whitened and rested her hot face against the sun-warmed bars. If she squinted hard enough at the dusty windows she fancied she would see the German prisoners moving inside and they would notice her and stop what they were doing and cluster at the window, seeing her as a brief reminder of what they were missing back home.

Holding onto the fence, she closed her stinging eyes. She felt old and heavy. She was exhausted. She desperately wanted to go home to bed, close the curtains and slip out of the day unnoticed, but she couldn't face seeing Elisavet again, not right now, anyway; she'd had as much emotion as she could deal with.

She walked slowly around the perimeter of the camp, killing time. She reached the road and plodded along to the Spar shop where she wandered up and down the aisles and in the end bought a Battenberg cake. She went to the library, sat at one of the tables, and broke bits off the cake surreptitiously while reading the local papers. What a world, the things people got up to, bad and good. After a while she felt it was safe to go home.

The kitchen smelled of Flash. The white envelope lay on the table where she'd left it and when she picked it up she realised immediately that Elisavet's cash was still inside. 'Hello?' she called out cautiously.

No reply.

She went from room to room, and each one had that wonderful glossy purity about it that Elisavet brought to her home. Which meant she'd cleaned, but hadn't taken the payment. Because of the Royal Doulton boy, of course.

Cora checked the pedal bin for the pieces but it was empty apart from a fresh bin liner. 'More complications,' she said aloud.

She looked in the kitchen drawer for Elisavet's card from Mr Patel's, with the address, 15 Queen's Lane, the phone number and the instruction: *Ask for Jelisaveta*. She picked up the phone and it occurred to her that, in the circumstances, Elisavet might not want to take a call from her.

She put the envelope and the money in her bag with a sigh, and reluctantly postponing the peaceful comfort of home, she left the house again.

Heading to Elisavet's, Cora stopped on the Old Bridge that crossed the River Ogmore. She leant her weight against the sun-warmed stone, grounding herself for a few moments, watching the silver river tumble on its ceaseless journey towards the sea.

She always found the bridge's great age and permanence profoundly reassuring. It put her troubles into perspective, knowing it had been here for centuries before she existed, surviving floods and bombs, horses and footfall, and would be here long after she had gone.

It was on the pilgrims' route to St David's Cathedral and she imagined tired feet driven by light hearts as they trudged over these cobbles in their quest for help with life's difficulties. Treading the same path, she straightened up with determined optimism and patted the bridge wall fondly. 'Old friend.'

Queen's Lane was a thoroughfare rather than a destination. For some reason the house numbers went up on one side and down on the other, no rhyme nor reason to them. Number fifteen was in the middle of a terrace. The small front garden was paved over, green with moss and decorated by a rusted bicycle frame chained to a drainpipe.

Cora rang the bell and listened to it echo inside. It was some minutes before the door was opened by a skinny, bare-chested man in baggy jeans who looked dazed, as if he'd just woken up.

'Who are you?' he asked her accusingly, as if he'd been expecting someone different altogether and she'd appeared under false pretences.

'Is Elisavet in, please?'

'Number three,' he said, pointing with his elbow and jerking his head for her to come in.

Cora hadn't given any thought to where Elisavet might live. It took her a moment to adjust to the shabby gloom in the hall. She'd assumed it would be some spotless haven, clean and shiny, rather than somewhere with scuffed skirting boards, a plasterboard wall punched in and a door with a splintered lock.

The shirtless man stood in his doorway, watching her suspiciously with his thumbs curling in his belt loops as she knocked on the door of number three.

There was enough of a gap that she could slide the envelope under the door and she was bending down to do just that when the door opened and Elisavet was standing over her.

Crouched, Cora saw a wheelie suitcase lying open on a single bed with an orange bedcover. Despite its narrowness, the bed seemed to take up half the available space and all Cora's grief, fear and indignation over that spiteful sweep of the yellow duster faded as she straightened up with the money in her hand. 'You forgot this.'

The balance of their relationship shifted again.

Who was this woman? Cleaning lady, lawyer, refugee. Each time, Cora had adjusted her manner to suit, but now suddenly she had the peculiar feeling that she'd slipped into Elisavet's skin: she could feel her dark hair loose around her face, her chin high and stubborn, her eyes old and angry at fate.

Cora saw herself through Elisavet's eyes – a mature, grim-faced woman with a quizzical look, holding out the white envelope like a summons or a sacking or a request for compensation.

'Thank you,' Elisavet said and took the envelope from her. The edge of the sticking plaster was curling on her finger.

Cora opened her mouth to say not at all, she'd earned it, but she didn't want to say the wrong thing so she took a deep breath and, with an immense effort of will, managed to say nothing.

Elisavet's dark eyes were wide and unblinking, as if she too was on the brink of a sentence. She chewed the inside of her cheek, creasing the corner of her mouth.

Their gaze met, flickered uncertainly, settled.

Cora gave a nod and turned to go.

'I'm sorry,' she heard Elisavet whisper as she closed the door.

The bare-chested man gave her one last, suspicious look and closed his door too.

'Right, that's it,' Cora said briskly once she was back on the road again. 'If I don't talk to someone right now, I'm going to explode.'

* * *

She stopped at Gladdie's on the way home.

Gladdie came to the door wearing a blue-and-white-striped butcher's apron and holding a paintbrush between two fingers like a cigarette. Her pink hair was anchored back from her face with three hair grips.

'Come in! I'm making my own greetings cards, I am, Cora,' she explained. '£1.99 your birthday card was, and I bet you hardly looked at it.'

'Of course I looked at it! It said *To a Special Friend*. Some kind of a patched-up stuffed toy on it, holding a bunch of flowers.'

'Oh.'

'It's on my windowsill.'

'Is it?' Gladdie was gratified. 'Fair play then. I take it back.'

'I've come about Elisavet, I have,' Cora said, following Gladdie into the kitchen.

Gladdie groaned. 'I knew it was something,' she said gloomily. 'She hasn't been stealing, has she? Because I tell you what, Cora, I don't want to know. She's marvellous in the bathroom. She's got my grout looking like new.'

'Of course she hasn't been stealing,' Cora said irritably. 'The opposite, in fact.'

'She's been leaving you things?' Gladdie asked smartly, swishing her paintbrush in a murky mug of water.

'She forgot to take her wages. So I took them round to her and she lives in this hostel in Queen's Lane, in what I can only describe as a boxroom. Awful for her,' Cora said. 'She used to be a lawyer.'

'She said she did, but she could say anything, couldn't she?'

'And she's a long way from home,' Cora said, trying to justify Elisavet's behaviour to herself, but from now on, when Elisavet was around she'd be walking on eggshells. She leant over the table to look at the card that Gladdie was painting: lurid splashes of red against a brown background. It looked like a bloody hunting scene in a dark forest. 'Is that what I think it is?'

'It's a robin.'

'Oh, right. Anyway, I think she's unhappy, and – she's a stranger in a strange land. We should do something to cheer her up.'

'Feel free!' Gladdie snorted. 'Don't you think I've tried?' she asked. 'I've been jovial till my cheeks ached. And Megan's baked a fruit cake for her, but she wouldn't touch a slice. I'll tell you something though, she looked happy enough at your party, didn't she?'

'Did she?' Cora hadn't noticed, so this statement came as a pleasant revelation. 'I suppose she's lonely.'

'Bound to be,' Gladdie said. 'Anyway, what I was going to say before you interrupted was that I'm starting an art club and I'm going to invite her to join, for company.'

This was news to Cora. First she'd heard of it. 'What do you know about art?'

'Excuse me! I'm a prize-winning artist, Cora.'

'Are you? Since when?'

Gladdie left the kitchen and came back moments later and handed her a gilt-framed watercolour in a green mount of the back of her bungalow with the curtains shut. The emerald lawn was neatly cut, and in the foreground a pink rhododendron bush was in full flower.

'Turn it over, have a look at the back.'

A white sticker read:

The Garden.
Original watercolour by Gladdie E. Griffith.

BRIDGEND AND DISTRICT AGRICULTURAL SHOW, August 1987. THIRD
PRIZE section F Art class number 39, watercolour.

'Third prize,' Cora said soberly. 'My word, there's a modest boast for you.'

'I'd forgotten all about it, to be honest,' Gladdie said, 'but Elisavet gave it a good clean and once I'd seen it with new eyes it gave me the inspiration to start the class. I'll expect you and Megan to come. And Elisavet. Just the four of us to start with, unless it gets popular.'

'You can leave me out, I can't paint a picture to save my life,' Cora said.

'What are you talking about?' Gladdie said, exasperated. 'It's not about painting! We can show her the countryside, take her to the beach, bring her out of herself. Even you can put a few daubs on a sheet of paper and call it abstract.'

Cora studied Gladdie's watercolour critically at arm's length. It was a nice enough representation of Gladdie's garden, but no masterpiece, which was encouraging. 'Abstract,' she said thoughtfully, putting the picture on the table. 'I could manage abstract. But you're not going to start being bossy and critical with us, are you?'

'No,' Gladdie said. 'As if!'

Cora thought of Elisavet's small room with the narrow bed. It was true, she could do with getting out a bit. They could show her the countryside and open her up to all the loveliness of it.

'All right then, as it's in a good cause you can count me in.'

9

On the first morning of the painting class, they went into town for art supplies.

The reason for them all to go was so that they could buy their own materials in WH Smith. This was agreed after a short discussion in the shop because Gladdie had suddenly started worrying about the expense.

'And after all, I'm not charging for my expertise,' she said, looking aghast at the prices on the painting sets.

'Good, because we wouldn't pay you anyway,' Megan replied. 'Elisavet shouldn't have to contribute if we're doing it for her. Let's get four of everything and split it between the three of us.'

They agreed that's what they would do and Megan put their purchases into her straw bag and they went to meet Elisavet on the bridge.

'There she is,' Megan said triumphantly.

That was disappointing because Cora had bet her a pound that Elisavet wouldn't turn up. Half-hoped it, really. Cora and Elisavet hadn't really spoken to each other since the incident of the broken Royal Doulton figurine after which Cora had sworn herself to silence. And the opportunity hadn't arisen since then because she made sure she was out when she came and she left Elisavet's wages on the table in a white envelope as usual.

The memory of that gesture, that sweep of the arm, still stung. She wished it didn't. She wanted to forget it. She wanted to forgive. But there was Elisavet with her dark hair coiled and pinned up in a mock tortoiseshell crocodile clip, wearing all black as if she belonged in an art gallery.

'She's obviously looking forward to it,' Gladdie said smugly. 'See how happy she looks!'

Elisavet was curved like a ship's figurehead, her arms on the balustrade, her head held high, facing into the wind. It was an exaggeration to say she looked happy, but there was no doubt she seemed relaxed.

She turned to face them. 'This bridge,' she demanded when they got close, 'tell me, what is it called?'

'It's called the Old Bridge,' Cora said. 'We're very imaginative when it comes to naming our bridges.'

'The Old Bridge,' Elisavet said thoughtfully, nodding. 'I like this very much.'

'It wasn't always called that,' Gladdie chipped in with the air of someone in the know. 'When it was first built it would just have been known as the Bridge, I expect.'

'It's a scheduled ancient monument,' Megan said. 'A bit like us.'

'Ah.' Elisavet absorbed this fact with her usual seriousness. 'In Prizren, in Kosovo where I come from, there is a similar bridge in the old town. It is much like this, very old, made of stone,' she waved her hand, 'with these same cobbles to walk on.' She added with pride, 'It is one of our cultural heritage monuments.'

No wonder Elisavet looked relaxed, Cora thought, coming across some-thing wonderfully familiar in an unexpected place.

'Is it? Fancy that!' Megan said. 'What is your bridge called? Something exotic I expect?'

'Yes.' Elisavet's dark eyes shone with humour. 'It is called the Old Stone Bridge.'

They laughed because it was funny, and pleasing to know that the bridge's comforting charm was Elisavet's home from home too.

* * *

Gladdie's painting class was taking place at her house. She put on her butcher's apron which had a smudge of red paint on it, a badge of honour. 'We're going in the garden, as it's sunny.'

'Nice day for it,' Megan said. She put on her loose, navy fisherman's decorating smock which was polka dotted with cream emulsion. Her grey hair was parted in the middle, and growing out horizontal in a grey, lemony dishwashing-liquid scented storm cloud of frizziness.

Cora had no intention of getting paint on herself. She was wearing her normal everyday clothes, specifically a pair of red drawstring trousers and a floral blouse.

They followed Gladdie out to the back of the house where she had set up four chairs behind a trestle table on the lawn next to the pink rhododendron bush. In front of the table stood an easel displaying her third-prize-winning framed watercolour of the garden. For inspiration, Cora supposed.

Elisavet's eyes were seeking Cora's.

Cora looked away. *I'm not just hurt, I'm still angry with her*, she realised, not only because of that deliberate act of destruction but because Elisavet had assumed she'd had an easy life in an 'it's all right for you' attitude. She felt totally misunderstood. How could this woman presume to know what kind of lives they'd had? Their upbeat amiability belied the fact that the three of them had come through tragedy, drama and trauma too. Course they had. You couldn't avoid it. It was called living. It was the way life was, fraught with challenges and regrets.

She watched Gladdie busily rearranging four yoghurt cartons full of water on the table, placing them alongside four mismatched chipped tea plates, a mug of paintbrushes of various sizes, some A4 sheets of paper from their sketchbooks and several tubes of watercolour paint.

Megan caught her staring and let her raised eyebrows speak for her.

'What?' Cora replied defensively.

'Look at Gladdie, bless her, she's in her element being a teacher again.'

She was, too. Cora sat down at the end of the table on one of Gladdie's dining chairs. The back legs began sinking into the lawn. 'Abstract,' she reminded herself aloud, picking up a paintbrush.

'You like abstract?' Elisavet asked, sitting down next to her.

Cora hesitated. 'Yes. You?'

'Of course. It's more interesting, don't you think?'

'Yes, I suppose so.'

'Abstract doesn't tell you what to think, it makes you think for yourself.'

'True enough.'

Elisavet looked from Cora to the painting of the garden that Gladdie had propped up on the easel to inspire them.

Definitely not abstract, Cora thought, waggling her paintbrush at a wasp to discourage it, and she wondered if they were rather subtly taking sides.

Of course, she'd seen Gladdie's greetings card of a hunting scene, or a robin, which, while not being strictly abstract, was definitely open to interpretation.

After chewing the end of the brush she decided to paint the rhododendrons. She squirted red paint and white paint in two short parallel lines on the plate, where they lay in stripes like toothpaste, and mixed them together before applying to paper in therapeutically exuberant pink swirls. This didn't take long.

After half an hour, Gladdie strolled around the table to check their efforts, and she said happily over Cora's shoulder, 'Is that me?' and made a humming sound of approval.

Cora stared at her creation for a moment and resisted the urge to say: I don't know, is it? She had just been about to add dashes of green for the leaves but it was much more fun to find she'd been painting Gladdie instead. 'I might enter it into the Agricultural Society competition,' she said, sitting back. She looked across the table at Gladdie's blue and yellow oval, obviously an Easter egg. 'What's that?' she asked before committing herself to praising it.

'A blue tit. I haven't finished it yet.'

Cora put her paintbrush in the yoghurt pot and folded her arms with the satisfactory sensation that she was back at school, having found the exam a lot easier than she'd expected. The sun was warm on her face and the rhododendrons hummed with insects.

To her left, Megan was painting the gnarled trunk of Gladdie's oak tree. She was touching up the features of an old man's face in the bark. It looked like her pacifist father, Idwal.

Cora turned to look at Elisavet's creation. Using a ruler and a pencil, Elisavet had drawn black squares like a crossword grid. Cora narrowed her eyes and tried to let the picture speak to her. Hello? Anyone there? No. Nothing.

Elisavet put her pencil down and turned to Cora.

Cora's stomach tightened with a sudden pang of guilt because Elisavet looked deeply unhappy. She tried not to notice.

'Forgive me,' Elisavet said softly. She touched Cora's arm, her slender fingers brushing the floral sleeve.

Cora glanced desperately towards Megan and Gladdie, but they seemed to be caught up in their own personal worlds of art. It didn't mean they weren't listening.

Cora knew it would be the easiest, most sensible thing in the world to nod and agree, yes, I forgive you, but she clung on to her indignation as if it was the one principle that defined her, because it wouldn't be the truth and she didn't.

Her own solid stubbornness surprised her as she was normally quite a nice person. She rubbed her eyes as a sense of déjà vu suddenly destabilised her. This was how her mother must have felt when she'd kept the shotgun ready by the back door, waiting for the day she could kill a German and pay back the hurt.

Cora was paying back the hurt now, and why not? Because let's face it, when it boiled down to it, Elisavet had deliberately and spitefully broken something she knew was special to her. That she didn't know about Owen wasn't the point.

Elisavet leant to one side and picked up her bag from the grass, put it on her lap as if she was about to leave. Good. But she carefully took out a bundle wrapped in newspaper and held it towards Cora. 'Here. Take.'

Cora took it. It didn't weigh much. She could guess what it was. She could guess, but at the same time she was reluctant to look.

'Open it, please,' Elisavet urged her.

Cora unwrapped the sheets of newspaper and as she thought, it was the Royal Doulton figurine. Elisavet had glued it together but there were small pieces missing, and the gaps were letting in gleams of sunlight.

Cora cradled it in the palm of her hand. She felt tearful. It was damaged. It was never going to look perfect again.

'It must have taken you a long time to mend it,' she said after a long moment, glancing at her, keeping her voice low and under control. She felt the emotion choke up her throat. She wanted to cry for Elisavet's unhappiness; she wanted to cry for everything else that would never look perfect again.

'What I'll do,' she said, almost to herself, 'I'll put it back on the mantel-piece where it was, and I'll look at it and see the cracks and then I'll stop looking at it and I'll forget about the cracks, I'll just know it's there. I'll know what it stands for.' That was the truth of it, she realised. The gluing together stood for putting things right, or trying to, as best you could.

It was her turn, now, to put things right. She met Elisavet's anxious eyes and cleared her throat. 'Thank you.'

Elisavet nodded. She pencilled over the black squares of her drawing with deliberate concentration, her head bowed so the shadows hid her face, and after a few moments she said in a dead monotone, 'My fiancé wrote. He broke up with me that day.'

'Fiancé?' Well now, this was news. Cora dabbed more pink paint on the flower that had become Gladdie's head.

'Too many problems knowing me.' Elisavet's eyes rimmed silver with tears and the holy, innocent look was replaced by hurt confusion. 'All these years we grew up together, we went to the same school, our parents were friends. And then all of sudden it changed, and his family wouldn't speak to us because they are Serbs and I'm the enemy now.'

'Ah.' Cora frowned. She was beginning to see the picture, like the magic painting books that were popular when Gwyn was a child, all black and white until you wetted the paper and the colours showed through. She wrapped the figurine up in the newspaper. *Too many problems knowing me.*

I know exactly what it feels like, Cora thought, when love causes too many problems. She wanted to tell Elisavet that, but whether she could find the right words to explain it was another matter entirely. 'Do you remember that old notebook of my husband's, written in 1944, that we found in the tin box?' she began awkwardly, jerking her head in the vague direction of home.

Elisavet glanced at her and gave a brief nod. 'The book that he wrote in German.'

'Yes. You see, Frank was a German.'

Elisavet chewed her lip. She was a smart woman, quick.

'Oh?' She lifted her eyebrows and instantly understood the bigger picture. 'But in 1944, Germany and Britain were at war, no?'

Cora nodded, feeling secretly gratified she still had the power to surprise. 'Yes, exactly. He was a prisoner of war. So there we are,' she said, 'if it helps.' She wasn't sure it did, but she didn't want to labour the point. Let Elisavet make what she wanted of it. After all, Cora wasn't Gladdie, who always wanted to teach a person something – considered it her duty to, actually, whether you wanted to learn a thing or not.

Elisavet frowned. 'And the German loved you?' she asked in a tone of disbelief.

'Well, I was younger then, obviously,' Cora said quickly, 'and not bad looking as it goes.'

'Of course.'

'Anyway, I'm thinking of getting a dictionary, see if I can make sense of what he wrote or at least get the gist. He mentions my name a few times. It would be nice to see things from his point of view.'

Elisavet pursed her lips and went back to sharpening the stub of her pencil as methodically as she did everything else.

It seemed to be the end of the conversation and Cora sat back, tilted her head up and watched the clouds creep slowly over Gladdie's roof, sliding shade on it.

Elisavet tapped her arm. 'I don't do anything on Friday nights. I know German. I can tell you what the book says if you want,' she said softly.

'Can you?' Surprised, Cora felt a rush of excitement, as though Frank had suddenly got in touch with her after a long absence. 'Oh! I'd like that!'

'What are you two whispering about?' Megan asked brightly, holding her paint-puckered tree trunk at arm's length. Without waiting for a reply, she turned it to show them. 'What do you think?'

Cora nodded. 'Nice. It looks like your dad.'

'Interesting texture to the face,' Elisavet agreed.

Gladdie wiped her hands on her painting apron and hurried over to add her own judgement, as hers was the one that counted. 'Hm. Good effort, Megan, fair play. What have you drawn, Elisavet?' she asked her in an encouraging, teacherly tone. 'What are they? Squares? Modernism, is it?'

'Windows,' Elisavet said, pointing towards Gladdie's house.

'Oh, yes,' Gladdie said, comparing them. 'Fair enough. But where's the glass?'

Elisavet stared up at her and shook her head. Her voice trembled. 'No glass.'

'Oh. Never mind.' Gladdie added encouragingly, 'It's quite difficult to draw something you can see through, isn't it? That's why in my painting, look, you'll notice I've drawn the curtains in instead. A little trick I came up with. Anyway, it's something for you to think about.'

No glass? Cora glanced at Megan and knew she was thinking the same thing. There was no glass in the windows because of the war. Gladdie could be surprisingly dense sometimes.

'How's the blue tit coming on?' Cora asked her.

'See for yourself,' Gladdie said. She peeled it carefully off the table and held it up.

'What are those red things?' Megan asked.

'Wellingtons. Had to give him wellingtons, see, because the toes came out wrong. But I think it works, don't you? Glass of wine, anyone?'

Elisavet glanced at her watch. 'I must go,' she said. 'I have a client.' She picked up her bag and hoisted it over her shoulder. 'Maybe another day.'

'What a shame! Your windows are coming on so nicely, very lifelike,' Gladdie said, walking with her back to the house.

'A client! Hear that, Cora? Elisavet's two-timing us,' Megan said, scraping at a flake of brown paint on the front of her smock. 'Do you think she enjoyed herself?'

'Hard to tell.'

'Not exactly the life and soul, is she?'

'Not exactly, no,' Cora agreed.

'What were you whispering about?'

'This.' Cora lifted the newspaper bundle from her lap and unwrapped it to show her. 'She mended it for me.'

'Oh dear, your little evacuee,' Megan said, taking the piece of china and running her thumb along the glued cracks. 'It's been in the wars, hasn't it?'

'Indeed.' Cora gave a dry laugh. 'Good choice of words.'

'A bit of overzealous dusting, was it?' Megan asked, propping it on the table.

'Mmm. You could say that.'

They had been friends too long for Megan to let that pass. 'So could you, so why didn't you?' she asked mildly. 'Deliberate accident, was it?'

'What do you mean?'

'The fact that she's taken it upon herself to glue it together. Why would she otherwise?' Megan picked it up and held it to the light. It glowed with sunlight, candlelit. 'What's Gwyn going to say?'

'That it can't be helped, something like that, I expect.' He'd given it to her in memory of the uncle he never knew. He was a lovely gift giver, was Gwyn, Cora thought.

'I'm surprised you didn't put it away somewhere safe when she came,' Megan said.

'I know, I should have.'

Megan looked towards the house again. 'Where's Gladdie with that wine she promised us? Here, you'd better wrap this up again.' Seeing her expression, she gave Cora a sympathetic smile. 'I know, love. It's a shame. I know what it meant to you and so does Gwyn, bless him. But you've got to look at it long-term, see. To Fiona it's just a naff ornament, a bit of kitsch, and when you're dead, sure as eggs she'll have a clear-out and drop it off at the Oxfam shop in Wyndham Street along with all the other things you love.' She paused and added, 'Mind you, they might not take it with it being chipped and all.'

Strangely enough, the idea cheered Cora up. She laughed. 'You're right. Or she'll hire a skip and dump everything in it.'

Funny how perfectly acceptable that idea was in old age.

When she was a child, like most children, Cora had believed in that godlike childish manner that the world existed for her and because of her, and everything was solid and permanent. But then the boys they'd known from childhood became men and went off to fight with a great deal of fanfare and never came back. And from then on everything was transitory. More or less everything. Because although she didn't know it then, the concept of the enemy was transitory, too.

She should have told Elisavet that.

She realised that the remarkable thing about Elisavet was that she had the knack of letting them see old things through new eyes, Cora thought, taking a fresh look at Megan's painting of a tree trunk resembling her father.

And suddenly, with a flash of clarity, Cora wondered if it was serendipity that had made her stop and look at the advert in Mr Patel's window.

10

NOVEMBER 1944

On the day the German prisoners of war were arriving in Bridgend, Cora and Megan walked up Station Road arm in arm. Cora saw Megan's father, Idwal, wearing a sandwich board as he waited in the cold wind outside Bridgend railway station. He had the energy of a man who was filled with passionate expectation.

'What's your dad saying?' she asked Megan.

'Love thine enemy,' Megan said, jamming her hat on her dandelion-yellow head because her springy hair had a tendency to take charge and lift it off. She'd inherited her hair from her father.

Luckily, that was all she'd inherited, Cora thought, because Idwal was considered a harmless lunatic, shouting his message of peace to the war-torn world, whereas Megan was always calm and sensible.

Cora saw that his sandwich board had the two messages written on it in black paint, *Love thine enemy* on one side and *Bless them that curse you* on the other. They were radical messages in the circumstances, Cora thought.

'Why is he wearing a sandwich board as well as shouting?'

'It's for the hard of hearing,' Megan explained.

Cora gave her a sympathetic look. As the crowds gathered on the pavements, she watched Idwal jump around frequently like a boy playing hopscotch so that both sides could be seen and his message of hope appreciated. Now and then the sandwich boards clapped him hard enough to knock the breath out of him, which was a relief. 'He's going to wear himself out, doing that,' she said.

'Just ignore him,' Megan said, frowning.

For her sake, Cora tried her best to, but it wasn't easy because he was making a spectacle of himself.

The crowds were gathering for the arrival of the special train with its large consignment of German prisoners of war. Very hush-hush, it was, and everybody knew about it, so they had come to see the enemy for themselves.

Cora was nervously looking out for her mother. When she saw her coming up the road in her black felt hat and sensible shoes, with her handbag secure in the crook of her elbow and her lips pressed white with distaste, she couldn't help thinking there was something to be said for Idwal's message of peace.

Gladdie came running to join Cora and Megan, and stopped dead when she saw Idwal.

'If your enemy is hungry, feed him; if he is thirsty, give him something to drink!' Idwal roared, shaking his fists like an Old Testament prophet.

'Poor Idwal,' Gladdie said. 'Delusions of grandeur.'

Poor Megan, too, Cora thought, but she didn't say it. Idwal had been a perfectly ordinary farmer right until the Germans started bombing Cardiff in 1940 and he took the blame for it on himself.

No matter how unlikely it sounded, or how loudly people mocked him when he repeated his story, Idwal had got it firmly into his head that he himself was the real reason the Luftwaffe was targeting them and there was no talking him out of it. It was personal between him and Lord Haw-Haw. Lord Haw-Haw knew the area. He'd lived there for a while, see, Idwal had explained to Cora earnestly, and he liked a drink.

Idwal's story was that he had met Lord Haw-Haw, alias William Joyce, in the Red Dragon pub one market day when the man was surrounded by a little group of farmers because he had the type of accent that made his words sound authoritative and worth listening to, and well, you never knew.

That impression wore off the longer he spoke, and the deep scar that curved from the corner of his right cheek to his earlobe looked very much like a sneer, but it was hard to shut out that upper-class voice, and eventually Idwal could take no more of it. He lost patience and told him he was talking rubbish. Did a fair impression of him too, he would add modestly in the telling. *Tawking rubbish, old chep*. It caused a lot of amusement at the time, which was gratifying, but William Joyce didn't like it one little bit and he jumped to his feet and threatened Idwal with his pointing finger. 'I'm not going to forget this, sir, you wait and see!'

The way he said it, spit flying from his thin lips with the force of his words, Idwal swore it sounded more like a curse than a threat. And sure enough, not long after that, Lord Haw-Haw escalated the disagreement with the help of the Luftwaffe.

Coincidence? Idwal didn't think so, and no one, not even the minister, could convince him otherwise.

A guilty conscience is a terrible thing to live with and it weighed heavily on Idwal's shoulders. He replayed this story over and over to Megan and to anyone else who had the time, inclination, or misfortune to listen, looking for some loophole to his own arrogance so that he could genuinely change the outcome before it was too late. He deeply regretted going into the Red Dragon that day and losing his patience.

Kneeling in his Anderson shelter one night with his knuckles pressed into his forehead and the bombing disturbing his prayers, he had a sudden spiritual revelation. God spoke to Idwal in his own voice, the voice of a Welshman, and Idwal made a bargain with God that he would become a pacifist so that God would put an end to the war.

Megan told Cora she hoped the experience might wear off him eventually, like most rash promises made to God in the heat of remorse, but four years ago, that was, and Idwal wasn't put off by the fact that peace was taking longer than he imagined. He was content to be patient because the Lord, being eternal, worked on a different timescale from man and quite right too.

While for Idwal all of this made perfect sense, he was generally regarded by those who'd always known him as having gone a bit *twp* in the head with a touch of shell shock from the bombing, although they agreed he was harmless for the most part.

It wasn't any consolation to Megan. She worried. Her father had, on occasion, been beaten up by irate squaddies on account of his message of peace. Dabbing his face with antiseptic after one of his escapades, she told him she hoped they'd knocked some sense into him, but no, after getting to his feet, Idwal had a habit of chasing after his attackers with the aim of converting them.

And now here Idwal was at Bridgend station in his sandwich board, wanting to make peace with the Germans.

Megan turned to Cora and shrugged helplessly. 'What can you do? He won't listen.'

Cora gave Idwal a wave. 'Shall we go and say hello to him?'

'No,' Megan said, pulling her back. 'Let's stay here where we are. I love him, but he's embarrassing. And he keeps wanting me to stop working in the factory and help him on the farm instead. He says we're just making things worse by keeping the war going and retaliating tit for tat. He thinks we should talk to the Germans and shake hands and be nice. There's no arguing with him.'

Cora and Gladdie didn't mind staying on this side of the road at all because to be honest they had a better view of Idwal from here without appearing to stare. All that jumping! Cora huddled deeper into her coat and marvelled at his energy.

'I wonder what the Germans will make of him when they arrive?' Gladdie asked with a grin. 'They'll think he's our secret weapon.'

Cora was very nervous about the arrival of the Germans, and a cold wind shuddered through her as if she was about to be indelibly and voluntarily tainted with evil.

She'd come here defiant, her anger smouldering quietly and undetected under the surface like a peat fire. On a daily basis, she filled those hundreds of large, shiny shells with TNT, and she was efficient about it because, in her imagination, all the enemy soldiers shared one familiar face and one hectoring voice: that of Adolf Hitler, the Implacable and Merciless.

And now she had come to see the enemy for herself. But this was the point that troubled her: the enemy was also going to see her, and she was a coward at heart. 'I've changed my mind about it. Let's go,' she said to Gladdie, clutching her sleeve.

'Don't be daft,' Gladdie said irritably, shaking her off. 'I'm not missing this for anything.'

Across the road Cora's mother, Jane, had gone to stand near Idwal, preoccupied with her own thoughts. It was only when the train pulled in and Idwal jumped one hundred and eighty degrees with the clack of his boards frightening the life out of her that she was jolted into reacting.

'Fool!' her mother said furiously, and all the waiting people jostled to get a good view of what was happening, pushing Idwal to one side.

The first people they saw were the British guards, looking solid and dependable in their uniforms. A cry went up from the crowd: 'Well done, lads!'

And shortly after that came the moment they had been waiting for and dreading.

The Germans were here.

Smart and fearsome the officers were in their grey and black uniforms and heavy boots, and they kept on coming, hundreds of them, carriage after carriage, lining up in the station yard, shoulders back, and not the slightest bit intimidated by the guards or the watching crowds. It was their attitude that alarmed Cora most – they looked as straight-backed and proud as victors.

'Blow me down,' Gladdie said, leaning heavily on Cora's shoulder. 'Look at them! We've got no chance.'

'Swastikas,' Megan said soberly. 'Well, good luck to my dad and his peace mission, that's all I can say.'

'What exactly does SS stand for?' Gladdie asked.

'Brutality.'

'Oh, right.'

'Why have we brought them here to Wales, of all places?' Cora asked, chewing her thumbnail. 'It's like inviting wolves into the sheepfold.'

Some kind of noisy argument was erupting in the station between the German SS officers and the British guards. It had been hard to make sense of it at first, because the British guards were shouting orders in German and the Germans were protesting back in English. The words 'Geneva Convention' and 'sod the Geneva Convention' were being batted back and forth.

'Ructions!' Cora said, curling her cold fingers up into the warmth of her sleeves. Men were still pouring off the train, hundreds of them with their kit bags slung over their shoulders and cases in their hands. The platform was crowded, and the SS officers stood firm at the funnel end of the station like a cork in a bottle.

When the guards ordered the prisoners to form ranks they did so smartly enough but there was nowhere to go.

Disturbed by the almighty racket outside his window, Mr Hill, the stationmaster renowned for his short fuse, came out of his office in a terrible temper to find out what was going on.

He was a fair man though, furious with both British and Germans alike, and he commanded them all to leave his station immediately with the power and authority that his status gave him.

The crowd held its breath.

But marvellous, it was! The SS officers picked up their bags and began to goose-step sharply out of the station. Dew, but their faces were hard and their eyes were cold. After Sieg Heiling energetically they began to sing some defiant marching song.

Behind them, also singing and marching but with less patriotic vigour, was the tired, motley rag-tag of ordinary battle-bruised soldiers. They stared straight ahead, eyes blank and faces set. Cora watched them from the pavements with despair in her eyes.

She hadn't been prepared for the unexpected novelty of seeing so many ordinary men her own age trudging from the station, carrying their possessions, heads down, defeated, humiliated, lost in a world of their own misery.

Or trying to get lost in it, she thought; except for one man near the back of the line. He didn't look defeated at all. He was looking around with intense interest, like a sightseer, goose-stepping as energetically as the rest of them. Fair hair showed beneath his grey cap, and his grey eyes were bright and keen.

Cora stared at him. There was no good reason why, out of all of the Heil Hitlering river of fifteen hundred marching men, this one should catch her eye. There was nothing particularly distinctive about his features – he had a bland, regular face – but he looked as pure and vital as an angel.

She glanced at Megan, but Megan didn't seem to notice. Turning back, Cora saw him again immediately as if he was lit up, every thundering goose-step bringing him closer to her, until he was shielded from her line of sight momentarily by one of the guards.

As he came back into view, the German sensed her gaze, caught her eye and gave a sudden smile.

Instinctively Cora smiled back, woman to man, smile to smile, as if she knew him, body language familiar to them both, and then above the noise of jackboots, a familiar voice screamed in fury:

'Murderers!'

It pierced the air with hate and there was a scuffle as Cora saw her mother knock his cap clean off his head.

'You bloody, bloody murderers!' Jane screamed, and was pushed to one side by a guard.

Oh, lor. Cora's heart turned over clumsily in her chest.

The soldier stumbled and tried to get his cap back, and a murmur of approval rose from the crowd.

'Your mam said bloody,' Megan observed to Cora in sympathy.

'I know.'

The young German's grey eyes were desperate, then he was prodded onward by his marching comrades and now she could only see the back of the soldier's bobbing bare head and ruffled fair hair.

Cora had the impression of the train pulling out of the station and curving around the track out of sight, taking him with it. Oh, Mam, she thought in despair, because she'd seen her mother's naked agony for the first time.

The way her mother coped with trauma was to put her feelings into cold storage.

After Owen went away, their lives had gone on pretty much as usual and it was a blessing to Cora that Dio hadn't been driven to wearing a sandwich board, and that her mother hadn't taken to her bed like Megan's mother had. Their normality had made her normal too.

But now she'd had a glimpse of her mother's true feelings and she wished she hadn't. It was like seeing her parading naked through the town and Cora was hotly ashamed on her behalf. And now she began to wonder what was going on in her father's head that he didn't want anyone to know about.

More uncertainty in an uncertain world.

Cora tried to push through the ranks of marching men to reach her mother but she was stopped by a guard who blocked her way. In between the bobbing heads Cora caught glimpses of her mother like snapshots, as if she was seeing her for the first time: vulnerable, looking older than her years, her hair turning grey, chapped hands worn red by housework.

'Get back, Miss,' the guard ordered.

'Can't you let me through? My mother's upset. They killed my brother.'

'They killed a lot more people than him,' the guard said tiredly.

Cora returned to her friends. They watched the procession of prisoners and guards until they marched out of sight.

'So that's the enemy,' Megan said. She sounded puzzled, as if the enemy was a disappointment.

Gladdie was staring at the prisoners blankly and she started fiddling with her watch as if this was the kind of thing that happened all the time.

Cora saw the soldier's cap on the ground, trampled and filthy now, and kept her eye on it. The British guards were taking up the rear with their rifles, and one of them kicked it to one side. Cora ran across, and picked it up. She pressed it to her nose, smelling the soldier's hair oil in the fabric, and stuffed it in her pocket.

Her mother, Jane, was back on the kerb next to Idwal again, staring into thin air, her face stiff. Everyone was moving on except them.

Cold? Oh, she was cold all right. Jane had always had the ability to freeze people out, and now she'd frozen herself out. She was in a trance, as if she was hoping no one could see her because she'd made a spectacle of herself.

'I never thought it of you, Jane,' Idwal, the pacifist, said askance, and his gaze went back to the tail end of the noisy procession stomping past the shops on their way to Island Farm Camp.

Cora went to put her hand on her mother's arm but she could feel the crackle of her mother's mood icily close to the surface. 'Let's go home,' she said.

'I can't forgive them,' Jane said to her in a deep, throbbing voice, 'and I don't care if I burn in hell for it. You can't forgive someone who doesn't repent, can you? I looked into their eyes, Cora, and what I saw there—'

'Shh, I know,' Cora said quickly, because she too had looked into the eyes of the SS officers and what she'd seen there was contempt.

'I knocked a German's cap off,' Jane said proudly, her mouth twisting with bitter pleasure. 'He looked too pleased with himself by half.'

'I know, I saw you do it,' Cora said, keeping her voice neutral.

'Good.' They stared at each other nervously, eyes glittering, corrupted by their own anger.

'Tell you the truth now, both of you, I thought it was uncalled for,' Idwal said. He looked down at his sandwich board as if to remind himself of its message. 'Love thine enemy,' he said, and his thin face was troubled. 'But you know, having seen them close up like, I'm not at all sure they want to be loved, not by us, anyway,' he said slowly, flattening his hair with his hands. 'I get the feeling that to them, *we* are the enemy.'

'Fool,' Jane snapped.

Idwal lifted his shaggy eyebrows away from his honest brown eyes. 'I know. Hard to believe, isn't it? Here's Megan. Hello, bach,' he said brightly to his daughter. 'I thought you hadn't seen me from over the road.'

'Hello, Tad. You missed an opportunity there,' Megan said. 'You should have written your sign in German and converted the lot of them.'

'Have it bilingual, you mean?'

'Yes. Works both ways,' she said.

'So I would be telling the Germans to love us.' He thought this radical idea over for a moment. 'That puts a different complexion on it altogether.'

'I know, Dad. I wasn't being serious.'

Cora felt different, charged, disturbed. She had expected to feel triumphant at the Germans being marched to prison but instead she felt sick, as if she'd fallen into bad company and was regretting it. 'We'd better head back, Meg,' she said to her. 'Where's Gladdie got to?'

'She's gone after them. Her dad said to keep an eye out because they're duty bound to make a break for it, on Hitler's orders.'

'And Gladdie's gone to put a stop to it, has she?' It was meant to be funny, but as soon as Cora said it she knew it wasn't funny at all because they could see for themselves that the prisoners far outnumbered the guards and the guards looked tired, as if they'd seen too much of the war already and they'd had enough of it. 'They'll get shot if they try anything,' she said.

'Yes. Let them try.' Jane's eyes were hard behind her glasses, and in her new, deeply vengeful, unmotherly voice she added, 'I'll shoot them myself in two shakes of a lamb's tail.'

'I know you would.' Cora felt depressed. Her mother had been broken for the past four years and they had pretended not to notice the cracks. Well, she could see them now plainly enough and it was an ugly sight. She wanted to look away.

The war had tipped them up and spilled them out and it was hard to untangle themselves from who they had been before it. From now on, she thought, they were always going to be uncertain about their own selves and who they were, and how they were capable of thinking and acting. Cora had always thought she had a solid core of decency in her, that she knew right from wrong. But how was one really supposed to know?

As they headed back home, she crushed the faded cap in her pocket and then she smelled her fingers. The spoils of war, she thought. The cap was softened with wear and weather. Her heart broke when she thought of the soldier's bright smile, brief and so quickly erased. She pondered on her mother's choice of victim, kicking a man when he was down.

She would have been better taking revenge on the SS officers if she'd wanted to make a point, and sent their caps flying instead. Maybe the idea didn't occur to Jane straightaway, that was the best explanation, but to be honest those men at the head of the two columns didn't look the sort to take violence lightly.

It was the soldier's sudden happy smile that had caught the attention of both of them in different ways and for different reasons.

And even worse, the shouting and the well-aimed blow hadn't settled the score for Jane at all. On the contrary, it seemed to have stoked her to a greater fury.

For a moment Cora shivered. She had a vision of Jane's emotions as rampant, raging things, animals to be kept subdued as brutally as possible by whatever means available, with chains and whips to bind them and tie them down.

But it was too late now.

Jane had tasted violence and liked it, and she was hell bent on revenge.

11

1992

When Gladdie came back into the garden she was carrying three mugs of tea on a tray and she had taken her painting apron off.

'What happened to the wine you promised us?' Megan asked, stacking the china paint palettes on top of each other to make space.

'The wine was for Elisavet, to help cheer her up. I'm not wasting it on you two because you don't need cheering up.'

'I don't think wine would have worked anyway,' Cora said. 'She's got a broken heart.'

Gladdie put the tray down with a rattle. 'Rubbish! What's given you that idea?'

'She told me,' Cora said.

'Oh,' Gladdie said shamelessly. 'I guessed it was something like that.'

'Gladdie, you fibber!'

Unperturbed, Gladdie handed her a mug and asked, 'Who broke it, did she say?'

'Her fiancé, back home. He told her she's the enemy now,' Cora said. 'Where did Gwyn say she was from?'

They shook their heads, couldn't remember.

Megan sipped from her mug. 'If you promise a person a glass of wine, Gladdie, a cup of tea is a terrible anticlimax. And can we drop the art club now? I'm not cut out for it. Don't try to persuade me with encouraging words because it's not going to work.' She was still irritable, and not just about the wine.

'Elisavet said we think life is a joke. She doesn't realise that because we're old we've learnt things.' Cora added ruefully, 'Mainly that it *is* a joke.'

Gladdie was reluctant to let the art club go. 'If we keep up with the art club we can teach her all the things we've learnt.'

Cora had a sudden pleasing vision of them as three old gurus with Elisavet sitting by their feet on the grass, eager to learn the secrets of life. It didn't, of course, take into account their different personalities, nor for the fact that she wasn't sure they had learnt much of anything except the importance of keeping going. And that wasn't even something you had to learn – one had no choice in the matter.

'Bad idea. Nobody likes to have lessons forced on them,' she added. 'Elisavet won't like being preached to. We have to learn things for ourselves.'

'And you won't be subtle about it, Gladdie, that's the problem,' Megan pointed out, 'I know you, you'll ram it down her throat like the art. Good effort, that's what you said about my tree trunk with my father's face in it, and I call that condescending, considering you painted a blue tit wearing red wellingtons. Give me a hand to get up, will you, Cora.'

'The horse liniment not working for you?' Gladdie asked innocently.

Cora held Megan's hands and with her assistance, Megan got out of the chair, gritting her teeth.

They collected their things together. If they were together for any length of time they tended to get cranky with one another. Cora picked up her bag and for a moment she wondered why she had some old newspaper in it, and then remembered what was wrapped up inside it. 'We're better behaved when Elisavet's around,' she observed.

'That's true,' Gladdie said. 'So what are we going to do about the art class? Same time next week?'

No one could accuse Gladdie of not being a trier.

'I'm not promising,' Cora said. 'I might have better things to do.'

'If I come, and it's a big if, I'm bringing my own wine,' Megan decided.

The three of them knew that it was settled, and they would definitely come, but they enjoyed a rebellion from time to time.

'That's sorted then,' Gladdie said. 'Don't forget your paintings.'

'Frame it and don't say I never give you anything,' Cora suggested. 'Tell you what, Glad, I'll sign it for you if you like.'

'No, *you* frame it,' Gladdie said. 'I'm serious. We're going to have an exhibition at the end of the summer.'

'What?' Megan threw her hands up in disgust. 'You didn't tell us there was going to be an exhibition!' she protested. 'I might have known. Trust you to try and show us up, it's typical of you. You said it was just for fun and to help Elisavet.' She jerked her head meaningfully towards Elisavet's empty chair.

'It *is* for fun,' Gladdie said, 'but it might as well be two things as one thing. And look on the bright side – you might have improved by then.'

'That's it, I knew you'd insult me sooner or later,' Megan said firmly, wiping her hands on her smock. 'I'm hanging up my paintbrush.'

Cora gave Megan an arm to lean on and with a grunt, Megan picked up her damp, puckered painting. 'See you later.'

'See you later,' Gladdie said.

12

Flapping her painting to dry it as she walked home, Cora was surprised to see a red car parked in her drive. Gwyn's Fiona was sitting inside it, alone, her arms resting on the steering wheel, squinting at the house as if she suspected Cora was in there hiding from her.

Cora tapped on the window. 'Hello, stranger! What are you doing here?'

Fiona jumped, startled, and unfastened the seatbelt. It retracted with a clatter. She got out of the car, tugging her beige skirt down modestly. She looked flushed and unhappy.

Uh-oh.

'Come inside and have a cup of tea,' Cora said. 'I was going to make a sandwich. I've been to Gladdie's, I have. Painting lessons.' She waved the painting, to show her.

'That's nice,' Fiona said without enthusiasm.

'You've obviously got an artist's eye,' Cora said, unlocking the front door. 'Come on in.'

Fiona's misery seemed to seep out of her pores. She sat at the kitchen table while Cora looked for somewhere to put her masterpiece. She laid it on the draining board for now, and thought about pegging it out on the washing line to dry. She switched the kettle on, took two mugs out of the cupboard, put a splash of milk in both, rinsed the teapot, all the while playing for time in the presence of the very silent Fiona, with a rolling stream of questions going through her mind. Best not to jump the gun, though. Give her time.

She put the mugs on the table and waited for the kettle to boil. Then, having run out of excuses for stalling, she sat down at the table with the teapot, folded her arms and waited.

Fiona tossed her blonde hair away from her face with a twitch of the head. 'Has Gwyn spoken to you?'

Her heart sank. 'What about?'

'I *knew* it,' Fiona said. 'He promised he would.'

Cora imagined a tangle of visions and misfortunes and settled on the worst of them. 'Has he lost his job?'

'No. Why? What have you heard?'

'Nothing. I just thought...' Cora had never been alone in Fiona's company before. Gwyn had always been there, like a cushion, making things comfortable between them. She didn't know of anything they had in common, apart from him. 'You'd better tell me what you've come to say, otherwise it will be a wasted journey for you,' she pointed out, pouring the tea.

'It's Lottie,' Fiona said. 'She's causing trouble between us.'

'Really?' This was unexpected. 'How is she causing trouble?'

'Well, she's always there, isn't she? Hovering, keeping an eye on her dad. She doesn't like me, she's made it clear. And I can't say anything to her, can I? Gwyn keeps telling me it's her home. Well, it's my home too, he doesn't seem to realise that.' Fiona rested her hands flat on the table and frowned at her engagement ring. She took a deep breath and looked hopefully at Cora. 'Listen, I know she stays with you sometimes. I was thinking – maybe you could ask her to move in with you permanently.'

Cora paused with her cup halfway to her lips.

'I mean,' Fiona continued more confidently now, warming to her plan, 'let's face it, no offence, Cora, but you're not getting any younger, are you? Lottie can keep an eye on you, kill two birds with one stone, you know what I'm saying? It will be nice for you to have the company, won't it?'

'I have plenty of company and I don't need anyone to keep an eye on me.' Cora felt a wave of dislike wash over her. 'And Gwyn's right. It was her home first.' Seeing Fiona flush under her make-up, she tried to soften her tone. She didn't want to be the cause of any conflict between Gwyn and Fiona. Fiona made Gwyn happy, that's what she had to remember, that was the important thing. But it was obvious that Gwyn was no longer making Fiona happy and she was sad about that. 'I know it's difficult—'

'Exactly. It really is,' Fiona said, her voice wobbling.

Cora breathed in deeply through her nose. 'Lottie hasn't said anything about coming to live here. I don't think it's ever entered her mind.'

'Yeah, and you know why? Because she wants to break me and Gwyn up.'

Cora stirred her tea slowly. 'I don't think she does, you know. She loves her dad and she knows you make him happy.'

'Do I?' Fiona asked in a high, tremulous voice. 'So why doesn't he do something about it? He's infuriating!' She picked up her mug, gulped down her tea noisily, then slammed it down on the table.

Careful! Cora wanted to say sharply. You had to respect people's things!

For a moment she thought of Elisavet with her sweeping yellow duster and wondered if her other possessions would be safe. 'I'll have a word with Gwyn and Lottie,' she said. 'Look, obviously this situation isn't easy for them either. It can't be, can it? Tensions in the family can lead to all sorts of unhappy outcomes. I should know.'

'Thanks.' Fiona bit her lip and tried to smile. 'I knew you'd understand.' She got up, rinsed her cup under the tap and put it rim down on Cora's masterpiece lying on the draining board.

13

Cora phoned Gwyn to invite them to supper on a Tuesday evening when the house was still spotless from Elisavet's endeavours.

'The three of us?' Gwyn asked.

'No, I thought – just you and Lottie, this time.'

Silence. Then: 'Ah.'

Cora wondered about the way he said 'Ah,' whether it was with disappointment or understanding. 'The thing is, Gwyn—' she began.

'I know,' he interrupted her. 'Fiona is picky about her food.'

'Well, yes, she is, a bit.' It was true, she was. Fiona had developed a habit of sniffing her food before eating it and then making all sorts of faces once she'd put it in her mouth. She had become proud of being fussy, but Cora felt it reflected badly on the rest of them for enjoying the food Fiona had decided wasn't up to scratch. She wondered if this fussiness had rubbed off on Gwyn and decided to be specific. 'I'll make pasta with a tomato-based sauce, Parmesan cheese and bread rolls.'

'Delightful!' he said. 'See you Tuesday.'

'Can't go wrong with that menu,' she said aloud. Fruit salad to follow. And then she'd broach the subject of Fiona's visit. It was always easier to digest difficult news on a full stomach, she'd found.

She gathered up the birthday cards from the windowsill and put them in a drawer.

She wasn't sure what the supper would achieve, except that it was easier to get these things out in the open, talk about them, hopefully put things right. Her loyalty and her love were always first and foremost with her son and granddaughter, but the more she thought about it, the more she could see it from Fiona's point of view. Gwyn had loved Regina and you couldn't divorce the dead.

Mind you, that whole business of Fiona telling her she was getting on in years had tarnished her sympathy for her somewhat. Getting on in years? We're all getting on in years at exactly the same rate, she thought. Should have said so at the time.

The previous year Fiona had been happily talking about the wedding; she'd been checking out venues and considering colour schemes with swatches of fabric. Cora was enjoying it. Everyone loves a wedding! But then she'd looked at Gwyn, sitting on the sofa saying nothing, just listening to his fiancée with a helpless expression, as if he was being carried away from shore by a rogue wave to a distant horizon.

'Should I buy a hat?' Cora had asked brightly.

'Not yet,' he'd replied, equally brightly.

Oh, Gwyn bach.

Personally, she'd never thought that long engagements were a good idea. She felt that marriage vows should be promised in the first crazy flush of love, before practicalities came into the picture; before a couple started weighing up the cost of a wedding versus a deposit on a house, for instance.

So she'd kept quiet, being diplomatic.

That might have been a mistake. She had discovered over the years that we set a lot of store by what people think, even if it was something they just said off the cuff. What was just her opinion might have sounded to Gwyn like an instruction to marry Fiona. If she'd said something, they might have been married by now and Lottie would have given up trying to come between them, if that's what she was doing.

Dew, listen to me, power mad, she thought, believing I've got more influence than I actually have. It was a trait she saw clearly in others, like Megan's father, Idwal, thinking he was responsible for Cardiff being bombed because he insulted Lord Haw-Haw in a pub, but normally she was able to ignore in herself.

* * *

Gwyn and Lottie came on the dot of six thirty on Tuesday, all smiles and as happy to be there as she was to see them.

'Come in, come in,' she said, draining the pasta.

'Something smells good,' Gwyn said.

'It's only pasta, it is,' she said, taking off her apron.

When Cora invited people to come for food, she didn't like to keep them waiting. She handed the wine bottle and corkscrew to Gwyn to open, no good reason for that, she was perfectly capable of opening her own wine bottles but in her opinion you could take independence too far sometimes. 'Sit wherever you like. I've got a sauce ladle here somewhere,' she said, looking in the cutlery drawer. 'Here you are! Dig in!'

She joined them at the table where they looked expectantly from one to the other.

Gwyn was wearing a blue floral shirt, very jazzy, and Lottie was wearing torn jeans and two black ribbed vests, one on top of the other. Her hair was in a high ponytail and she looked very young without make-up.

Cora wished she had invited them because she enjoyed their company, and not because she had a mediation to perform. However, she never wanted them to feel obliged to come as a duty, and so she was sparing with her invitations. She thought again of Fiona saying she was 'getting on'. The cheek of her.

'What are you thinking?' Lottie asked her, one inherited eyebrow quizzically raised, transferring her fork to her right hand in the American style.

'Me?' For a moment, Cora hesitated and then she put her cutlery down. Get it out of the way, she thought. 'Tell you the truth it's Fiona, it is. She came to see me.'

'Did she? Why? What for?' Lottie asked warily.

'She said that in her opinion, your house isn't big enough for the three of you. That was the gist of it, anyway. Getting it off her chest, like.' She glanced at Gwyn. She'd always found it difficult to know what he was thinking, and now, to her relief, his grey eyes as he looked back at her were calm and untroubled. 'I know you love her, son.'

He looked faintly surprised. 'Well, yes.'

'And Lottie, she talked about the possibility of you coming to live here. I didn't know if that was her idea, or yours.'

'What?' Lottie's angry expression said it all. 'Why would she say that? I've got absolutely no intention of coming to live here!'

'Lottie!' Gwyn shouted. 'Don't be rude!'

'It's all right, Gwyn,' Cora said quickly, her face burning.

Lottie dropped her fork into her pasta bowl. 'Sorry, I didn't mean it that way. I'm furious with her for discussing us behind our backs! She's not right for you, Dad, she's an airhead,' she said indignantly. 'I don't understand why you can't see it for yourself. It's not as if she tries to hide it.'

Cora sprinkled too much Parmesan on her pasta in agitation and wondered how on earth it was that Gwyn hadn't noticed the atmosphere in the house. It had spread here now, like smoke, the kitchen was heavy with it. She bitterly regretted getting involved at all. Fiona should have left her out of it and they should have worked it out between them. It was underhanded, now she thought about it, because like it or not, it had made her take sides, although she didn't know whose side she was taking.

Gwyn frowned and stiffened for a moment. He opened his mouth as if to argue and then he shook his head to clear it. 'Fiona doesn't mean any harm, it's just the way she is,' he said to Lottie. He frowned. 'I didn't know you two didn't get on. Why didn't you say something?'

Lottie's eyes filled with tears and she wiped them away roughly with her napkin. 'It doesn't matter,' she said desperately, and took a deep breath. 'Ignore me. Like Grandma says, as long as you're happy.'

'I'll talk to her,' Gwyn said. He rubbed his face with his hands and shook his head. 'I thought you'd like having another woman in the house.'

'Why?' Lottie replied bitterly. 'To replace my mother?'

Gwyn winced. 'No,' he said. He added softly as if he'd just realised it, 'No one could replace her.'

And there it was, out in the open. As soon as he said it and the way he said it, Cora understood the situation clearly for the first time. She wondered why she hadn't seen it before. Much as Cora loved her granddaughter and felt sorry for her son, she suddenly felt even more sorry for Fiona. Fiona had been bright and carefree when she and Gwyn first met, a lovely girl. She was a new beginning, a fresh start, but now they had tangled her up in their guilt and loss – yes, she'd done it herself, too – treated her as a poor replacement for Regina. No wonder she had become so particular about things, and so self-centred. They hadn't seen her for the person she was, only for who she was not.

He ought to marry her. She would feel secure if she was his wife, Cora believed that very strongly. Being alone was fine. She wasn't lonely, she had friends, but nothing could compare to a good marriage in her view.

They carried on eating in silence, silver clattering against china, and then Cora said brightly, 'Gladdie's started an art club because she won third prize at the Agricultural Society Art Show.'

To her relief, Gwyn started to laugh. 'Is that your painting, stuck on the fridge?'

'Yes.' Cora sipped her wine and said craftily, 'What does it look like to you?'

'Strawberry mousse,' he said.

'A nudist beach,' Lottie suggested.

The three of them stared at it speculatively for a moment.

'Well, there we are,' Cora said happily. 'The joy of abstract is that it's whatever you see in it.'

Gwyn grinned. 'Did Gladdie tell you that?'

'Yes. She's educating us.'

'Who else is in the club?'

'Megan and Elisavet.'

'Elisavet? How is she doing?'

'We haven't got her to smile yet, if that's what you're asking.' Cora ate her last mouthful of pasta and put her fork down. 'She's living in a hostel at the moment. It's difficult for her.' Her face clouded over. 'Her fiancé has told her it's over because they're on different sides of the conflict all of a sudden.'

'He's broken up with her?' Gwyn looked startled. 'She said his family weren't happy but he was supposed to be coming over here to join her. She couldn't wait to see him again. She misses him.'

'They've split up because of a *war*?' Lottie asked with the wholehearted innocence of a girl who had never had to experience one. 'That's so random.'

'Is she still cleaning for you?' Gwyn asked.

'Yes.' Cora looked at him, expecting him to ask her whether Elisavet had supplied her references yet. 'The art club is for her, really. Gladdie thinks she's lonely. We're going to show her around, take her to beauty spots, cheer her up.'

'Aww, Ma,' he said, and his eyes were gentle. He scraped back his chair and got up rather abruptly. He rested his hands on Cora's shoulders and kissed the top of her head.

Being loved and understood. The bliss of it soothed her to her soul.

'It makes no sense! If they love each other, how can they suddenly be enemies?' Lottie demanded, looking from her father to her grandmother.

'Good question,' Cora replied, reaching for the fruit salad, and then she realised Lottie was serious and waiting for an answer. She put the serving spoon down again, and thought about Frank's notebook. 'I suppose the question of who the enemy is depends solely on your viewpoint,' she said.

14

That Friday evening as promised, Elisavet turned up right on time. Her dark hair was loose, and she was wearing a blue T-shirt and jeans as if it was her night off.

Cora took her through to the front room and handed her the black leather notebook which was still warm because she'd been pressing it against her heart like a Bible. The mended china boy was on the mantelpiece, next to the lump of clay.

She lit a large church candle in the hearth as it was too warm to make a fire. 'Come and sit here,' she gestured, because it seemed only right that Elisavet should sit in Frank's chair to speak his words.

She went to the kitchen and poured a glass of wine and put it on the little mahogany table next to Elisavet because the occasion seemed to call for it. She did it very carefully and respectfully, like a ritual, wanting everything to be done properly. There! And then she settled down in the chair opposite to listen.

Elisavet opened the notebook and began to translate.

November 1944
'Hands up! Schnell!'
I was face to face with the enemy, standing in the rot and decay of the

ditch, paralysed by terror, facing interrogation, torture and death by a British bullet.

I wanted to raise my hands in surrender but adrenaline had petrified me. I couldn't move them and they hung down uselessly like lead at my sides.

'Move! Schnell!'

The voice was fading now, and I woke with a jerk to find my heavy hands were up after all, my fingers caught tightly in the luggage rack webbing over my head, and I was not in the ditch, nor crushed in a cattle truck with fifty other men, but alone in a comfortable railway carriage in enemy country. Weary men were streaming by along the platform.

So here we are, we have reached our destination, wherever here is, impossible to tell because the station signs are painted over.

I took my bag down from the luggage rack and as I did so I noticed the small, printed sign fixed beneath it: Great Western Railway. To my surprise the map detailed all the road and rail links along the route, a map that had obviously been overlooked by those in authority who should have known better – lucky for me!

I took out my fountain pen and copied the map on the inside of my cap as meticulously as I could, a wavering line of coast on which I wrote the words: Newport Cardiff Bridgend Port Talbot Neath – the word 'port' had me buzzing. What good fortune! Port equalled freedom!

I smoothed my hair into place, adjusted the worn grey field cap on my head, opened the door into the corridor and joined the men stepping down onto the platform into this chilly November day.

Milling around in the station, hundreds of defeated men shuffled from foot to foot to keep warm. The lucky ones. An old man told me so in Calais before we were divided into groups, separated from our close comrades indiscriminately.

'Lucky? How do you make that out?' I asked him, genuinely wanting to know.

'You're a good-looking chap, life will be kind to you,' the old man said cheerfully. 'And more importantly – we're alive, aren't we?'

Barely, in his case, I thought now. The optimistic man was skin and bone, scooped up by Hitler to make up numbers in our depleted ranks.

I licked my dry lips, thinking of the biscuit and the cup of tea that the *guards had handed out when we got on the train. I'd let the biscuit dissolve blissfully on my tongue, making it last.*

On the station platform we were all thrown together, the German Army, Kriegsmarine, Waffen SS and Luftwaffe, the SS claiming superiority, and all getting frustrated because further up the platform there was some kind of a commotion going on. The Nazi officers were refusing to carry their own kit bags because it was beneath their dignity to take orders from a Britisher of a lower rank like common soldiers.

A year ago, I would have approved of this approach. Rules were rules! Now, I looked around warily, trying to gauge the reaction of those around me and wishing we could just get on with it. I caught the eye of a young lad in a filthy uniform. The lad was crying silently and his tears were leaving clean tracks down his cheeks to his jaw. Young, but not too young to fight, just as the lucky old man was not too old.

All welcome! Roll up! Roll up!

'They're going to shoot us,' the lad said fearfully, gasping out the words between sobs.

Which is exactly what I was thinking myself, because that's one sure thing we knew about the British: they interrogated you and then they shot you.

But so far I hadn't seen any prisoners shot although I was initially suspicious that the tea and biscuits were to be our Last Supper. 'No, they won't,' I reassured the kid. 'Geneva Convention.'

Suddenly a bad-tempered, self-important official in a dark uniform with gold braid burst out of the ticket office in a state of fury. In a strange accent, he ordered us to vacate his railway station at once.

The Nazi officers saluted him, satisfied that their request for a superior officer had been granted. They followed his orders to leave the station immediately and we started moving at last.

Lining the road ahead of us I could see the local civilians silently watching from the kerbside.

Their silence unnerved me. It was worse than the obscenities of the French and the spit of the Belgians. These people were not angry, but disappointed.

Me too, I thought.

I had started to wonder if the whole mess of war had been wasteful and pointless, but I goose-stepped along anyway because that was what I'd been trained to do, and as I marched I glanced at the faces in the crowd.

The silence was broken by a strange man shouting hoarsely: 'Love thine enemy!' Behind us in the station the guard whistled and the steam hissed and the train began chugging noisily along the railway track, and I remembered the map I'd copied into my cap. It was such a wonderful stroke of luck, my one bit of good fortune in the darkness of chaos, that I smiled to myself.

A young woman on the pavement responded by smiling back at me. She was an unusual woman, with vivid green hair and a bright yellow face, but her smile was sweet and sympathetic.

BANG!

The blow landed hard and unexpected on the back of my head, like being hit by a stick. It knocked my cap off. My map! The stick was in fact the bony arm of a furious, middle-aged woman, yelling at me: 'Murderer!'

I stumbled, trying to retrieve the cap and the men behind me laughed grimly and marched into me, shoving me forward because everyone liked a bit of sport, a bit of fun at someone else's expense.

My unexpected hope for the future, my means of escape had gone, it had gone just like that. 'Hey you! Keep up, will you,' a British guard encouraged me, with no particular ferocity.

The wild man in the sandwich board was still shouting: 'Love thine enemy!'

The SS officers at the front started singing patriotically, drowning him out, and the rest of us took it up: 'Deutschland, Deutschland Uber Alles'.

I too belted it out tunelessly, and the crowd was a wary audience for fifteen hundred stubborn, defiant voices as we marched to our new home in Island Farm, POW Camp 198.

Here, Elisavet stopped reading and closed Frank's black notebook. She placed it carefully on the mahogany table next to her now empty wineglass and looked up at Cora.

Don't stop! Cora wanted to urge her, because for the past hour or so she'd been full of the thrill of Frank's story and lively and young again. But remembering she was mature and sensible, she smiled gratefully.

'Thank you, Elisavet. Lovely!' She rapped her chest with her knuckles, mimicking the thud of her heart. The candle flickered on the hearth. 'Took me back, it did.' She smiled, because she felt so at home in the past she didn't want to leave it. 'Can I get you anything?' she asked hopefully. 'More wine?'

'No, no,' Elisavet said, shaking her head. Her dark hair slinked around her shoulders. She got to her feet. 'I can translate more the next time if you like.'

'Oh, can you? Great, thank you, that would be—' Cora felt tears of gratitude rush hot and unexpected in her eyes, and she blinked them away. 'I'd like that,' she nodded, and she followed Elisavet to the door.

She watched her go down the path and when she was out of sight Cora stayed in the doorway listening to the night noises with a sense of dislocation. She frowned, wondering what was different. Then she realised that it was the sound of peaceful quiet.

Silence is a luxury, she thought. The war had been full of constant noise, from one source or another.

Funny how the past held on to its place in a lifespan like a museum of the memory, always open to be revisited and reviewed.

She closed the door.

And relived, she thought.

15

1944

The factory was noisy and monstrous, but Cora was warm in her overalls, thinking about the soldier's cap as she worked. It was a relic of the soldier's war: dust, blood, hair oil and gun oil.

Concentrating hard on the monotony of filling the pellets, Cora found her mind flying free, reliving conversations, and the radio tuned in and out of her consciousness. She had long since stopped registering the sharp smell and vivid colour of TNT. Time passed by playfully as it pleased, dragging sometimes and leaping forward at others, and any diversion was a welcome marker to peg the day on, to distinguish it from the previous day or the one to come.

She found herself thinking of the fair-haired man who owned the cap, and the cap was their connection. She thought about him a lot that day. Her mother had hit him while he was defenceless, and she kept coming back to that uneasy sense of shame and guilt.

What Cora remembered most about the moment the Germans arrived was her mother's accusing scream.

It seemed, looking back over the moment, that everything else was hushed, frozen by her mother's brutal sweep of the arm as her anger tore out of her.

Cora had the impression that the faded cap momentarily blotted out the hazy sun as it sailed through the air. Didn't, of course, because it was instantly trampled on.

And she remembered the triumphant look that Jane had given her, knowing that her daughter would be on her side.

And I was, then, Cora thought. I sort of was, because of Owen.

But then she remembered the shock of the blow and the desperation in the prisoner's eyes and felt only pity for him.

* * *

Back home after work, she took the cap out again and sat on her bed, wondering what to do with it. It was worn and the grey had faded to pale blue, and when she held it to her face she breathed in the smells of earlier days. There was another smell, too, the smell of him, the man. Her body reacted to it, it was a good smell and she hummed with appreciation and then wondered about the safety of her soul. She put the cap into her pocket, evidence of her mother's wild behaviour, and her own perfidy in picking it up again, the souvenir of a good-looking man.

She couldn't keep it and it wasn't hers to throw away.

There was only one person she could think of to talk to about it. Love thine enemy, as Idwal would say. Probably didn't mean it literally, though. She went to the window and looked out across the familiar countryside, the bare trees, the fields waiting to be ploughed, the dense dark woods, the mountains in the distance, all faded shades of grey and brown, briefly lit by an unexpected flash of sunlight through a gap in the clouds.

Later, she watched for Idwal coming home from the pub, hunched against the cold.

When she saw him, she hurried outside and asked him if she could have a word.

Idwal lit a cigarette he took from behind his ear and screwed up his eyes to look at her through the smoke. As an afterthought, he offered her one from behind his other ear.

'No thanks,' she said, surprised that he'd offered. What she liked about Idwal was that he had his own opinion about things and he didn't much care what people thought. 'You know when my mother smacked that soldier, knocked his cap off?'

Idwal nodded, frowning.

'Well, I picked it up afterwards,' Cora said, and she could feel the colour rush to her face. 'But now I've got it I don't know what to do with it, see.'

Idwal's face smoothed out with relief. 'That's it?' he asked her as if a burden had lifted from him. 'That's your problem? Dew, I thought it was going to be something terrible.'

'Like what?'

'Nothing specific, but you hear all sorts these days,' he said cryptically, and now that he no longer had to use the smoke as a screen to shield behind, he stubbed his cigarette out on the sole of his boot and put it behind his ear again. 'I'm very relieved it's something simple. You'll have to give the cap back to him. It's his, after all, and they don't have much in the way of possessions, going by the size of those kit bags.'

She thought about it, and it made perfect sense. 'But how do I do that? I don't know his name.'

'You know where he lives though. You pass the camp every day,' Idwal pointed out. 'Keep an eye out for him. You're bound to recognise him eventually.'

* * *

It was true, Cora, Megan and Gladdie did pass the camp every day on their way to and from the factory because it was a short cut along the edge of the field, and also because it reassured them to see the prisoners safe behind barbed wire. They agreed without bias that the Germans weren't as wholesome as the GIs nor as seductive as the Italians. Of course they weren't. These prisoners were dangerous fanatics, everyone felt that.

'And the way they look at us,' Gladdie said indignantly, 'as if we've dropped from the moon.'

'As if they'd never seen yellow women before,' Cora said. 'With green hair.'

'And hair as bright as an orange. They've lived very sheltered lives.'

'Somewhere in Germany there must be women doing exactly the same job as us, writing messages on the shells same as we do.'

'Only we do it better.' Cora squinted at the dark yellow sky. Clouds were approaching from the hills in a dense grey line. 'It's going to snow,' she said with a shiver.

After Idwal gave her the advice that he did, she'd been looking out for the man with fair hair as she passed the camp. 'Here,' she would say to him, throwing him the cap. 'I think this is yours.' And she would watch his eyes brighten. She imagined apologising to him on behalf of her mother. But she wasn't sure that one could apologise for another person. She could only apologise for herself, for not throwing the cap back to him when she'd had the chance. She imagined explaining to him about Owen and at the same time, remembering that he was the enemy, and the words the guard said to her: *killed a lot more people than him.*

16

1992

It is a terrible thing to have a conscience, Cora thought the next time Elisavet came to clean.

In the same way that she had wanted to return the cap to the soldier all those years ago, she wanted to make things right for Elisavet today, because she was grateful to her for translating the notebook.

It was a failing of hers to want to make people happy.

There was obviously no chance of Lottie moving in with her and she still felt vaguely insulted by the sharp refusal, even though it had been Fiona's idea in the first place, not hers.

'I'm just off, Elisavet,' she said.

Elisavet was cleaning the bath vigorously and Cora stood awkwardly in the doorway with her bag over her shoulder.

Elisavet straightened up to face her and blew a strand of hair away from her face. 'Okay.'

'Listen – I've got a bedroom going spare here. It's yours if you want it. It might be more comfortable than living in Queen's Lane.'

For a moment, Elisavet looked blank. 'I am comfortable,' she said defensively.

'Yes, I know. What I'm asking is, would you like to live here, in this house?'

Silence. A frown. Then: 'Live here with you?'

'Yes.'

'Thank you, but no. I like to be private,' Elisavet said, and she went back to cleaning the bath.

* * *

Megan answered the door with her hair tied up into two fluffy grey bunches. 'I'm trying out a new style,' she explained, puffing them up like pom-poms. 'What do you think?'

Cora glanced at a sceptical Gladdie and then took another look at Megan's new style. 'If you want my opinion, Meg, you look like an elderly Mickey Mouse.' Cora was still smarting from Elisavet's swift refusal. First Lottie, now her! It stung. 'But it suits you,' she added quickly to soften her opinion. 'Sorry, I'm feeling out of sorts today. Out of the kindness of my heart I told Elisavet she could move in with me and she said no, she likes to be private. I'm not that bad, am I?' she asked. 'You'd move in with me, wouldn't you, Megan?'

'I don't know.' Megan pursed her lips. 'Depends on the circumstances.'

'Go on then. Name them.'

'If my house fell down, for instance. In a storm in the dead of night. And I was desperate. Then yes, I'd consider it.'

'I'd move in with you, Cora,' Gladdie said encouragingly, 'as long as we had a rota for shopping and cooking and TV viewing and that sort of thing. I've got my Dymo label maker, we could label everything so there's no confusion.'

Cora thought about it briefly. 'There's a lot to be said for living alone,' she decided.

'Elisavet's very unhappy, there's no doubt about that,' Megan said. 'I heard her crying in the kitchen as if she'd lost all hope. I told her there was always hope, that she shouldn't worry because people can change – thinking of Enid, I was. It's funny, before that I hadn't thought about her in years but it was the sound of her crying that took me back.'

The three of them sighed in unison. There was a story to boost the spirits and give you hope! You would have to have a heart of stone not to be cheered by it, even if Enid did suffer the worst fate anyone could imagine.

'I always thought Enid was the closest Bridgend had to a film star,' Gladdie said.

'Beautiful, she was,' Megan said, 'like Rita Hayworth with her copper hair.'

Cora agreed. 'She shone her glow on us. Men looked at us differently when we were with her.'

Enid had dived headfirst into the war years as if it was her element, as if she was born to freedom and glamour. But the trouble was, at the time Enid didn't care at all who she splashed on the way in.

* * *

The following week, Gladdie said she was taking the art club to the Royal Ordnance Factory memorial in the centre of town to give Elisavet a taste of local history and inspire her with the interesting story of Enid. They would be painting in the wild, she said, making it sound as if they were on safari, and so they would need to take sketchbooks.

The three of them walked from Island Farm Avenue through green fields and along the leafy path by the side of the clear, rushing River Ogmore. They were meeting Elisavet on the Old Bridge.

From a distance they saw Elisavet leaning on the bridge wall waiting for them, her dark hair blowing in the breeze. Behind her, framed by a narrow alley, was a glimpse into the centre of the town.

Cora always felt the arched stone bridge was a portal into a different world.

'There she is with her sketchbook, bless her!' Gladdie said. 'She's in for a treat!'

Cora had been wondering a lot these last few days about what they had learnt during their long lives, if anything, that was worth talking about. It wasn't a question that could be answered easily, but Enid was a perfect example. Beautiful Enid. It was a love story turned on its head if ever you needed one! And it was a way of telling Elisavet more about themselves without being self-centred about it.

The Royal Ordnance Factory memorial was situated on New Bridge, the next bridge along from Old Bridge. They were taking Elisavet to see it because it was a tribute to their work during the war years. The list of names was surprisingly short, considering the thousands of people the factory had employed.

The inscription on the slate read:

Remember with great gratitude all those who worked at the Bridgend
Arsenal and especially those who were killed there.

'That's us,' Cora said. 'We worked there.'

'We weren't killed there, obviously,' Megan added helpfully to Elisavet, making a joke.

Cora gave her a look. It was no use trying to make jokes with Elisavet. She was very literal because it wasn't her first language.

'This place, ROF 53, this is where we made munitions,' Gladdie told her. 'We were filling shells. Bombs,' she clarified. 'It's gone now, of course. It closed down after the war.'

'Okay.' Elisavet's dark hair blew across her face and she tucked it behind her ear.

It was one of those days when Elisavet looked young, Cora thought. Maybe it was the housework that aged her, or maybe it was them. They were an acquired taste.

Cora wondered how old she actually was but for some reason she couldn't just ask out of the blue because that would seem as if it was something that mattered. It didn't, particularly, it was just curiosity. 'We had a friend, her name was Enid. She came to Bridgend from North Wales.'

'Beautiful girl,' Megan added warmly, 'with hair like a newly minted penny.'

'Older than us,' Cora said. Funny how age mattered even if you tried to pretend it didn't. 'She came to Bridgend to get away from her father, who was a drunk. You know what I mean, an alcoholic?'

Elisavet nodded seriously. 'Yes, I know it.'

'She was looking for a husband and she fell in love with Temperance. Mostly because of his name. Ha ha! I'm joking. He was much older than she was, round faced, lively, and the truth was, she could have had anyone she wanted, so he was happy. She was like a beauty queen, wasn't she, Megan? Made to a better standard than the rest of us. Taller, prettier. She turned heads. When she was fifteen she had attended the Home Training Centre to learn domestic skills, which was four months of being told how to cook nutritious meals, how to launder shirts, how to darn, knit and sew, how to clean the house. The Ministry of Labour had set the scheme up in order to make women more employable as servants, or wives, which was much the same thing in those days. It was compulsory, wasn't it, Gladdie? If you were unemployed.'

'Don't get me started,' Gladdie said, fanning herself.

Elisavet was clutching her sketchbook, frowning at them.

'To be fair, that's got nothing to do with the story,' Megan pointed out.

'It's got a bit to do with it,' Cora said, 'because Temperance could see she was good wife material and that's why they got married. If you don't like the way I'm telling it, Megan, why don't you tell it, then?'

'See, ultimately,' Megan said to Elisavet, 'the Ministry of Labour made girls into better wives so they would have a man to look after them, you see? When Enid met Temperance she could see the advantages of marrying him because she'd been trained for it and he was a good earner. It was a means to an end.'

Elisavet frowned and tossed her hair away from her face. 'Your friend Enid,' she asked them, 'she didn't mind staying home and being a wife?'

It was an interesting question.

'Oh, yes, she minded,' Cora said.

17

1944

Enid didn't want to be a housewife, she wanted to work in the factory with Cora, Gladdie and Megan. Temperance was dead against it, because he liked having her at home. They turned up together at Cora's after tea, both looking for an ally. Cora was washing her father's shirts in the sink, and she left them to soak and dried her hands on her apron.

She was dog-tired because a machine had broken down and she'd had to work faster to make up her quota. She closed her eyes and she could still see the hard beauty of the rows upon rows of gleaming shells, and feel the camaraderie of the women and their sympathetic smiles. It had been a good day on the whole because at lunchtime Gladdie had started a jive class to teach them the steps that she'd learnt from Charles, her GI.

Gladdie had got Megan to pretend she was Charles, which made Megan laugh herself limp. Cora smiled to herself. It was good to let off steam before getting back to work.

'Wakey wakey!' Enid was brandishing a newspaper around. 'They're advertising for women to work in the factory again. I'll be safe there, playing my part against the Nazis.' She slapped Temperance with the newspaper. 'Tell him, Cora!'

Cora looked at Temperance. She knew he didn't want Enid to go to work in a factory, of all places, partly out of pride and partly because he was afraid for her.

'It's true, they're always looking for more workers,' she said.

Temperance did a double take as if he'd only just noticed her. 'Dew, Cora! Look at you! Your hair's as green as ivy and your skin, well – you remind me of a daffodil, you do.' He turned to Enid. 'See? That's what Brackla does to you, it colours you unnatural. Trying to put her off, I am, Cora. She cares about her looks.'

'So do I,' Cora said ruefully. Budgies. *Who's a pretty girl, then?*

'I'll wear make-up,' Enid said. 'I'll be able to afford it if I work. The job offers good conditions and good pay, and we're killing that lot while we're at it,' Enid said, jerking her head in the direction of the singing from Island Farm camp. It had started in just one hut, but now the whole place was lively with marching songs.

Oh, but Enid was beautiful, Cora thought, with her copper hair curled back from her pale face, perching on the edge of Jane's kitchen table because she liked an audience.

Dio came in carrying the coal scuttle, letting in a roar of song before slamming the door on it.

'Did you hear the singing from the camp last night?' Temperance asked him. 'Incessant, it was.'

'Heard it?' Dio gave a grim laugh. 'Hard not to, isn't it?'

'You know, I've never thought of the Germans as being musical.'

Dio mulled it over. 'J. S. Bach was a German.'

Temperance nodded. 'Aye, that's true enough. But he's got a Welsh name.'

Of all the neighbours that Island Farm had housed since 1937, the Germans were by far the worst. They sang their loud, patriotic marching songs day and night, and their singing throbbed above the camp and became corralled by the mountains, creating a funnel of music over Island Farm Avenue. Although the prisoners were contained behind barbed wire, their voices weren't, and the noise was driving them mad.

Temperance turned his pleading gaze onto Dio. 'Tell Enid, will you? Munitions is no job for a married woman, is it? You wouldn't let your Jane work there, would you?'

'Jane's got no need to work there,' Dio said, defending his wife.

'Exactly!' Temperance said, throwing up his hands. 'Neither has Enid.'

He was usually a cheerful man, with a plump boyish face, full of an energy that he didn't always know how to channel constructively. He had been barred from Swansea football club for being rowdy. All the supporters were rowdy, truth be told, but his rowdiness was the loudest and he expressed his emotions freely, without the safety net of civility.

Enid said she was so utterly bored with her life she was glad of any diversion. Boredom was a terrible thing, it sapped the energy out of her. 'The hand that held the Hoover turns out shells,' she added, holding up the advert.

Temperance looked dismayed, because there was no getting away from it.

'If you don't like boredom you won't like the factory,' Cora said, resting her chin on her fist.

'Whose side are you on, Cora?' Enid asked sharply.

Dio crouched to put the coal on the dying embers. When he straightened he had a fringe of soot on his white hair. 'I've been thinking of getting up a petition to send to Hitler,' he said, 'asking him to put an end to the singing. I can't get to sleep when I'm on the night shift.'

'I'm not sure he's going to take much notice of a petition, Dio,' Temperance said doubtfully.

'Someone needs to put a stop to it anyway, because the rumours in the pit are that they're singing to drown out the sound of tunnelling.'

For a moment they all fell silent and looked at each other. It was an awful thought if it was true.

Cora stared at her father and folded her arms defiantly. 'The Germans can't dig a tunnel without making a mess,' she said logically. 'And they'd be digging through solid concrete floors. And then once they were through the floor, they'd have to start digging through clay.'

'I'm just telling you what I've heard,' her father said. 'And our chaps managed to do it,' he pointed out.

They fell silent for a moment.

'Little good it did them,' Temperance said. He lifted his chin and scratched the bristles on his neck. He glanced at the feeble flame in the grate. 'We should plan for it anyway, I suppose,' he said after a moment. 'We should work out what action we'll take if they do escape. We'll have to organise a committee, work out our roles. We should keep our shotguns ready at all times.'

Dio nodded. 'It's about time we took action.'

'Tell you what, we'll meet at our house.'

'Will we, Temperance?' Enid said, tilting her head. 'Heaven help us!'

'I'll pass the word around there's going to be a meeting,' Dio said. 'It will set Jane's mind at rest. It agitates her something awful that there are hundreds of them just a stone's throw away and she can't do anything about it. You know, because of...' He trailed off.

Cora knew the unspoken end of that sentence.

'I'll put the kettle on.' He headed for the stove and changed his mind. 'Tell you what, this calls for something stronger than tea. How about a whisky, Temp?' he asked, rubbing his hands together.

Whisky? Cora was suddenly wide awake and her heart plunged as she watched her father go into the pantry. He'd gone to fetch the decanter. She stared at him in panic.

Last May, when her mother was at the WI knitting socks for servicemen and her father was at choir practice in the pub, Gladdie would bring her GI Charles around to Cora's house. Very sociable it was, too, because Charles always brought a friend with him and a couple of pairs of nylon stockings. Why GIs had unlimited access to nylons she didn't know. It was a mystery.

Gladdie's Charles was a tall, good-natured man from Texas with a face full of freckles and bright red hair that was almost the same colour as Gladdie's, only natural.

The first time he came with the gift of stockings, Cora was so delighted that she felt she should be generous with him in turn. She had gone into the pantry to look for something, and standing on the shelf next to a half-full packet of dried milk was the crystal whisky decanter that her father had inherited from his father, whisky and all. Her father had never touched it, so it was full.

Cora removed the glass stopper, took a sharp sniff in case it was off, and blinked her watering eyes. Dew! She fetched the four small glasses that they'd used for egg cups before the war, poured whisky in each and handed them around.

'Bottoms up!' Charles said, and Gladdie giggled.

'Bottoms up!'

'Good health!'

Cora topped up the whisky decanter with water, and she clinked glasses with whoever Charles had brought with him as company for her, making small talk and getting the boy to tell her about America, that land of films and glamour, while Gladdie and Charles went to the front room to cuddle and murmur in private.

Now, Cora was full of dread as she watched her father come back into the kitchen and pour the whisky into those same glass egg cups, one for Temperance and one for himself, crouching to check the levels with scrupulous fairness before giving up and extravagantly filling them to the brim. As he poured, the crystal decanter threw rainbows of light on the tablecloth.

The whisky had been dark once, Cora remembered, but now it was pale as straw.

Oh, Lor, she thought, going back to the sink to rinse the shirts and letting the water drain out.

She braced herself as Dio choked on his drink.

Now I'm for it, she thought.

'My word! That's strong stuff!' he said, patting his chest.

A miracle! Cora relaxed and smiled at him, feeling drunk with relief.

'Takes me back,' Temperance said approvingly. 'It's good stuff, Dio.'

'Belonged to my father, it did.'

The back door opened and Jane came in, removing her black hat. She frowned at the sight of her husband and Temperance with the decanter between them, and Enid sitting on her table like a pin-up.

'Hello, Jane,' Enid said brightly.

Dio held up his whisky glass and looked at his wife through it.

'Hello, Enid.' Jane prided herself on being polite so she swiftly turned her irritation onto Dio. 'Drinking, is it?'

'Just a small one,' he said. 'We're planning what we'll do when the Germans tunnel free. They're singing to cover the digging.'

The words changed Jane's mood in an instant. 'I knew it wasn't for the love of music! Good!' she said. 'I hope they dig like the wind! And when the enemy gets out, we'll be waiting for them.'

The enemy. As if they weren't individuals, Cora thought, with their own families, their own beliefs. It was the way she said it that made Cora look at her small, broken mother with an awful foreboding.

'I've been praying for this to happen,' Jane said to her fervently, clutching her hat to her chest. 'They've been delivered unto us for a reason. So that we can pay them back for what they've done to us.'

'That's the spirit,' Temperance said.

18

1992

Even though the art class had started out that day with the best of intentions to share some of Enid's story with Elisavet at the factory workers' memorial, they had done a lot more talking than drawing.

Now it was starting to rain, making wet dints on Cora's sketchpad. Cora looked up at the sky suspiciously, and it was smudged by dirty clouds.

Megan looked up, too. 'See that, Gladdie, it's like a charcoal effect. I'm surprised you haven't pointed it out.'

Gladdie glared at her as if she was about to argue, and then she stared at the sky and called her bluff. 'You're right. Maybe we should get it down on paper while we can, I've got some pencils in my bag somewhere.'

'Or we could have a coffee until the rain passes,' Cora said. 'We could tell Elisavet more about Enid's love story.'

'This is a love story?' Elisavet asked Cora as they hurried to the Bridgend Cafe. 'About this woman who was taught how to be a good wife?'

'Yes, that's the whole point of us telling you. Thinking of your fiancé, we were, because love takes all sorts of unexpected twists and turns during war. You'll find that out for yourself, I expect. Is that a queue?'

At the cafe there was a bit of a last-minute rush to get inside because everyone had the same idea of having a coffee to get out of the rain. Gladdie elbowed her way in. Her asymmetric pink hair was a good distraction – people tended to stop what they were doing to have another look at her.

'Bit lopsided, isn't it?' the waitress said.

The four of them slid damply into a booth by the window, making the vinyl seats squeak.

'Did you all do wife lessons too?' Elisavet asked.

'Do you mean you can't tell?' Megan laughed. 'Ha ha! No, as a matter of fact we didn't do wife lessons. We worked in the factory instead.'

They ordered their coffees, and Gladdie said she fancied a scone, as it was still raining, so they all had scones, which came with cream and little jars of strawberry jam.

With so many damp people in a small space, the windows began to steam up.

'It smells like sheep,' Megan observed, 'with all these wet woollies.'

The door opened again, letting in a fresh breeze of rain-washed air, and the sound of happy laughter made them all look up at once. It was the kind of contagious laughter that made them smile, too, because it was nice to be part of it.

Cora's first impression was of youth, white teeth and wet blond hair. The young couple, looking business-like in navy suits, looked around for a table, and to Cora's surprise she saw that the wet girl was Fiona.

'Hullo?' Cora said, putting a question mark in her voice where it wasn't strictly necessary.

'Hi, Cora,' Fiona said with a smile. She nodded a greeting at Gladdie and Megan.

Megan had a mouthful of scone, as she waved at her full mouth to indicate.

'Hi, Elisavet,' Fiona said, giving her a wave.

'Good afternoon, Fiona,' Elisavet replied, her eyes brightening.

The wet blond man had spotted someone paying at the counter and he immediately pounced on the vacant table with the air of a triumphant hunter. 'Fiona!' he called to her, pointing at it in an exaggerated manner.

'Oh, well done,' she called back, going over to join him in a scraping of chairs.

Cora had never seen a man look more pleased with himself. She turned back to the table and looked at her half-eaten scone on her plate. She'd lost her appetite for it momentarily.

'Well!' Gladdie said, propping her elbows on the table. 'Fiona's back to her old self! Fancy!'

There was only five years' difference in age between Fiona and Gwyn, and Fiona's life had been blessedly straightforward. Her parents were still married, her grandparents lived only a short drive away, and she gave the impression of a person who'd always been loved. Perfect for Gwyn, Cora had thought at the time.

She tilted sideways to look at the man that Fiona was sitting with. He too, she thought resentfully, looked completely untouched by life, as if any worries he'd ever had had just slid right off him. 'I hope his suit's not wool,' she said.

'Are you going to warn Gwyn?' Gladdie asked her.

It had been Cora's first thought.

'Warn him?' she said, as if it had never occurred to her. 'I'll say we bumped into her in the coffee shop, if I remember.' She started eating the scone again because it was very unnatural of her not to finish it, and Gladdie would be bound to attach some meaning to it.

'And there you have it in a nutshell,' Megan said to Elisavet. 'Love, full of twists and turns, just as Cora said.'

19

1944

Cora was the first to arrive at Temperance's meeting of the anti-escape committee. She'd reached a decision during the night and had brought the soldier's crumpled cap with her in her pocket. She would be sorry to relinquish it but she would show some decency towards the prisoner, at least. She'd gone there early hoping to ask Superintendent May quietly if he could return the cap to its owner in the camp, it being lost property, like.

'Hello, Temperance. Is Mr May here?'

'Not yet. Come in, Cora, come, you're the first.' Temperance welcomed her gratefully and straightened the tie under his pullover. 'Enid's upstairs, getting changed for the meeting. Enid! Cora's here! Go into the front room, Cora. It's more formal, for the superintendent.'

He turned to the door to welcome Jane in as she wiped her feet on the doormat and closed it quickly behind her to mute the singing from the camp.

'Listen to them! Gloating! It's a terrible thing to have the Germans in our midst.'

Cora rubbed her thumb on the cap in her pocket. 'What will they do if they escape from Island Farm?' she asked. 'Head for the Channel?'

'They'll go on the rampage, that's what they'll do,' Temperance predicted. 'They'll steal our cars and our food and cut our throats and break into other camps to let their pals out. Then they'll swarm the countryside.' He wiped his mouth with the back of his hand. 'But don't you worry, girl, we won't let them get far. We'll stop them.'

'I'm not worried. I was just wondering.'

Megan, Idwal, Gladdie and Dio came into the house after congregating on the street. The arrival of the Germans in their own backyard, as they put it, had been an extraordinary event and they were keen to compare notes.

'Enid!' Temperance shouted up the stairs. 'Have we got enough chairs?'

Enid came downstairs elegantly as if she was lit by limelight, and joined the little group of neighbours in the cold front room, kept for best. The portraits of Temperance's parents looked sternly down at them from oval frames.

They all sat bolt upright on the best furniture, keeping their coats on and their elbows tucked in to make space. Dio and Jane sat on dining chairs, Temperance in the big armchair with his notes on his lap, Gladdie on a stool next to him and Megan sat on the sofa next to Cora.

Idwal was no use to the discussion, being a pacifist, so Temperance put him in a lowly position on the tapestry footstool. 'I hear you've already taken matters into your own hands, Jane,' Enid said to her, looking amused from the doorway.

'They needed putting in their place. Mind you, you should have seen the respect the Nazis gave to Mr Hill. He gave them a telling off, and they marched away as good as gold. You could have invited him here tonight.'

Temperance grunted. 'I did, but he said he was busy.'

'Pity, that.'

'Superintendent May is coming, though, if he's got the time.'

'If he's got the time? Of course, he's safe enough where he lives. When they get out, we're the ones in the front line, facing desperate men.'

'Be fair, Jane, he hates them as much as we do. His son's in the Far East.'

Temperance told them he had mixed feelings about May. He had taken it for granted that he himself would be the one to chair the meeting as it was his idea, but unfortunately for him, Bill May was a step ahead of him, or as Temperance put it, he'd jumped on the bandwagon. Of course, May had had the unfair advantage of advance warning of the arrival of the prisoners, and his plans were already underway and ready to be implemented, that's what he said.

May arrived only two minutes late, just at the moment that Temperance told them he would start without him.

Superintendent May turned up in police uniform with his cap tucked under his arm and a briefcase, so he looked official.

'Come on in,' Temperance said heartily, putting a brave face on things, although he gave the impression he wouldn't really have minded if Bill May hadn't turned up at all.

Cora had never seen two men look more different.

The policeman had a lean, lined, no-nonsense face, which gave him an unfair advantage. Temperance's own boyish face was round-looking, even when he sucked in his cheeks. In fact, it was the same shape that had won him a bonny baby contest in his early years. 'Still baby-faced!' his mother would greet him affectionately in chapel in front of everyone, pinching his cheek. As if it was his own doing, as if he'd decided to cling onto it to please her.

'This meeting is to discuss our strategy as a precaution, just in case the prisoners attempt to escape,' Temperance said as May sat on the sofa between Megan and Cora.

'Correction. We *know* they will try to escape,' May said. It sounded like a reprimand.

'Oh? How do we know that?'

'They've been ordered to. It's their solemn duty. Hence the need to be vigilant.' May was taking the Germans' escape seriously, and as it turned out, even more seriously than Temperance himself.

May had come clutching his own plans, ready-typed, with no discussion or voting involved, and he had already, he said, coordinated with the control centre.

Temperance was now bitterly regretting having invited May to the meeting at all.

His own plans for a plan were still a bit hazy and open to input and suggestion, whereas May had produced a folder out of his briefcase, with sheets of paper already typed up official-like. What's more, he told them, he had already discussed the matter of a possible escape with the camp's commander.

'I declare this meeting open,' Temperance announced belatedly, taking the upper hand. Then everybody spoke at once, not to him but to the superintendent.

'Are we safe?'

'Do we need a petition?'

'Are the Nazis dangerous?'

What a question! 'Of course they're dangerous!' Temperance shouted over everyone in exasperation. 'That's the whole point!' and Bill May raised his hands for hush as if he was addressing a mighty throng.

When they all stopped talking to listen to him speak, his voice was a mere whisper, as reverential as if he was in chapel. 'Ruthless, too,' he breathed, so softly you could hear a mouse snore. 'And they will, I assure you, attempt an escape. It's in their blood.'

Temperance stared at him, and cupped his hand around his ear.

Cora was not so much taken by his words, which were repetition of what he'd already said, but by his volume. This technique was a revelation. Temperance had always been keener on outshouting the opposition, but she could see now how quietness worked; everyone had been forced to shut up and listen to May just so that they could hear him speak.

'That's exactly what I told Enid,' Temperance said, vindicated. He tapped his pen against his notepad, feeling Churchillian. He raised his voice. 'We have to' – and lowered it again – 'stop them at all costs.'

'What's that? Speak up, man,' Dio said.

'Stop them at all costs!'

'How?' Cora asked. 'And why do we have to stop them? Isn't that what the guards are for?'

'No. Because there aren't enough of them,' May said.

'The Jerries have started a camp choir already, I notice,' Dio pointed out bitterly. 'That's a war crime in my opinion, throwing our own traditions back at us. The noise they made marching from the station! And they're not even musical. They're just loud.'

'Ah,' Bill May said softly, tapping the side of his nose. 'I've got some intelligence on the subject.'

'You would,' Temperance said under his breath.

'We have to listen out for them singing "Silent Night". If they start singing "Silent Night" it signifies that an escape is imminent. We have to listen out for it, every single man of us.'

'Who told you that?' Temperance asked enviously.

'The camp commander, Darling.'

'Steady on, Bill.'

'I don't mean you, Temperance, as you very well know,' May said irritably. 'Darling knows all their little tricks.'

'Why "Silent Night"?' Dio asked, sceptical.

Cora was just going to ask that herself. She looked at her father's black-rimmed eyes and his white hair, and thought he looked like a silent movie star, but she knew he couldn't help it. Mind you, when she looked at her own face in the mirror it sometimes took her by surprise. They could join a circus after the war, both of them.

'To lull us into a false sense of security,' Bill May said.

'But now we know about it, won't that give them away?' Cora asked.

'The thing is, they don't know we know. It's something we have to listen out for.' May glanced at his watch like the busy man he was, and shuffled the typewritten papers in his hand. 'To sum up. In the event of a suspected escape or an actual escape, the alarm will sound, Flight Lieutenant Martin at the RAF landing ground will lend us his guard dogs which have been specially trained to track down escapees. A three-mile cordon will be placed around the area and all pedestrians and motorists rigorously checked for their identity papers. As a last resort, in the event of the non-apprehension of the escapees, the army and the coastguards will be informed, but I repeat: this will be a last resort. This is something we in the police force can deal with ourselves. Your job, as residents of Island Street, is to keep alert and listen out for "Silent Night".'

They were silenced by disappointment.

'Not much of a job, is it?' Jane said after a moment, looking sour.

'Still. Each man has to do his bit. They're a wily bunch, you know.'

'Wily?' Temperance snorted. 'I'm not sure that's the word you're looking for,' he said disapprovingly.

'I'm not looking for any word, because I've already found it,' May snapped, putting his papers into his case and getting to his feet.

They glared at each other across the room and Temperance turned in appeal to the rest of the group. 'No need to rush off,' he pleaded as he accompanied the police officer to the door.

When he came back he could see they weren't intending to, not after being told their job was to keep alert as if they were children. The cheek of it.

They were on permanent alert, anxious, sleepless, nerves jangling, and had been since the start of the war.

Enid got to her feet. 'Is that it?'

'We haven't finished yet,' Temperance said. 'I'm not sure you realise the implications of an escape. With your looks, I dread to think what they would do to you if they escaped, Enid, truth be known. It doesn't bear thinking about.'

'Well, don't think about it then,' she said reasonably. 'And they can't get out, can they, not with the guards, barbed wire, the dogs, the tommy guns and all that security.'

'Dogs?' He pounced on the word. 'What dogs? They say they're getting dogs but I haven't seen any, have you? Silent dogs, are they now? What security? They haven't got searchlights, nor watchtowers. And how many guards have you seen? They can't be everywhere at once, can they? They're outnumbered by the inmates. And the truth is, the British are not the ones running the camp. You know who's running it?'

She stared at him. 'Who?'

'The Nazis,' he said.

'Oh. I'll put the kettle on,' Enid said, levitating gracefully from her chair, ankles crossed, without using her hands. She patted her auburn hair into place.

Temperance watched her go with a frown on his face.

Dio had been uncharacteristically silent throughout the whole meeting.

Cora turned to look up at him in concern. 'What are you thinking?' she asked him.

'If you ask me, May is a bit of a know-it-all. Condescending, like, and I'm disappointed in myself for saying it, but I think he's misguided. Why would they escape? They get fed better than us, they've got all the amenities they need and they don't have to fight any more. But if they do get out, they'll be sorry. I agree with Jane, see. An eye for an eye.'

'I hope they do escape,' Jane backed him up. 'I can't wait! All his talk of guard dogs and cordons,' she said with contempt, her hands jittering in her lap. 'My shotgun's ready for them by the back door.'

'You can't be too careful,' Temperance agreed.

Cora looked at Jane's once motherly face, now turned hard. She was wearing her black felt hat over her prematurely greying hair and Cora thought of the blow she'd aimed at the defenceless smiling soldier, and the look on the man's face as he flinched, and the look on Jane's face, too: vicious and satisfied.

She couldn't get it out of her mind. She wouldn't have thought her mother was capable of cruelty – she'd been a good woman, a Methodist. But Cora had the feeling she would shoot the prisoners in the same way that she shot rabbits for the pot.

It alarmed her to think her mother had hidden that side of herself all her life. Or maybe her ferocity had never been hidden but merely dormant, lying quiet and undisturbed until she called on it. She'd been so dignified after the loss of Owen that everyone agreed she was an example to them all, and they'd admired her for it. But it was all surface, like looking into a pond and only seeing the clouds and the sky.

The war was the end of everything good. What had happened to them, gathered here in this cold front room? The Welsh were renowned for their hospitality, it was the nation's best characteristic, one that they were proud of, woven into centuries of ancient storytelling. They were a nation that welcomed guests into their homes and hearts, but now they were all damaged and broken whether they realised it or not, herself included.

It worried her because she'd always seen them as preservers of tradition. She raked her fingers through her green hair and frowned.

'Love thine enemy,' Idwal was saying stubbornly, because of his pact with God. 'There, I've said it.'

'What's new? You're always saying it,' Jane said.

For the first time Cora studied Idwal and wondered whether he still believed it. 'Is there any point in loving your enemy?'

'It is a theological question, isn't it?' Idwal said. 'Love conquers all.'

Temperance came back into the room rattling the tray of teacups and Enid handed them around elegantly with a little dip of her knees.

'It's all right for May,' Temperance said. 'He doesn't live right next to the camp like we do. We could all be murdered in our beds by the time he's got his cordon encircling the area and his dogs at the ready. We need our own plan, that's my feeling.' He rubbed his jaw, mulling things over. 'When our boys escaped from Stalag Luft III the Nazis shot fifty of them to set an example. That's something to bear in mind.'

'Steady on, man! We're not Nazis, are we,' Idwal said quickly.

'But if it comes to it we'll stop them any way we can,' Dio vowed. He had wanted to join up, but there was no escape from the colliery for him. The country needed miners as much as it needed soldiers. His own father had died at the end of the Great War and Cora knew he wanted to do his bit in his father's honour. His belongings, a comb and a pair of dice, had been returned to his mother.

She'd been tight-lipped about the dice – gambling, see. She kept them in the front room in a drawer in the sideboard with a newspaper cutting about his death, and his two service medals and his Death Penny. 'If it comes to it we shan't shy away from the fight,' he concluded.

'We must protect our women,' Temperance added, glancing at Enid, who shivered with anticipation.

'It will be up to our own consciences how we behave,' Idwal argued, frowning at Jane. He added soberly, 'We just have to remember we have them.'

Jane snorted her contempt, water off a duck's back. 'Why should we have consciences, Idwal, when they don't?'

It was a good question.

'This business May mentioned about them singing "Silent Night" as they escape sounds nonsense to me,' Cora said, balancing her saucer on her knee. 'It won't be long until Christmas, and of course they're going to sing it. What are we going to do if they start practising it just to be festive? We'll never get any sleep if we're going to keep jumping out of bed to check if they're out.'

'That's true, Cora. May missed a trick there,' Temperance said, sipping his tea.

It was November when the German prisoners of war arrived, and with Christmas not far away, Cora felt it would be surprising if they didn't add 'Silent Night' to their repertoire. It was a bit of a disappointment, if the truth be told, for the beautiful song to be used in that way. But she understood why it might. It lulled ordinary people into a daze of sentimentality, it did.

Jane repeated her hope that the prisoners of war *would* escape, just so that they could successfully put their plan into action and pounce, otherwise all this talk would be a waste of time.

Cora glanced at Gladdie. So far, Gladdie had remained sitting on the stool, legs tucked under her, without saying a word, which was a rare event for her. Suddenly she got to her feet and spoke up passionately out of the blue. 'You know what I'd like to do? I'd like to take the whole lot of them down to the hospital,' she said, 'and lead them from bed to bed to show them the damage they've done. Let them hang their heads in shame!'

They fell silent. The mantel clock ticked steadily.

Idwal was the first to speak from his uncomfortable position of crouching on the tapestry footstool. He rubbed his knees. 'Exactly. You've hit the nail on the head, Gladdie. But I've no doubt in return they'd like to do the same to us,' he said mildly. 'We're as bad as each other. Their blood is on our hands too. We are all stained by the mark of Cain.'

His words put a damper on the evening, took the adventure out of it. They had been like happy children playing in the dirt and now they were suddenly faced with the consequences.

Temperance tried to rally them. 'May and his ilk can stick to their own devices, and we'll make our plans, separate and independent like, shotguns at the ready to defend ourselves and our women. I would defend Enid to the death. And I'm sure in your case, Jane, you will defend Dio.'

'Steady on, man,' Dio said, hurt by the comment.

'Sorry, I'm joking, like. It's May, it is.'

There was a general feeling that May had spoiled the evening by arriving late, going early, and coming up with plans that didn't involve them.

'Actually, Temperance, I don't want you to defend me,' Enid said, her voice clear pitched and higher than normal, her chin raised in defiance. 'I want to do my bit and defend myself. I want to work in the munitions factory. And I still don't actually understand, in the circumstances, why you feel I shouldn't.' That moment, it was a stroke of genius, Cora realised.

They all fell quiet and looked at Temperance curiously as he searched his conscience, and from the expression on his open face it seemed a painful process.

His attitude towards Enid was at odds with his warmongering. All Temperance's objections so far had been to do with how Enid's appearance would be altered, and there, that evening in his own front room sat three young women who were unselfishly putting their country before their looks. What did it say about him?

His emotions flickered across his face and he looked up in agony at the stern portraits of his parents on the wall and then at the enquiring faces of his neighbours.

Last of all, his gaze settled on Enid and his baby face melted with sorrow and love.

He seemed to know what was going to happen to her, but he was powerless to stop it. She was his life, but more important than that to her was her own life.

'You're right, of course,' he answered with a sigh.

Enid smiled at him and blew him a kiss.

But his sigh stayed with Cora. It was, she said afterwards, as if he knew in his heart the disaster that was to come.

20

1992

Waiting for Elisavet to come and translate on Friday night, Cora got everything ready for her the same as before.

She refreshed her lipstick and laughed at herself because she felt as if she was preparing for a romantic date with Frank.

There! The pillar candle was lighting up the hearth in shimmering gold and the ruby glow of the wine in the wineglass shone on the black book.

She went to the window, looking out for Elisavet, eager to see her and at the same time feeling strangely nervous because she had never before had access to Frank's unspoken past.

Despite her waiting, when the doorbell rang Cora shrieked in surprise. 'Sorry about the scream,' she apologised to Elisavet. 'I was lost in my thoughts, I was. Come on in.'

Elisavet nodded gravely as if she perfectly understood. She went into the front room and sat in Frank's chair, casting her eyes over the notebook and the wine with what seemed like approval. She picked up the book and stroked the leather cover in exactly the same way that Cora stroked it. It was smooth and tactile and it seemed to invite it.

'Okay, so,' she said.

Okay, so, Cora thought, and she sat back in the chair and closed her eyes.

When we arrived at Camp 198, left-right! Left-right! My personal belongings, except for my fountain pen, were taken away from me. I felt disorientated without them. Only my memories identified who I was to myself, and some were memories I was desperate to forget. I wondered if I'd died and was forced to relive recent events on a nightmarish loop in my brain.

I waited for my orders. I hadn't thought for myself for a long time now. I hadn't had to, the Wehrmacht had done all the thinking for me. Those in charge told me what to do, and I did it. It didn't matter whether I thought the orders were right or wrong, I carried them out regardless, and if ever the question: Am I going to survive this? arose in my doubtful mind, I told myself impassively to Wait-and-See.

Wait-and-See was my motto.

Life in Island Farm Camp was as regimented as it ever had been. The SS officers were in charge, every day had its own timetable, but the difference was that when work finished I had time to think, and what I was mostly thinking about was the yellow-skinned girl who smiled at me from the silent crowd, eye to eye, warmth to warmth, humour to humour.

For a split second she had made me real to myself again.

I went through the humiliation of writing a postcard to my family to say I was detained in a prisoner-of-war camp in Britain. It was humiliating because in the beginning I saw war as an adventure. I'd imagined myself returning home as a conquering hero, hoisted on the shoulders of my family and my grateful neighbours. Oh well. For them, it would be good news to know I was still alive and that they would see me again. They would be happy about that. At the homecoming they would open their arms to me, their eyes alight with joy.

The SS officers in charge of the camp still retained the motivating fire and zeal of the Third Reich. I wasn't so sure. Hiding my disillusionment, I kept quiet, listening more than I talked, getting the measure of my fellow inmates in the small room we shared.

We were strangers to each other, each of us trying to work out who the other was, who we could trust. Steffan, the boy who cried at the station, was in the opposite bunk above Kurt, a shell-shocked man my own age who barely spoke. And in the bunk beneath mine was Otto Fiegel.

Otto was older than any of us, in his late forties. He had a toothbrush moustache and a stern expression. He had fought in the Great War and was called up for military service again in 1939 and worked as a military construction and building official.

He could easily be a Nazi but I noticed he too kept quiet as the SS officers talked about the inevitable victory. He neither agreed nor disagreed, but kept his own counsel.

I saw him as something of a father figure. I trusted him, too. Behind the small round glasses, Otto had seen the world at its best and at its worst.

When I despaired at our situation, Otto clapped me on the shoulder and assured me that this was a holiday camp. Take it from him, he knew all about camps because he had made an unfortunate habit of being captured, he told me ruefully.

During the Great War he had been interned in Siberia and as a lasting souvenir he wasn't in the best of health. The experience had taken its toll and he was given a disability pension once he was released from military service in 1921. And twenty-three years later, here he was, back in captivity again.

Sharing my own information in turn, I told him about my extraordinary connection with the yellow-faced girl by the station.

'Don't start believing you can love the enemy,' Otto reprimanded me. He stroked his moustache and his glasses reflected the light. He had a way of thinking carefully about his words before responding, making it difficult for me to know whether he hadn't heard or whether he was still considering his reply in depth with his usual solemn attention.

I was lying on my narrow bunk thinking for myself, and forced to think of my family in particular, how much I longed to go home, when Otto handed me this little notebook.

'Write down your thoughts, it will help you,' he said.

I thanked him politely, although I didn't see how a notebook would help me at all. 'My thought is that we should think about escaping as soon as we can,' I said quietly, so that if the statement caused trouble I could deny I said it.

'Of course,' Otto replied, as if it went without saying.

I was encouraged. 'We are not too far from the sea and ports, and rail links – I know this because I copied a map in the railway carriage,' I said.

'Really? Show me,' Otto demanded.

I admitted awkwardly. 'I don't have it now, unfortunately.'

'Oh.' Otto smoothed his moustache with his finger. 'No matter. If you saw this map in the railway carriage, no doubt other men will have seen it too. Pity you lost it. It would have given you a role as a valuable member of the escape team. As it is, you have nothing to offer, you see, Frank. Priority will be given to those with a better chance of making it home.'

Singing started up again from another hut close by. The singing was not particularly musical, more like the united fellowship of a football crowd. 'This singing business...'

'It will cover the sound of digging when we start on the tunnel. Also,' Otto added, polishing his spectacles with a faint smile, 'it's a good way of annoying the British. And who doesn't want to do that?'

21

1944

Cora was sitting on the sofa unravelling an old red cardigan and listening to the radio: *Sincerely Yours* with Vera Lynn. She jumped as Gladdie burst in.

'There's a letter come for me,' Gladdie said, waving it at her.

Cora put the cardigan down. 'Who's it from?'

'US Military Hospital, Bridgend. Do me a favour, open it and tell me what's in it, will you?'

Cora looked at the envelope curiously. She fetched the letter opener, slit the envelope and unfolded the letter. She scanned it quickly. 'It's from Charles! Or at least, it's written on his behalf.'

When the GIs left Island Farm Camp, it was a chapter closed, brief as a daydream. For the sake of their sanity, that's how they'd seen it.

Cora knew that Gladdie hadn't heard a word from Charles since he left, and although D-Day was a triumphant success according to the news, Charles's long silence had spoken of a different truth.

Gladdie bit her lip anxiously. 'How is he? He's back then, is he, all in one piece?'

Cora let out a deep, quivering breath. *Please visit me if you can spare the time. If you come, be prepared*, he said. *I'm different from how you remember me.* 'Not quite all in one piece, by the sound of it,' she said. 'Here. You'd better look at it yourself.'

Gladdie read it, taking her time, reading the implications as well as the words, biting the edge of her nail.

'I should be glad he's alive when I thought he was dead,' she said. 'Maybe "thought" is the wrong word. I'd assumed I would never see him again and I'd tried not to think about him so he was as good as dead to me. It wasn't that hard. I cut him out of my mind so firmly that I haven't even dreamt about him, not once.' She skim-read the letter again. 'I wish he'd said what was wrong with him in plain English. I'm different? What is that supposed to mean? He could at least have given me a clue, it's only polite.'

'Good-looking boy with his freckles and red hair,' Cora said. She looked at Gladdie and smiled. '"Deep in the Heart of Texas"!'

'Yes.' Gladdie smiled too.

Charles had made a good impression on them. Heavens knows how he managed it, Cora thought, but when Gladdie's mother had invited him for Sunday tea not out of hospitality but more to get the measure of him, Gladdie said he had got her singing 'Deep in the Heart of Texas' with gusto, and the four accompanying claps had been thrilling and perked them up over the sparse fare of tinned salmon and sliced cucumber in vinegar.

'Deep in the Heart of Texas'! They knew all the words. In the factory it was banned from *Music While You Work* because there was a danger that the clapping of the workers might set off the detonators but they had sung it all the time when walking home.

'What are you going to do? Are you going to visit him?' Cora asked her.

Gladdie sighed and flopped down limply on the sofa, as if all the strength had gone out of her. 'I don't know, truth be told. What bothers me is that it's not his handwriting so—' She shuddered and finished the sentence, 'I don't know what to expect, Cora. I'm squeamish at the best of times, always have been, I don't know why.'

It was true. It drove her mother mad the way she checked the lettuce for earwigs before eating it, and wouldn't eat a raspberry without first examining it for grubs, or bite into a windfall apple in case there was a worm.

Be grateful, girl!

'There could be all sorts of reasons that he couldn't write it himself,' Cora said.

'Such as?'

'He might be too weak to hold a pen.'

'Too weak?' Gladdie brightened for a moment and then thought about it. 'He wouldn't say he looked different if that's all it was.'

'No, you're right. But you're only going to find out if you go and see him.'

'And then what, Cora?' Gladdie shook her head. 'What if he expects me to stand by him and look after him? That's what it will look like if I go there, as if I've gone to see him because I care about him. I did, I loved him a little bit, back then. It was fun, having them around. It was glamorous, wasn't it? But we knew they wouldn't be here for long. It was a snatch of happiness; we knew that and we didn't mind, see? Like catching a dandelion seed from the air and making a wish.'

'He was a charmer, though,' Cora said.

'Aye, he was that.' She sighed. 'What should I do?'

'Don't go, if that's how you feel. Anything could have happened, the letter could have got lost or for all he knows you could have moved away or got married. Just because he's written to you it doesn't mean you have to reply, does it?'

'But it's a coward's way out, don't you think?'

Cora grinned. 'Yes, but you are a coward, Gladdie. You're scared of sheep.'

'That's true.' Gladdie laughed and grabbed her hand, crushing it in hers. 'Thanks, Cora. You're right. I don't have to see him, do I?'

'Of course not. And it's not as if he's on his own in there, he'll be with his pals, and he's got nurses to look after him. It was probably a nurse who wrote the letter.'

'Yes. A nice nurse, who has taken pity on him and who doesn't mind – that he looks different.' Gladdie took a deep breath and let it out slowly, the tears silvering her eyes. 'I don't want to be a coward.'

'Go and see him, then. But you don't owe him anything.'

'No.' Gladdie sat forward and warmed her hands at the shifting fire. The ashes were turning grey. She was silent for a few minutes and then she covered her face with her hands and said through the gaps in her fingers, 'I did it with him, you know.'

Cora was confused. Then: 'Oh!'

Gladdie opened her hands like blinkers. 'Only once.'

'You never said!' And then curiosity about the details got the better of her. 'Where?'

'In the Capital Cinema air raid shelter.'

Cora let out a laugh. She grabbed a cushion and hugged it. 'Boring film, was it?'

'*Beau Geste.*' Gladdie was smiling too. 'Gary Cooper and Ray Milland. We were having a cwtch in the back row. Beau Geste was fighting tribesmen when the message *Air Raid Sirens Have Sounded* flashed up on the screen and we all piled into the shelter and Charles put his arms around me and said, casual like in my ear, "Shall we take up where we left off?"'

'No!' Cora was looking at her curiously and asked the only thing she'd ever wanted to know. 'What was it like?'

'Quick. The funny thing was, with the sirens going off it felt urgent at the time, the most important thing in the world, and even though there were people all around I didn't care, I just wanted to do it with him there and then in case it was the last thing we did. We weren't the only ones at it,' she added defensively.

The war had made some people more fearful and made others more reckless, and maybe the recklessness was just another form of fear.

'I know. I know what goes on,' Cora said.

'What am I going to do?' Gladdie asked her as she clutched Charles's letter. 'I'm torn between doing the right thing and not doing anything at all.'

* * *

A couple of weeks later, Cora went with Gladdie to the American Military Hospital so Gladdie could visit Charles.

Cora sat on the wall outside the hospital to wait for her in the sunshine, and it was no time at all before Gladdie came back out, her face oddly misshapen, lips pressed together.

They walked back to the Old Bridge in silence.

Gladdie stopped in the middle of the bridge and rested back against the stone balustrade, tilting her head to look up at the sky. The tears hung balanced in her eyelashes.

Cora kept quiet, waiting, listening to the loud, protesting roar of the river as if it was raging at the unfairness of life.

After a while, Gladdie blinked hard and turned to Cora, shaking her head. 'He's being repatriated.'

Cora tucked her arm in Gladdie's and they walked slowly home.

That's all Gladdie ever said. Never told Cora about the difference in Charles, and Cora never asked.

Deep in the Heart of Texas, clap clap clap clap.

22

1992

I lay on my bunk with my hands behind my head, safe from sudden death, no more battles to worry about for now. Our main subject of conversation was how to plan our escape. It bonded us. Planning gave a person a future to work towards.

'It should be easy enough,' Steffan said.

'Shhh!'

His voice hadn't broken yet so we were always telling him to keep quiet. The guards were likely to search the hut, thinking we'd smuggled a woman in.

'They've got no watchtowers and no searchlights. If you ask me, the easiest way to escape is to pole vault out of here.'

I laughed. 'Have you got a vaulting pole you haven't told us about?'

'It would be easy enough to fashion one.'

'Really? Would it? And then what?'

'Then we vault over the barbed wire, obviously.'

'I mean, what happens beyond the barbed wire?' Otto asked. 'We'll be caught and shot.'

'No, we won't. Look.' Steffan reached into his pocket and unfolded a creased sheet of red paper on which was printed, in German and English:

SAFE CONDUCT

The German soldier who carries this safe conduct is using it as a sign of his genuine wish to give himself up. He is to be disarmed, to be well looked after, to receive food and medical attention as required, and to be removed from the danger zone as soon as possible.

Dwight Eisenhower
SUPREME COMMANDER,
Allied Expeditionary Force.

I laughed at his naivety. 'It's worthless, trust me. I lit my cigarette with mine. The British will stop you politely at gunpoint, read it, and then shoot you. But you'll die a hero,' I added, 'which will be a consolation to your parents.'

Otto was sitting with his hands dangling between his knees. He looked up at Steffan and said, 'No pole-vaulting, son. We will work together and dig a tunnel. A tunnel is the only way to organise a mass escape.'

'Who cares about a mass escape? As long as we four get out we'll be happy.'

Otto let out a laugh. 'You think four of us can dig a tunnel by ourselves?' He stamped his boot on the solid floor. 'Getting through this will be a challenge in itself. But luckily for us, we're well positioned. It's not far from here to that field beyond the wire.'

I jumped down from my bunk and went over to the window and looked out. It was getting dark and the mist was settling gently, erasing the fields beyond the camp. 'It's about forty metres or so.'

'Exactly. This is not a job for three men. Twenty might do it, on a rota system, and even then it will take a few months.'

'A few months?' Steffan repeated shrilly. 'A pole vault would be quicker.'

'What's the hurry? What else do we have to do with our time? Do you have plans or something? Somewhere you need to be? There is a lot to organise. We will need identity papers, compasses, maps, civilian clothing and enough food to last us for the journey.'

Steffan sighed. 'If you're absolutely confident then we'll try it your way first. Where do we start the hole and what do we use to dig it with?'

'Obviously we start it under the bunks where it will be hidden from view, it's only common sense.'

'What makes you an authority on tunnels?' I asked him curiously.

Otto smiled. *'My occupation. Before the war I worked for Organisation Todt. I'm a civil engineer,'* he said.

Every day was the same as all days: cold, full of routine and nothing else. No mail for me again in the Red Cross delivery, no response to my postcard, and the disappointment gave me an ache in my guts. I wondered fearfully what had happened to my family. I had a burning need to hear from them.

Those lucky ones who received letters lay on their bunks to read them, lost for now in the world as it used to be, and they were silent afterwards.

I put my head over the side of the cot to look down at Otto, who was folding his letter away with a frown.

'Any news?'

'Yes.' Otto smoothed his brown moustache thoughtfully. *'I am happy to report that the mighty Germany Army continues to pulverise London off the face of the earth with waves of V2 rockets and in addition, the Russian Red Army is wisely surrendering. That is, according to my wife.'* There was something ironic in the way he said it, and he grinned.

'Hitler will be pleased,' I replied seriously, in case it was a trap.

A twitch of the eyebrows, that's all. Otto the engineer was not a soldier and he was not in the best of health today. His eyelids were rimmed in red, as if he had coloured them.

'In the event that the German Army doesn't liberate us, I think we should start work as soon possible,' he said conversationally. *'We will need somewhere to dispose of the clay, and tools to dig. How about signing up for gardening duty, Frank?'*

'Why? The ground is frozen and it's cold out there.'

Otto continued to look at me patiently.

'Ah. Yes.' Suddenly, I understood.

I volunteered to tend the vegetable patch near the perimeter. There were no other takers. It was a cold winter and the ground was hard, but it used up my energy, kept me warm, I had access to tools, and digging the dirt from the tunnel back into the earth was as good a way as any of disposing of it.

But I was happy with my new job for another reason, too.

I had watched the yellow-faced girl pass the camp with two yellow-faced friends on their way home from work. One of the girls had straight, orange hair, and the other girl had frizzy hair that was a vivid yellow: Budgies, the guards called them, not only because of their colouring, but also, I thought, because their laughter sounded like little birds.

When local people walked past they ignored us, but the girl who had smiled at me glanced my way, looking at me with her wide, clear eyes and then looking away quickly as if to spare my feelings. That's what it seemed like. That's what I told myself, because I hoped she understood how humiliating it was for me to be trapped here, being guarded by the enemy instead of fighting them.

I wondered a lot about the coloured hair, whether it was something to do with the orange sticky clay or if it was a national characteristic. I would like to ask.

As inmates of Hut 9 we had little in common, but we were united in wanting to escape. The shared enterprise made it easier to live together in cramped conditions. During our first discussion, it was agreed that Luftwaffe and U-boat personnel had the best chance of making it back to Germany because they could steal a boat or an aircraft, not for their own sakes but because Germany needed them.

I was neither a sailor nor an airman and therefore not included in the escape party. I was a Landser, an old-fashioned word that was a throwback to the Great War. But I was as keen as anyone to go home and find my family. I had almost had a ticket out of there in the form of the railway map which I had lost, and I cursed my bad luck every day.

It was early afternoon and already getting dark. The wind was sharp and the frosty grass crunched under my worn soles.

The singing started again in one of the huts nearby and I hummed along. A pale mist was layering the fields, and above the black and distant hills the sky was sprinkled with stars.

I looked at them with longing and I had the awful sense of time passing, and it frightened me to feel my life slipping away from me as though there was something I needed to do urgently before it was too late.

I picked up my spade and tried furiously to penetrate the hard cold earth, at the same time digging over old ground in my thoughts, determined to use up enough energy to sleep dreamlessly, undisturbed by snores and Steffan's sobbing.

The handle of the spade was icy in my palms. I could only think about escape.

The power of the will could get a person so far, and patience was the one thing I had learned from the war – maybe the only thing I'd learnt. How bloody easy it was to be constantly waiting to be told what to do, when to eat, what to think.

I tucked my frozen hands under my armpits, looking out at the fields and the hills fading to grey as night fell.

Through the tangled curls of barbed wire I saw two women moving along the path, their coats catching the breeze. The girl with the yellow face and green hair. I only needed a glimpse of her to make a day worth living.

As I watched, there she was, coming up to the wire. In the twilight her skin was grey and her hair was grey and her coat was black and her hat was black but I knew it was her. My spirits rose.

'The girl was you, I think,' Elisavet said to Cora, closing the notebook.

'Yes,' Cora said, nodding, her eyes filling with tears. 'It was me.'

23

1944

Cora was huddled against the cold, exposed, with a fitful northerly wind gusting as the mood took it. It was evening. The camp was low-lit, and two rows of coiled barbed wire separated their two worlds of heaven and hell, although which was which Cora wasn't sure. 'That's him,' she said to Megan. She knew him straightaway. 'The one that's digging.'

The man with the innocent face was turning the earth over with quick, deliberate movements. The back of his bent neck looked smooth, vulnerable. He was wearing a grey jacket and badly fitting trousers held up with twine.

Megan stared at him, silent for a moment. Then she said: 'How do you know it's him?'

'I recognise him,' Cora said. She watched his jaw muscles tighten, sweat shining his brow despite the chill of the day. 'Hey,' she called out.

He turned and she pulled his cap out of her pocket.

He didn't respond at first in the dark but she held it up to show him.

'I've got your cap,' she shouted, waving it at him.

He wiped his forehead with the back of his hand, his eyes narrowed, and then he saw what she was holding. His face lit up and he grinned.

He stopped digging and walked towards the fence. He quickly looked around to check for guards and then he took a paper aeroplane out of his pocket. He smoothed it, straightened the tail and held it like a dart. With a few practice moves of his forearm he got the feel of it, and launched it over the barbed wire towards her.

Cora watched it swoop, lift, dive, and the wind caught it and sailed it over the barbed wire. She ran to catch it, laughing, bumping into Megan and breathless with excitement. 'Sorry!'

'What does it say?'

She unfolded it and held the message towards the light from the camp to read it.

HELLO MY NAME IS FRANK.

'Hello, Frank!' she called to him. 'I'm Cora.'

'Cora,' he repeated.

'I've come to give you your cap back.'

'He probably doesn't speak English,' Megan said. The cold wind was taking her breath away.

Frank pointed at the top of the fence, and Cora knew they were thinking the same thing.

'I'm going to throw it to him,' Cora said, holding on to her hat.

'We can't, see. The wind's going to take it and it'll get stuck on the barbed wire,' Megan said sensibly, 'and that will be that. We'll have made it worse, not better. Come on, let's go. You know, Cora, he said goodbye to that cap when your mother swiped it off his head. You're just teasing him with it. Look at his face! Bless him. You've given him hope, now.'

The speakers that were hooked up around the camp suddenly crackled and squealed into life, startling them.

The German didn't move. He stood there listening as the news blared out about Allied advances.

Cora glanced at Megan, feeling the shame wash over her. 'Fancy listening to that every day, us rubbing it in.'

Megan agreed. She said ruefully, 'Listen to us! Whose side are we on?'

'The civilised side, I hope.' Was there such a thing during war? She turned her back to him and kicked up the dead leaves. 'I should have thought this through. I didn't think about the wind. If I throw it to him now, at best it's going to come straight back to us. Let's try some other time when we're better prepared.' She turned around again. 'We'll come back,' she called out.

He didn't move.

'He doesn't understand you,' Megan said. 'Let's go. We're going to get a bad reputation, you know. We'll go to court and be fined for fraternising. And it would kill your mother to know you're hanging around the camp. Or,' she added wryly, 'she will kill you.'

She was right. 'It's my mother that deprived him of it in the first place. I'm just returning what's his,' Cora said, justifying herself. 'There's nothing wrong about that.' She called to him, 'Do you speak English?'

He nodded. 'A little, yes.'

'I've come to apologise. Believe it or not, we're not all bad, you know.'

They looked at each other through the barbed wire, the impossible barrier between them.

As she turned to go he said quickly and apologetically, as if he wanted to keep her talking a bit longer, 'I hear that London is being destroyed by our rockets.'

She turned back to look at him, wishing he hadn't said it. Because that was the impossible barrier, the unarguable fact they were on different sides. 'Yes, I've heard it too.'

A moment later he almost faded from sight as a cloud covered the moon. 'I'm not sure it's exactly true though. I'm going now.'

'Goodbye, Cora.'

'See you, Frank.'

In the huts the singing started up again.

24

Since their conversation in the dark, Frank had occupied a lot of space in Cora's thoughts. She had gone over their conversation obsessively, word for word, because he didn't seem like a dangerous man. Mind you, there were some English people in the public eye who would vouch for Hitler being a decent enough chap, once you got to know him, and good impressions couldn't always be relied on.

'Stop talking about him. You're asking for trouble,' Gladdie said.

'I feel sorry for him, digging on his own in the dark. I don't know why he bothers, nothing's going to grow there. I want to get his cap back to him. I want to make his face light up.'

On Saturday night she talked Gladdie into going with her to a pub with a bad reputation where no one knew them. It was dimly lit for safety reasons and blue with smoke. It was where the guards went, and they were the main cause of the bad reputation – they were looking after Nazis so they tended to get angry about it in drink. Nazis were for killing, not for cosseting.

In the gloomy blue light of the bar of the New Inn, she and Gladdie got their stout and sat at a small table feeling conspicuous and needing to find a guard to talk to.

'This is a stupid idea,' Gladdie grumbled, lowering her head and sitting hunched. 'Everyone's looking at us.'

'We'll just have one drink and try to enjoy ourselves.' Cora folded her arms. 'Why shouldn't we?'

Gladdie looked at her sceptically. 'Why shouldn't we? Arguing with yourself, are you now? I wouldn't know where to start.'

'I'm arguing with my mother in my head, I am.'

'Well, tell your mother to apologise to him then.'

Cora picked up her glass and saw movement out of the corner of her eye.

One of the guards had got to his feet. Bingo! He was young, cocky-looking, and he limped over to their table and sat down heavily. It was his limp that she recognised.

'Good-looking girls like you shouldn't be drinking alone,' he said cheerfully. He held out his hand. 'The name's Arthur. Budgies, are you?'

'Yes. I'm Cora and this is Gladdie.'

'What's wrong with your leg?' Gladdie asked him abruptly.

'Got my calf shot off,' he said. He sounded apologetic.

Gladdie recoiled. Ever since visiting her GI she had been repulsed by war injuries.

'You want to see it?'

'No thanks,' she said, waving her hand, 'you're all right.'

But he was already standing and rolling up his trouser leg to show them. His sock was held up with a rubber band for a garter. 'I bet you've never seen a leg like this before,' he said, resting his foot on his chair.

It looked as if a predator had bitten a chunk out of it, Cora thought. The gouged scar tissue where his calf muscle had once been was pink, puckered and totally hairless. He stared down at it, baffled, as if it had only just happened to him. He tugged his trouser leg down to cover it again and looked at them, trying to read their expressions. He sighed. 'That's me done for, isn't it,' he said.

'What do you mean?'

'I used to have a way with the ladies.'

'You're not doing too badly, you know,' Cora said to him.

'Aren't I?'

'We're talking to you for starters.'

He gave a fleeting, wistful smile. 'Aye, you are. Don't mind me, I just wanted the company. I'm not looking for a date. I've got a girlfriend, see.'

Cora took a sip of her drink. 'You're a guard at the camp, aren't you?'

'Who told you that?'

'We've seen you as we walk past.' She didn't tell him how she recognised him. She took another sip of her beer, wondering how to get to the point. 'What are they like, the prisoners?'

He shook his head wearily. 'Don't ask. The Nazis won't accept being told. They want to be in charge. They *are* in charge. Live and let live, I say. They might not rule the world but they rule the camp all right. They're welcome to it.'

Cora looked into her beer, dark as honey. The conversation wasn't going the way she hoped. There must, after all, be some good and decent prisoners in amongst them but that was the wrong way of thinking. It was Them and Us. But this was her chance and she was going to take it. 'Arthur,' she began hesitantly, 'there's a man digs in the garden.'

'And the singing,' Arthur groaned. 'Don't talk to me about singing. It's enough to drive you bloody mad, but we don't stop it because it's good for camp morale, keeps the violence in check.' As if her statement had taken its time to arrive in his consciousness he said, 'A German? What are you asking about a German for?' Arthur sat back in his chair, studying her. He gave a slow smile, understanding. 'Taken a shine to him, have you?'

'No, of course not, it's just – I want to give him something.' It sounded more mysterious than it was, so she added, 'He dropped his cap at the station and I'd like to return it to him.'

'No, you don't, take it from me, you want to burn it. It'll be riddled with lice.' Arthur's expression altered, hardened and there was a gleam in his eye. He leant forward on the table, his face inches from hers. 'It's illegal to fraternise, didn't your mama tell you that?' he asked in a mocking tone.

Cora sat forward too and met his dark eyes close up and almost out of focus. 'I know.'

'Thought you did. What's it worth to you,' he asked, 'if I give him the cap?'

The men in Cora's life were good men, hard-working, chapel-going. They feared the wrath of God in the hereafter, and in the here and now, the wrath of their wives.

But she had also come to know the men in the factory, a different type of person altogether, rough, more like Arthur. She was conscious of Arthur's size. He was bigger than she was, with an aggressive confidence that implied he knew all about her, knew her better than she knew herself. 'It depends on what you want, doesn't it,' she replied.

He dragged his thumb along his lower lip. All his bluster seemed to leave him and he looked away from her. It was a few moments before he spoke again. 'It's my leg. You think it's ugly. I could see it in your face.'

'I wasn't—'

Gladdie chipped in helpfully, 'Don't worry about her, she always looks like that.'

'It's true, I do,' Cora agreed. 'It's just my eyebrow, nothing to do with you.' It was instinct that had made her recoil from his mutilation but she hadn't been repulsed, just shocked. She'd felt sorry for him with that rubber band holding up the sock on his skinny, half-eaten ham hock of a leg. 'It doesn't look too bad at all, really,' she said.

He squinted at her. 'I'm scared for my girl to see it. It'll put her off me.'

'No, it won't. She'll be all right.'

'You think so?' Arthur asked desperately, rubbing his hands over his face, his voice momentarily muffled.

'Yes.'

'Prove it,' he said. 'Don't get me wrong, I'm not looking for any funny business. Just touch it for me. Put your hand in the hole.'

She didn't like the way he put it, but it wasn't a big thing to ask. It wasn't a date, or a kiss. She'd told him his injury didn't look too bad and it was true. It wasn't the mutilation that made her hesitate, it was the intimacy of it, the shabbiness of touching this stranger in return for a favour. It made her feel bad for both of them.

The dim light of the bar outlined his face blue, and she realised she'd hesitated too long. His face had closed up again as if the night had fallen over him.

'Go on then,' she said. 'Roll up your trouser leg.'

He did so, keeping his eyes lowered as he crossed his leg over his knee. He carefully eased the rubber band around his ankle and pushed the sock down.

She hesitated. 'Does it hurt?' she asked him.

'Not really.'

Cora hovered her warm palms above his puckered skin, full of pity for his embarrassment. She laid them down on the gouged skin. There. It was not such a big deal as he seemed to think. It was only a big deal to him, and to no one else. She felt sorry for him now. She could feel his leg warming up beneath her hands and presently she put her fingers into the dent where the skin was baby soft. 'There,' she said. 'Your girl won't care about it, I'm sure. You don't have to worry.'

Arthur pulled up his sock protectively and smoothed his trouser leg down. 'Have you got the cap?'

She took it out of her bag and noticed for the first time the doodles inside it, like a jigsaw.

She looked at it more closely.

'Checking for lice?' Arthur asked with a laugh.

Cora saw it was a map of South Wales: Newport, Cardiff, Bridgend, Port Talbot, Neath written and marked neatly. And a vertical line to the left, with a lot less detail, had the word Eire written next to it in large letters. Cora realised with a lurch of alarm why the prisoner had been so keen to get it back. Can't go far without a map, can they? she thought.

It also meant that Temperance was right, it was the prisoners' mission to escape. And theirs, as locals, to stop them, not to help them get away. Her skin stung with the chill of the knowledge. No wonder Frank was so happy to see her! 'I've changed my mind,' she said, putting the cap back in her bag.

'I don't blame you, it's asking for trouble.' Arthur tilted his head thoughtfully. 'Makes no sense though. You're filling the shells to blow them up and at the same time you're worrying about a cap?'

'I know it doesn't, you don't have to tell me.' Cora finished her beer. 'Thanks, anyway,' she said.

'Toodle-oo.' He waggled his fingers as they left.

Back outside in the chilly air, Cora turned up her collar and tried to make out Gladdie's expression in the frosty dark. 'What?'

'Why did you change your mind?'

Cora shrugged, her heart still pounding hard because the map was a huge deal and she'd promised Frank she would give it back to him. But she couldn't, now. Because Frank didn't know they were anticipating an escape, and ready, at the first wail of the siren, to give chase with dogs and pitchforks and shotguns in the deadly tally-ho of a human hunt, getting their own back at last for all the grief and agony and destruction that they'd endured over the last years.

'Arthur might burn it because of lice or forget about it, or give it to the wrong man,' she said.

'I told you that you were taking a risk, didn't I?'

'You did.'

'He's right, too. We're hypocrites, happy to kill them when it suits us.' Gladdie sounded depressed.

'We're not exactly happy about it. It's our job, what's hypocritical about that? It's only temporary and when the war is over the factory will close and we'll go back to our normal lives: housework, marriage, children.'

'Will we? You're assuming there will be some able-bodied men left for us to marry,' Gladdie said, blowing warmth into her cold hands. 'They'll all be like Charles. Broken.'

Cora was thinking about the German again, the way his serious face had lit up suddenly so that she'd responded without thinking. Like when someone waves from a train and you wave back even if you didn't know them. It was what people did.

They were on the bridge when they heard the singing, and the sound was echoing into the night. His voice was one of them, and it was a strange thought.

She was glad she still had his cap. Part of her wanted to keep it, like a souvenir of his bright smile, and the smell of him.

25

When they got to the factory they had to take off their everyday, 'dirty' clothes and change into 'clean' clothes, differentiated from each other by their shift colour, all of them looking the same in their overalls with turbans on their heads and rubber boots on their feet, as if they'd been churned out themselves by the machinery around them. Enid was the exception. She was tall and slim and she looked good in overalls and she suited a turban with her small, lovely face.

'You know, this is the best time of my life,' she said to Cora one day when they found themselves on the same shift.

Cora laughed. 'You must have had a terrible life then,' she said.

'It's nice not having to ask Temperance for things. He's careful with money and he expects me to be, too. The longer the war lasts the better, as far as I'm concerned.'

'You don't mean that,' Cora said. 'Temperance is all right.'

'I know he is. It's just that I never imagined marrying a man like him. I imagined falling in love with a good-looking man who would light my cigarette for me without being asked, and take me dancing.' She smiled. 'A man like Tyrone Power.'

'You don't want much, do you,' Cora said, because she'd fallen in love with Tyrone Power, too, after seeing him in *The Mark of Zorro* in the Empire.

'How about you? Who is your ideal man?'

Cora thought of Frank and said, 'Tyrone Power, of course.'

Enid laughed. 'You can have Tyrone Power, and I'll have Les Pugh.'

In the factory she could feel the men's eyes on her, admiring and appraising. And she liked it, knowing that there was no harm in it. Innocent fun, it was and everyone knew it.

At least it was innocent until Les turned up.

Dew, he was a good-looking man in his white overalls, with hair as red as hers, and from the start he'd made a beeline for her, as if they were already made for each other.

Cora saw him looking at Enid's hands for a wedding ring as she worked. Most women taped theirs up, to save the metal causing a spark, but Enid had decided to take her wedding ring off for work. Seeing she wasn't wearing one, his eyes had locked on hers, bright green and open and expectant, as if she was the surprise that he had been waiting for all his life.

She hadn't encouraged him, cross her heart and hope to die, she truly hadn't. Even Cora could vouch for that.

* * *

Cora caught them in the washroom.

Enid looked startled to see her. 'Hello,' she said, looking quickly towards the cubicles.

Les strolled out from hiding, his hair shining red. He seemed to pause mid-step, like a fox catching a scent of prey. 'Hello, Cora.' Lipstick smudged his mouth.

'What are you doing in here?' she asked him, her voice high pitched with surprise.

'No harm done,' he said, stepping towards Enid. 'If it had been anything funny we would have gone into a cubicle to do it, that would be the sensible thing to do. But we had no reason to because we weren't doing anything wrong. Hush yourself,' he said, and he winked at her. 'It's innocent enough.'

Cora had been desperate to go to the toilet but now, with him in here, she didn't feel she could go, it didn't seem right. She looked from him to Enid.

Enid had this look on her face, imploring like. 'You understand, don't you, Cora?' she asked softly. She smiled and pressed herself up against Les as if she was moulding her body into the shape of him.

'What she means is,' Les said, pushing her away, 'I had some contraband hair grips to give her that she didn't realise were still in her hair when the searchers came to check.' He shuffled his fingers in his pockets and pulled a couple of hair grips out. 'See? Told you.'

Looking from one to the other, Cora said, 'Well, you can give them to her now, can't you.'

Her heart was pounding as if she'd been running but she wasn't the one in the wrong. 'Anyone could have come in here. You're lucky it was me.'

'A bit holier than thou, aren't you?' Les said, looking amused.

'She's not really,' Enid said, letting him go and turning to the mirror again. She licked her finger and smoothed her eyebrow flat. 'She's got a passion of her own, or so I've heard.' She turned her face towards Cora and smiled sweetly.

Les grinned. 'Nice one, Niddy.'

Niddy, Cora thought in astonishment. He calls her Niddy. For some reason that was more intimate than hiding her hair grips. She didn't think about it long because by now her bladder was just about bursting. To hell with Les. She went into the cubicle, slammed the door and sat down heavily on the wooden toilet seat, closed in by the thin, scuffed walls. She saw Les's shadow creep past the door.

When she came out, Enid was leaning against the washbasin.

'Nothing fishy about it, honest, swear to God. It's true. Les really was giving me back some contraband hair grips that he'd kept for me.'

Cora's silence in the echoing washroom with the familiar smell of carbolic soap sounded like a shriek.

Enid began repairing her smudged lipstick. For a moment their eyes met.

'It's nothing, Cora, it's only a bit of fun, that's all,' she said. 'Same as you.'

The carbolic soap was cracked and hard as a pebble. Cora gave up on it and held her hands cupped under the flow of water. 'Same as me?'

'You know what I mean.' Enid gave a sly smile. 'I've seen you looking out for your German as we pass the camp. I know who he is, he's the one out there digging in all weathers. I'm not judging. It gets us through the day, doesn't it? I'll keep quiet if you do.'

'It's none of my business whether you keep quiet or not,' Cora replied, holding her hands under the tap and trying again to get a lather out of the hard soap. 'It's up to your conscience, not mine.'

'High and mighty!' Enid fell quiet. 'You've no idea what Temperance is like.'

'I've got a pretty good idea. I've known him a lot longer than you have, Enid, and he might be boisterous but he's a decent man at heart so don't blame him for your actions. Leave Les alone, can't you?' she said irritably.

'Tell him to leave me alone,' Enid said with her chin in the air. 'I can't help how he feels, can I?' She was full of excitement because he had kissed her and she wanted to talk about it, but she turned back to look at herself and pressed her palms against her cheeks, framing her pretty face. 'I'm getting a transfer to the detonators section. I don't want my face going yellow. I don't know how you can stand it, looking in the mirror and seeing yourself like that, I really don't.'

'Dets?' Cora looked at her in surprise. 'You know they call it the Suicide Club, don't you?'

Enid looked smug. 'I've been given permission to. The powder is no good for me, it's irritating my skin.' She pushed her sleeve up and showed Cora her yellow wrist. It was mottled with nettle rash. 'See?'

'Let me have a look.' Cora took her arm and looked closely at it. 'You want to stop scratching, for a start,' she said.

'I can't help it, can I? I'm sensitive, I always have been.'

Cora let Enid's arm go. 'This wouldn't have anything to do with Les, would it?'

'It's just a bit of fun, that's all.'

'Not for his wife, it isn't,' Cora pointed out.

'She doesn't have to know.'

'No, but she will though, won't she?'

Enid turned, the anger flaring up in her. 'You sound just like Temperance,' she said, annoyed. 'I'm not a fool, Cora, and I wish you'd keep your nose out of my business.'

Cora flushed. 'Does he know you're going to the dets section?'

'I'm going to tell him tonight. I don't think he'll care one way or the other, truth be told. Keep quiet about Les though, will you?' She gave Cora a sweet, insincere smile. 'And if you do, I'll keep quiet about you. Got that? See you later.'

Cora held out her hands under the cold tap, willing herself to steady before she left the cloakroom and started working on the shells again. She felt as if she was shaking all over. She was insulted by Enid's threat, because she wouldn't in any case tell. Who was she supposed to tell? She didn't even want to think about Enid and Les, far less talk about them.

But the comment about the German prisoner bothered her.

The war had brought with it its own immorality. Life wasn't playing fair with them and they weren't playing fair with life. There was no point in behaving well for the sake of the family's good name when they could be blasted out of existence at any moment. It was better to die having lived a full life. That was the way to die easy.

The images of death came out of Enid's talk of going to the dets section, like a shadow falling over them. It seemed to Cora that Enid was getting careless – in her job, in her marriage.

When she got back to her bench, her relief said accusingly, 'You've been a long time.'

'Sorry. Something I ate,' she lied.

She was aware of Enid looking at her from her workbench and she pretended not to notice.

I'm like her. I'm getting better at deceit, she thought.

26

1992

That winter was bitterly cold. Grey clouds tumbled towards the hills in the overcast sky. Sometimes when it grew dark I watched as they revealed their red and gold lining. This always made me catch my breath with awe because despite everything that had happened it gave me a religious surge of hope that things could yet be well.

Disposing of the clay was one of the hardest parts of our escape mission, and as time went on the plot of ground was beginning to look bulky and disturbingly like a mass grave. But it didn't deter me because I could look out for Cora who was living in the world beyond the wire.

Digging the clay into the hard ground also meant I was using up my fierce resentment constructively. My ears tingled with cold and the digging warmed me up, and I went at it furiously, not just for the love of work, or an appreciation of the evening sky, but in the hope of catching a glimpse of Cora, the girl I was in love with. In love? Well, that's how I thought of it anyway. I knew the pattern of her shifts, I could tell her mood by her walk, and I tried to always be there when she passed.

I liked the idea of this gradual courtship, there was something old-fashioned about looking out for each other and pretending not to, about glancing at each other for a moment and looking quickly away.

I had tried to imagine that she was Bavarian but the fantasy only lasted briefly before I dropped the idea. She was who she was, a Budgie, exotic but friendly. I leaned on my shovel and watched Otto stagger over with a large cooking pot.

We looked around. No sign of the guards.

'Go ahead, it's all clear.'

Otto removed the lid with a flourish. 'Look what I have brought for you!'

'Tasty,' I said, and grinned.

Otto emptied the clay at my feet. 'You're doing a fine job, my friend.'

He let the empty pan dangle by his side, then he too looked beyond the wire at the bare trees and the fields and the distant hills beyond. 'Desolate, isn't it. Have you any idea where we are?'

I jerked my head. 'Over there is the west, where the sun sets. The sea is that way, too.'

'To the west?' Otto turned westward hopefully, as if he expected to see it, but there was only the worn track at the edge of the field leading to the rows of white houses. 'Is that what you would do, head for the sea?'

'Yes. That's our best chance although I know nothing about boats.' I looked at Otto hopefully. 'How about you?'

Otto shook his head. 'My days of escaping are over.'

'Well, with any luck, mine are just starting. Steffan is going to head for an airfield and steal a plane.'

'He makes it sound easy,' Otto said sceptically.

'Maybe it will be. Not everything in life is hard. You take things too seriously sometimes, old man.'

'Of course. One should, you know.'

I glanced at my watch. The girl would be coming by any minute and I wasn't that keen on having to share her with Otto. 'Haven't you got a job to go to?' I asked.

'Of course. I have my cooking pan to clean.'

'Well, go and clean it then, will you,' I said, giving him a nudge. 'You're holding me up here.'

'Am I?' Otto chuckled to himself. 'Something's going on with you. You're acting strangely.' He looked beyond the wire. 'Ah. I see now what has caught your eye.'

The women were coming into view along the worn path, walking home from work. Otto watched them for a moment. 'One is prettier than the others,' he observed. 'The tall one with bright hair.'

'No, not her, the green-haired one. You just wait, you'll see she has an eye for me too.'

I leaned on the handle of my spade and we stared at the girls, willing them to turn and wave, but the girls ignored us, holding their hats on in the wind.

'Wishful thinking,' Otto said, amused.

'You've frightened them off.'

'It's for the best,' Otto said philosophically. 'I have a wife.'

I laughed. 'I know you do. But I don't.'

'There's no future in it, anyway,' Otto pointed out. 'Wait till you get home. You'll be in clover, there will be four women for every man and you can take your pick.'

It was an appealing thought, until you realised why that was.

I watched Cora, the green-haired girl, and her friends until just before the path curved beyond the trees. She still didn't turn to wave and then she was out of sight. I felt a sick ache of disappointment and squeezed the bridge of my nose. Now I was going to have to wait until tomorrow. I kicked a lump of clay in frustration, fragmenting it. 'I just want to get out of here.'

'And jump on a boat?'

'That's right.' I knew Otto was laughing at me.

Otto took out his cigarette packet, Eckstein Number 5, and shook it. He was down to his last two. He offered one to me. 'If the British catch you escaping, they will shoot you,' he said, suddenly serious again. He was very pale and intense. 'Doesn't that bother you?'

'I don't think about it.' There was something strange in the way that Otto said it, and before I lit up, shielding my match from the wind, I hesitated and said, 'Are you feeling all right, old man? You don't look well.'

Otto put his cooking pan down carefully and cleaned his glasses with his handkerchief. 'A touch of dizziness, that's all. It comes and goes.'

I felt a renewed sense of urgency. 'The sooner we get home, the better,' I said.

27

1944

Megan's dog, Shep, was waiting for them by the factory gates again that evening. They were on the late shift and the night was cold and the sky was clear, with a thin segment of a new moon glowing in the darkness.

Cora shivered. The black dog seemed bothered about something. Cora whistled to him, but he kept his distance. He didn't like a fuss made of him.

When he saw Megan he pricked up his ears and immediately turned around and headed purposefully along the road, mission accomplished, whatever the mission was.

She watched him blend into the darkness. Gladdie and Megan came through the gates together, laughing, and Enid was with them.

Enid gave Cora a smile and a wave. 'I've decided to walk home with you, see what you're up to,' she said archly.

See what I'm up to? That was the trouble with a guilty conscience, Cora thought resentfully. You could read too much into things.

She was tired after the day's work, longing to get away from the noise, the concentration, the rhythm, the repetition, *Music While You Work*, and now, her cheeks stinging with the cold slap of winter, she was longing to get back into the warmth again.

'I'm looking forward to Saturday,' Megan said, rubbing her hands together to warm them before plunging them into her pockets.

'Why? What's happening?' Enid asked. Their footsteps echoed in the frosty street.

'We're going to the Angel Ballroom to jive.'

'Can I come too?' Enid asked eagerly.

Megan laughed at the idea. 'You and Temperance?'

'No, just me.'

Megan grunted and Gladdie pushed in between her and Enid. 'Listen, you're asking for trouble, you know.'

'Am I?' Enid was silent for a few moments. Then she tossed her head. 'I just thought it would be fun. You're always telling me it's fun. And I've got my own money now so I might as well enjoy it.'

'You don't want to push your marriage too far, Enid. Think of your vows,' Gladdie urged her.

Enid laughed. 'I'd rather think of myself for a change.'

'Fine. But what will you do when the war ends and you're a housewife again, and Temperance won't have you back?'

Cora and Megan glanced at each other, because it was a good point. The way things had been before the war, with the men earning and the wives looking after them, that had been the only way to live, the right way to live, that's what they'd believed then.

'So what if he won't? I don't need him to look after me any more. I can look after myself,' Enid said. 'I've found that out, at least,' she said.

A bus passed them, lit up inside and crammed with workers and Enid turned to look at it hopefully.

Looking for Les, Cora guessed.

When they reached the fields, Cora saw a dark figure standing alone in the moonlight, angular as a scarecrow, and perfectly still.

Cora narrowed her eyes to see better, only half-listening to Gladdie's debate on whether to go to the Angel Ballroom or the Star Hotel to dance.

As they got closer, Cora realised it was her mother, and she was pointing her shotgun at the camp.

'Mam!' she called out in alarm.

Jane swung the gun away from the camp and mounted the barrels towards them. They stopped where they were and stood bunched together, scared and uncertain.

'It's us, Mam,' Cora said, her voice pitched high with fear.

It seemed a long time before Jane lowered the gun and broke it. 'Shooting rabbits, I am,' she lied as she pocketed the cartridges.

28

1992

They were standing by the cenotaph in the middle of Bridgend, reliving the past with their sketchbooks in their hands, when Cora saw her son Gwyn coming over the bridge, talking to one of the town councillors. 'Hey! Gwyn! Over here!'

He looked around, saw them, said something to the town councillor and came across the road to join them, blue tie flapping, with the kind of honest grin that you gave when you were happy to see someone.

'Is this the art club?' he asked.

'It's supposed to be,' Gladdie said, 'only Cora has taken us on a long trip down memory lane. We're filling Elisavet in as regards local colour.'

Gwyn looked at Elisavet, head tilted, his smile gentle and amused. His hair ruffled in the breeze. 'Lucky you.'

For a moment her dark eyes softened as she held her hair back and looked at him. 'Lucky me,' she agreed.

Cora tried to imagine what would have happened if she herself had said 'Lucky you,' to Elisavet in that way. Well, she would have broken something, probably. But Gwyn was like that, he talked to everyone, he liked people, and as a result, they in turn liked him. He gets that from me, Cora thought.

It was an age thing, that was the truth. The young spoke a different language. Elisavet and Gwyn were of a generation which didn't blindly adopt the opinions of their elders. They challenged them, which was no bad thing because, thinking of her own mother, Jane, parents weren't always right.

'Do you want to see our little efforts?' Gladdie asked him, handing him her spiral pad quickly in case he said no thanks, he was fine.

'Interesting,' Gwyn said.

Cora didn't have anything to show him because she hadn't drawn anything at all. 'I didn't bother drawing anything either,' Megan said, looking at the war memorial. 'It's a statue of a half-naked woman and the inscription is meaningless unless there's a name on it that you recognise.'

'You're right, I was just thinking that myself,' Cora said. 'Let's have a look at your picture, Gladdie. What's that? Lor! It's not another bird, is it?'

'It's a pigeon. It's been sitting at the top of the statue all this time.'

Cora looked at the drawing suspiciously. 'No footwear on him? Lost his wellies, has he?'

Out of the corner of her eye she caught Gwyn and Elisavet exchanging a glance. It was intriguing and also slightly annoying because she felt as if the meaningful look they shared was about her but didn't include her. It was the kind of glance that people exchanged when they knew each other well and something had similarly amused them. She wondered if Gwyn and Elisavet knew each other better than she'd realised.

She looked at Megan, and Megan was staring at her, eyebrows slowly raising in a query.

Cora shrugged equally slowly. *No idea!* It was none of their business anyway, she reminded herself.

Now Gwyn was looking at Elisavet's sketch.

She'd ignored the war memorial too. She'd drawn the shoppers hurrying by in Dunraven Square, all heading in the same direction.

'Was this in May?' Gwyn asked Elisavet.

'Yes, when it started,' she said.

It was as if they were speaking in code!

And when Gwyn said it was nice seeing them all but he had to get back to the office, it took all Cora's willpower not to run after him and ask him what on earth was going on.

* * *

Elisavet left them soon afterwards to go home and the three friends headed back to Island Farm Avenue. They stopped on Old Bridge to discuss the one subject on their minds.

'Did you see that look?'

'You can't set too much store by a look,' Cora argued. It put Gwyn in a bad light if he was cheating on Fiona, because that made him too much like Les, who had come fresh into her memory after all these years and who they hadn't thought much of at the time and thought even less of now. 'Gwyn's friendly with everyone. You know what he's like.'

'Perhaps he's heard about Fiona,' Gladdie said.

'Heard what?'

'About her enjoying herself with in the cafe with a man. And she was enjoying herself, Cora, you can't deny it.'

'Never mind, I'm not going to interfere. It's none of my business. It's none of yours, either, Gladdie. Just saying.'

Gladdie grunted. 'If you ask me, Elisavet suits him better than Fiona.'

'I'm not asking you.'

'What if she wants him to go back with her to the war zone, Cora?' Megan asked. 'That's what she was drawing, wasn't it, crowds running from the Serbs. Gwyn saw it straight away, which was quick of him. It was only when he mentioned May that I saw what it meant.'

'It passed me by completely.' Cora felt her stomach plummet at the thought. 'So they weren't shoppers going by in Dunraven Square?' she asked hopefully. 'After all, art can be anything you want it to be.'

'Bless you,' Megan said and gave her a kindly pat on the shoulder.

'A war zone,' Cora repeated. 'I'm pretty dim sometimes.' She expected Gladdie to make some smart remark, but she'd become thoughtful too.

'Remember how we carried on through it all, acting normal? It was strange because in between the times when life wasn't normal, it was perfectly normal, wasn't it?'

'It was imperfectly normal,' Megan said.

Cora frowned. 'Gwyn's an adult,' she pointed out. 'He's allowed to do what he wants.' In theory, that was perfectly true, of course. But the idea of him leaving was awful; it appalled her. 'Anyway, her fiancé might have a change of heart. That was the whole point of me telling her about Enid, love against the odds, giving her a bit of hope, like.'

'Ahhhh!' Gladdie and Megan said in unison, enlightened. 'Love against the odds!'

'We wondered where you were going with it,' Megan said.

29

1944

Les was married, of course.

He had a nice wife, Sara, and she was waiting for him outside the factory at the end of the shift one evening.

Gladdie saw her first and pointed her out. 'That's Sara, Les's wife,' she said.

Gladdie knew everyone personally, or at worst, once-removed.

Cora could see that to be honest, looks-wise, she wasn't a patch on Enid. Her nose was big, her chin was weak, her brown hair too straight under her hat. She looked painfully unhappy, and Cora's heart went out to her.

'She's looking for Les,' Gladdie said. 'Come on, let's go and talk to her.'

'No, don't,' Cora said quickly. She *knew*. And that meant that other people would know, too, which was sickening to think about but that's the way it was. It was impossible in a town like this to avoid gossip, because people shared everything: opinions, outrages, scandals and fears.

'What are we going to say if she asks us about Enid direct?' Megan asked Cora, keeping her voice low. The conversation was interrupted by Gladdie calling them over so Cora and Megan traipsed reluctantly behind Gladdie, keeping a bit of distance.

'Hey! You two! This is Les's wife,' Gladdie said cheerfully.

'Oh! Really?' Cora said, feigning surprise. 'Hello!'

'We know Les,' Megan said, turning her collar up against the cold.

'I've come about his sandwiches, see.' Sara was strangely furtive as she said it.

It was an odd thing to come about, Cora thought.

'I give him his sandwiches every morning, wrapped up in brown paper.' Sara looked at them with an expectant expression on her face as if it was something she thought they would know. 'I don't like him going to the canteen. Someone's started a dancing class.'

'That's me,' Gladdie said. 'Don't worry, it's just a bit of fun.' She added quickly, 'Les doesn't come to it though, it's girls only.'

'He says I should save myself the trouble of making sandwiches, but I'm his wife, aren't I? I do it out of love.'

'He doesn't deserve you,' Megan said.

Everyone saw this coming. In the factory the women far outnumbered the men.

'It's unnatural to have men and women working together so closely, it's asking for trouble. He's different now. When he leaves for work he kisses me on my head, here,' Sara said, pointing to her forehead. 'If the factory was bombed, that's all I'd have left to remember him by. An eye roll and a dry kiss.'

Suddenly, as if she'd gone completely mad, Gladdie swiped Sara's hat off her head.

Sara shrieked and Gladdie flapped her hands and picked it up, apologising.

'Sorry, I was just having a look what you were pointing at,' she said. 'Oh look, there's Les!'

They turned to see Les, yes, and there was Enid, too, knees bent, blending in with the crowd of women waiting for their bus.

Les hurried over to them. 'What are you doing here?' he asked his wife. 'Don't you trust me?' He tilted his head and gave her a strange smile, half guilt, half mockery.

'No, I don't, Les Pugh,' she replied, pushing her face in his. 'No getting away from it, I'm not much cop to look at, not from any angle. But I'm a good person, I try to do right by others, I don't misbehave, I take communion in chapel without hypocrisy and I can leave through that wooden door with my head held high, with no fear of being struck down by a disapproving Almighty.'

Not like you, her tone implied.

'Good for you,' Les said heartlessly, as if he didn't care two hoots about being struck down by the Almighty.

'And I'll tell you this, I'd rather lose you to a bomb than to a woman,' Sara said.

It was a heartless thing to say, in Cora's opinion. They'd lived in fear of a bombing raid, and no one really knew how the Luftwaffe had managed to miss the factory so far, all nine hundred acres of it, when they'd managed to demolish so much of Cardiff's residential area. It was surprisingly incompetent of them, she thought.

'Steady on, girl,' Les said, winking at them to pull them over to his side. 'What are you trying to do, kill off the lot of us?'

'Dew!' Sara said with relish. 'Imagine it! The explosion would rattle the windows! And then I'd be widowed and free to grieve for the man I wanted you to be. Poor old Les!' She blinked. 'The boys would miss you, I suppose.'

A bus trundled past, tugging their clothes and warming their legs with exhaust fumes.

'Well,' Gladdie said, clapping her gloved hands together, 'we'd better be off! We'll leave you to it! Good night, Sara! Good night, Les!'

They hurried away.

'Thanks a lot, Gladdie,' Cora said when they were out of earshot. 'What if she'd asked us outright about Enid?'

'She wouldn't, because she doesn't actually know anything, she only suspects. That's what I was trying to find out.'

Their footsteps were noisy on the frosty pavement and the air was chill.

'Poor woman,' Megan said. 'She looked so upset, I wish Enid could have seen her. She might have thought twice about flirting with Les if she had.'

30

Cora couldn't get near to the barbed wire fence because the guards were patrolling back and forth along the fence with unaccustomed diligence. She was frustrated, waiting by the trees, waiting for them to leave. Her hands were aching cold in her gloves and she had a bout of violent shivering while the dew froze on the dead leaves, anchoring them to the mud while the daylight dimmed. The wind sounded as rough as the sea.

Frank was digging the hard ground steadily to the clang of his spade. He was a good worker, it told her a lot about him that he dug with so much energy. From time to time he glanced quickly in her direction, checking if she was still there.

The guard finished his cigarette, flicked it through the fence in a red burst of sparks and moved further around the perimeter.

Frank sent a paper plane soaring and looping towards her.

It was almost dark now and she felt safer, shielded by the night. She dashed to pick it up before anyone caught her and unfolded the message.

The note said:

I THINK OF YOU ALWAYS.

It was practically a love letter, she thought happily.

They stood facing each other on either side of the fence, a vast distance between them, and she smiled with relief at seeing him again and the smile closed the distance up. 'I think of you always, too,' she admitted. 'I thought they'd never go. There are more guards around than usual.'

'They have found an escape tunnel in one of the huts,' Frank said, tucking his hands under his armpits for warmth. His breath was clouding through the double rows of wire.

Cora's heart jumped. 'Did anyone get away?'

'No. They hadn't got very far with the digging.'

'That's a relief!' She added quickly, 'I mean – not from your point of view, of course. I know much you want to get back.'

His face was in shadow. 'If I escaped, this would matter to you?'

'Yes, in a selfish sort of way. Because I would wonder—' She hesitated. 'I suppose I would always wonder what had happened to you,' she said softly. 'Whether you got home. You could write to me and let me know.'

Frank looked beyond her and didn't reply. She wanted to tunnel deep into his thoughts. The idea of him escaping frightened her on two fronts (*guns, dogs*), that he would be shot and she would know what had happened to him, or that he would get away and she would never know.

In the factory, when her thoughts turned to him in the rhythm of constant repetitious movement, in the jollity of the radio, she thought of him as being a distant figure standing motionless behind the wire. But when she was with him he was always moving, digging in the earth, keeping his energy flowing. Sometimes she felt it flowing through her too as she tried to keep warm on these winter nights.

He tucked his hands in his pockets. 'Soon it will be Christmas.'

She felt her throat tighten. 'Yes. Very soon.' She saw a shadow approaching. 'Guard,' she said softly. 'I'd better go.'

'I'll see you tomorrow, won't I?' he asked quickly.

'Yes.' She smiled at him.

Although she could barely see his face in the dark, she knew he was smiling and she felt a surge of happiness to know she could make him smile when there was little enough in his world to smile about.

* * *

A few days before Christmas, at the anti-escape committee in Temperance's front room, Cora was thinking of Frank under the watchful eyes of Temperance's parents who each had a sprig of holly tucked under their frames.

Idwal had noticed the holly, too. 'We should sing carols for them,' he said now to Temperance. 'Put them in a festive mood.'

Temperance looked up cautiously from his notes. 'For whom?'

'For the prisoners.'

'We could sing "Silent Night",' Dio said with a laugh. 'That will fool them.'

Temperance puffed out his cheeks. 'It's a bit risky, isn't it? Be sensible, man. May will come galloping up with dogs and reinforcements and shoot the lot of us.'

Enid was smiling vaguely, studying her hands.

Cora looked around the front room, wondering if anyone noticed the difference in Enid, but they seemed the same as usual, dutiful and bored, wishing the Germans would get a move on so that they could stop talking about what they were going to do to them and get down to actually doing it.

There was no talking behind their hands or sly winks to Enid or any of that nonsense. Cora was amazed, because you couldn't keep anything secret here, which was a very good thing because gossip curbed bad behaviour. Mind you, she corrected herself, if that were true then bad behaviour would be extinct as the dinosaurs, which it wasn't, and she herself was proof of that.

And having come full circle in her own argument, she felt nervous again. Her gaze drifted to Enid. She was different now, distant. All her lovely gratitude towards Temperance had gone. She had no need of him now.

Just at that moment the singing started up again from the camp.

'They're having a high old time in there,' Jane complained bitterly. 'They won't want to go home. They dress up and do shows, you know. They don't deserve to be treated as human beings.'

Dio said gloomily, 'The Nazis have got a reputation for that sort of thing.' He didn't say how he knew. 'It doesn't seem right that they're getting it easy in there. Plenty of food by all accounts, the Red Cross sees to that. If it wasn't for us, they'd still be across the Channel, fighting.'

'And the law is on their side. They're more worried about protecting them than they are about us,' Temperance said.

Jane's eyes brightened. 'That's because the authorities know exactly what we'd do to the Germans if we got hold of them.'

Idwal said, 'Come on now, Jane, it's the season of peace and goodwill to all men.'

'Germans excepted,' Temperance said. 'It's one of your pacifist ideas, Idwal, to sing carols to them and we're not doing it. It's in very poor taste to suggest it.'

The temperature dropped in the cold front room.

The meeting broke up immediately afterwards and they went home to warm up.

31

On Christmas Eve, three figures walked furtively in the starry dark to the field behind the camp.

Their collective breath formed a cloud over them, while the snow on the ground absorbed the light of the moon and returned it in a soft glow.

The three figures stood together by the barbed wire, and one of them took out his harmonica to give them the note.

And although there was singing in the prison camp, the huts on this side of the camp grew unnaturally quiet and gradually, on the other side of the fence, prisoners appeared like black shapes out of the darkness, outlined against the dim lights of the hut to listen to them sing.

And for this unseen audience the three sang wholeheartedly with sweetness and warmth, and had a quick discussion towards the end about whether they ought to sing 'Silent Night' in the circumstances or not.

But they felt it would be asking for trouble, and they ended with 'We Wish You a Merry Christmas' instead.

They hurried off home just as the guards appeared. They heard the prisoners clapping in the dark.

32

JANUARY 1945

After seeing her mother in the dark with her shotgun pointing at the camp, Cora's New Year's resolution was to give up Frank for both their sakes. It had been reckless of them to start a friendship, but still, she felt sick at the thought of cutting him out, rather than relieved. Frank put the colour back into her life. But worse than being jailed for fraternisation, she was afraid of them being caught by her mother.

A couple of dismal weeks later, Temperance sent out a note in block capitals to rally the anti-escape committee with the promise that there had been important developments, and Cora was keen to know what they were. If another escape tunnel had been found she would be able to relax, knowing Frank was safe where he was for a little while longer.

At the meeting, Temperance addressed them in his front room in his new, hushed speaker's voice, the one he'd learned from Superintendent May. 'I have some shocking news to tell you which has been given to me in good faith.' He added a warning. 'You'd better brace yourselves, because you'll never guess it otherwise.'

Dio looked at him sceptically. 'Shocking news? You don't look that shocked to me, mun. On the contrary, you've got a smug look about you and while I'm not keen on gossip, we can't all be like me. Spit it out.'

Temperance pulled a face. 'It's not gossip, come on! Women gossip. They gossip incessantly.'

'Which women?' Jane asked.

Dio glanced at her. 'He doesn't mean you.'

'No, what I'm doing is imparting information,' Temperance said. 'There's a difference.'

'I speak for us all when I say we're braced,' Idwal said, humouring him. 'Go on. Shock us.'

Temperance looked at each of them with intense concentration, to build up the suspense. Then he sat forward, his hands on his knees. 'The POWs are sending birthday cards to Hitler!'

Cora waited for him to say more, but that seemed to be all there was, and it was a bit of an anti-climax to say the least.

'That's it?' Idwal raised his eyebrows. 'Be fair. If anyone needs a message of good wishes, it's Hitler,' he said after a moment, running his hand through his hair. 'Birthday cards might do him good, spiritually speaking.'

Temperance stared at him in disbelief. 'Trust you to take the moral high ground with Hitler. I don't understand your thinking at all. They call him "The Mad Butcher", you know.'

It was true that after Owen was torpedoed on the children's liner, the headlines in the North Wales Echo read:

US calls Hitler 'Mad Butcher'

Temperance was so gripped by this apt description that he'd used the euphemism several times in Cora's hearing in the hope the phrase the Mad Butcher would catch on, but it never did. After all, everyone agreed the name Hitler seemed to sum the man up best.

Cora glanced at her father Dio. He was staring into thin air, probably thinking the same thing. 'On the other hand, look on the bright side! He's not going to read two thousand birthday cards, is he,' Idwal pointed out, 'even if they are full of many happy returns of the day.'

'They'll gum up the postal system while they're at it, you know,' Temperance said. 'Have you thought of that? It's part of their plan to make life difficult for everyone. It shouldn't be allowed.'

It was so cold in Enid's front room that Cora could see frost starting to form on the inside of the window from their breath.

They all agreed with Temperance that it shouldn't be allowed and stood up at once with an urge to go home and get warm.

'Lucky man, Hitler, to inspire such devotion,' Dio said.

33

1992

When Elisavet came to translate on Friday evening, her skin was flushed from the evening sunshine and it seemed to Cora as if she was slowly coming to life, thawing out.

Elisavet sat down in Frank's chair and flicked through the notebook pensively. 'I notice that Frank doesn't say you're the enemy,' she said. 'It's strange, don't you think?'

Cora hadn't given it a moment's thought, until now. 'You're right.'

She played with the string of pearls around her neck and realised how nice it was to be sharing his story with Elisavet. She was close enough to be comfortable with, but enough of a stranger not to take anything to heart. She said, 'You know, it means a great deal to me that you're giving me your time like this and I—'

Elisavet interrupted her, flicking her hand. 'Please. It's an interesting story.' She scooped her hair away from her face. 'Actually, I have started my own journal.'

'Good idea,' Cora said warmly. 'It's easy to forget things if you don't put them down.'

Elisavet nodded. 'It's for my family to know what it's like for me. It's important. Like Frank, no? He kept this book for you.'

'Yes.' Maybe he did keep it for her. It would be nice to think so.

Elisavet took a sip of wine and put the glass down. 'So. If you're ready, I will start.'

The main headache was disposing of the orange clay that they were digging out of the tunnel.

I had come to the limit of how much I could dig into the vegetable garden. We had tried flushing it away, but the drains couldn't cope and smelled bad when they flooded.

The boredom of the camp was making us intensely creative. Clay was the one thing that we had a surplus of and in a burst of divergent thinking we put in a request for modelling clay, to boost creativity and keep ourselves occupied, and to my surprise the request was granted and we blended it with our own clay, which we'd dug out ourselves, as a new way of getting rid of it.

The guards were pleased at the enthusiasm for pottery, and it was a revelation how many items you could make from a small amount of clay. Soon the hut was overrun with homemade ashtrays, figures, and trinket boxes. I, with still not a word from home, decided to sculpt my family, to make a diorama to remind me of them.

I started with my younger sister, giving her a big round head, a small round body, skinny legs and snaking ringlets for hair. The result was a crude figure, something primitive dug up by an archaeologist. I understood that archaeologists always liked to attribute meaning and importance to their finds, but maybe these ancient civilisations were just bored and trying to get rid of an abundance of clay. And no one had a head that was perfectly round, not even my sister. It looked cartoonish and ridiculous. I decided I could do better than that, do her justice.

I rolled the clay head between my palms, warming it until it was malleable again, shaped it, thinking of her. But it was painful to think of her because I missed her. I missed her innocence. I'd never thought it was something that you could long for, that you could yearn for the sweetness of life.

'Can I tell you something?' she would ask me, looking up at me with serious eyes.

'Of course.'

I hadn't always said of course. More likely I would say, not just now, can't you see I'm busy? When I saw her again, I would give her all the time she wanted.

It took me a while to shape her head, and then I tried again with her body. Her back was straight and her tummy jutted a little. Or maybe, with rations, it didn't any more. Her clay legs were too spindly to hold her and I laid the figure flat. Her face was a blank. With a matchstick, I poked two holes for her eyes, but the two grotesque empty sockets made me shudder.

I apologised to the effigy and smoothed over the holes again. I felt the features of my own face, pressing my fingers into the protective bone indent in which my eyeballs sat.

I had another attempt at her eyes, first of all making the sockets and then little balls for eyes. But eyes didn't bulge out like that, not in life, anyway, because they were half hidden behind eyelids. So now. Eyelids.

There was a lot of detail in the making of a human, I reflected as I pressed the sliver of clay eyelids over her clay eyes. I was pleased with the result. It didn't look much like her still, but it was her, that's what mattered. I pinched the clay to give her a nose, and poked two holes for nostrils. She had neat little nostrils, I remembered fondly.

Who to make next?

I wanted to replicate my father but I couldn't visualise what he looked like. It frightened me, the sudden blank in my memory. I shut my eyes. Come on, you can do it.

I tried to put my father into words, talk myself through it as if I was describing him to an outsider. Tall, with a long, studious face. That wasn't a description though. How could a face look studious? He only looked studious because of his spectacles, which told the world he did desk work, that he looked at the finer points of things in close-up detail, meticulously.

Not like me. I had no need for spectacles myself. My eyes were used to searching for the enemy and retaliating, or ducking as enemy planes darkened the brightness and dropped bombs, the sudden clear realisation that despite my proximity to my comrades, I was totally alone and close to God and hopefully my ascension to heaven would be swift.

It was a profoundly pious prayer, beguiling at the time. All I had to do was climb out of the trench, hold out my arms and wait for the bullets. Be done with it. Relax, it's nearly over now. I'm in His hands.

But each time I'd taken responsibility for myself again and kept on living, with the nauseous feeling that I'd made the wrong choice because it wasn't over at all, it was still going on and endlessly on.

I rolled the clay thoughtfully between my palms. My father had narrow shoulders and an apologetic stoop. The stoop was moulded by his desk work, his spine helpfully curving to bow his head and hold it closer to his papers. My mother had tried for a little while to correct the curvature of his spine with strapping, to pull his shoulders back. And every night she would unstrap him when he came home from work and I would see the vicious red welts cleaved into my father's soft skin.

I tried to remember my father's eyes. A fresh panic. I didn't know what colour they were. How could that be? The realisation saddened and frustrated me. Had I never, in all those years, looked into my father's eyes?

Those two circular glass lenses of his spectacles reflected everything, but the man himself remained hidden behind them. I felt a sudden panic as if my father had ceased to exist and I squeezed my eyes shut and willed him back into being. Show yourself!

And then I saw his smile, his gentle smile. I smiled back at him.

Yes. That's what I remembered.

I was still working on the clay model of my father when the two SS officers came into the room. I stood, saluted and sat down again. I'd very nearly captured it using the curve of my thumbnail. It wasn't a grin, it wasn't a beam, it was the gentle smile of a man who finds the world to be a good and decent place.

The officer waved a card and announced, 'You are all ordered to sign this.'

I said, without looking up, 'What is it?'

'Hitler's birthday card. It is a new initiative in order to cheer up the Fuhrer. We are sending him uplifting messages for his birthday in April.'

I had continued writing to my parents without any expectation of a reply. I hadn't received any news of them at all. It felt like an act of faith to keep sending them mail. But I didn't feel obliged to send Hitler anything. Our glorious leader had got us into this and I didn't feel the slightest bit inclined to send him a birthday greeting.

The officer handed me the template for the birthday card.

My Fuhrer,

On the glorious occasion of your fifty-sixth birthday, we send our personal greetings and hearty regards from your comrades in Hut 9, Camp 198. We are not downcast at our situation, because we continue to have faith in your power to lead us into victory with our heads held high.

May you continue to wield power and strength against our foes, until the realisation of the glory of our new empire, the Thousand-Year Reich. Our hearts believe in you!

Wishing you health and strength in your fifty-sixth year.

Long live the Fuhrer!

Heil Hitler!

'Leave it there,' I said, distracted. I had heard Hitler's broadcast on German radio that certain victory had unquestionably been forecast by astrologers.

All this talk of glory – our leader, I thought, had lost his mind.

'You can add a donation, if you like. Birthday money. A suggested a gift of RM327,230.'

I grinned – it was ludicrous, a joke. 'You think sending the Fuhrer birthday money is going to cheer him up him now?'

'What's that supposed to mean?' The officer's tone of voice was flat.

I shrugged. 'Never mind. Forget it.' There was always something. You didn't get a moment's peace in this place and I wanted to get back to making my clay family.

A hot voice in my ear, harsher now. 'You refuse to sign it?'

I flinched. 'No, I'm just saying – give me a minute, will you? I'm doing something.'

'Not any more.' Bam! The officer's fist flattened my clay father, wiped the smile of his face, the violence making the bench jump.

I leapt to my feet and responded with a ferocity that exploded from deep inside me. I aimed a punch, saw myself doing it.

My act of aggression was short-lived. Suddenly I was knocked to the floor and both officers were on me, kicking it out of me, every blow of the heavy boots delivering a sickening pain to my guts, my kidneys, my ribs. A final kick to the head sent sparks of light flashing behind my eyes and when they stopped kicking, one of them grabbed my hand and crushed it until the knuckles cracked, stuck a pen in it, signed my name.

I lay on the floor staring up at the rough brown underside of the bench through slits in my swelling eyelids. Couldn't make it out. Ow ow ow. My skull felt as if it had cracked open, spilling my thoughts, leaving them exposed, pain everywhere. 'Papa—' I said in a tight, frightened voice. My thoughts were mashed up. I had the wild sensation that they'd crushed my father in front of me.

Otto crouched over me. 'Hey. Let me help you up.' He put his arms around me, helped me onto a chair.

I whimpered in pain and looked at the bench in dismay. My clay father and sister, flattened. They've broken me. I was sipping in air, ribs hurting as I breathed. There's nothing good in this place, I thought. I wanted... I wanted...

What I wanted was elusive, like the fading of a happy dream.

The sharpness of the pain was subsiding into a throb, my head pulsing, each individual ache giving precedence to the loudest and most persistent from my ribs. I looked at the time, held onto the table and got to my feet unsteadily.

'Where are you going?'

'I have to go home. Where's my coat?' And with this desperate thought the curtain came down, the room went black and I passed out.

34

JANUARY 1945

'I haven't seen your gardener friend for a bit,' Enid said to Cora as they walked home from the late shift. The fields were white and aged with frost, and the cold wind hit them like a slap.

It was true, it had been days since she'd last seen him and she tried not to think about him.

She still had his cap, though. It was her lucky charm.

As they walked along the foot-worn path past the camp, their breath fogging the fields, Cora turned to look towards the vegetable patch out of habit, not expecting to see him there. But he was there, and her heart jumped with happiness.

His head was bowed and his hands sunk deep in his greatcoat pockets. He saw her and raised his hand.

She raised hers to him in return, a small quick gesture. 'Go on without me, will you,' she said to Enid.

* * *

She walked towards him, stepping through the brambles, and came up to the frosty, glittering fence with its crystal barbs, the brim of her hat a dark halo around her yellow face, frowning at him all the while. Something was wrong.

When she got close enough to see him properly she covered her mouth with her hand in shock. After a moment she said softly, 'Oh, Frank. What's happened? Who hurt you?'

He didn't answer.

She asked him more fiercely, 'Was it the guards? Because—'

'No.' He shook his head. 'Not them. The SS.'

Cora couldn't believe what she was hearing. 'Your own people?' she asked in astonishment. 'Your own people did this? You're supposed to be safe in there, safer than out here, at any rate.' Her anger burned through her. She had so many words of helpless fury and frustration to say to him that they piled up in her head like a word mountain.

'Why don't you hate me?' he asked her in wonderment.

'Because I can't,' she said simply.

He squinted his swollen eyes against the brightness of the frost and he tilted his head forward to see her better. 'What colour eyes do you have?' he asked her.

'See for yourself.' She stepped closer to the fence, took her hat off, shook her hair away from her face and let him look at her.

Their eyes locked. She found herself unable to breathe properly but for a different reason now.

'Grey,' he said. 'Like the sky.'

She smiled, tears in her eyes. 'Yours, too. Grey, like the sky.' She pursed her lips to blow him a kiss, but instead she blew him a long white cloud of breath and he did the same back to her so for a moment the condensation joined, mingled, dissipated.

'Hey, Cora! Get on with it!' Enid called over. 'I feel like a gooseberry standing here.' She came up as far as the brambles and stood with her hands on her hips. 'Hello! What's wrong with your face? Been in a boxing match, have you?'

'No – I—'

'Only joking. I'm Enid,' she said.

'Frank.'

'Frank.' She grinned. 'I'll be Frank if you'll be Ernest.'

He looked from her to Cora.

'It's a joke,' Cora said. She was aware of his gaze and as he looked at her she felt suddenly self-conscious about her one curved, humorous eyebrow that suggested life wasn't to be taken too seriously and the mustard-coloured freckles across the bridge of her nose and her ochre cheekbones.

Enid wasn't used to being ignored. Getting no reaction from him, she called over accusingly, 'You bombed Cardiff, you did.' But at the same time she stood with her hand on her jutting hip, ready for banter. When she had his attention again she tilted her head. 'Look at you! A fight, was it?'

'Yes.'

'Who won?'

He didn't answer.

Just then a guard came round the corner, lighting a cigarette, and then he saw Frank. 'You! Get away from the fence,' he ordered harshly. 'And you girls, clear off. I know your sort! I'll have you arrested!'

'See you later,' Cora said to Frank, putting her hat back on and tucking her hair into it.

'Hey! Why is your hair green?' he asked her.

Enid answered for her. 'Because she fills anti-aircraft shells to bomb you lot,' she told him gleefully, tossing her head. 'So put that in your pipe and smoke it!'

35

'Why did you tell him that?' Cora asked Enid as they walked back along the path, heading home.

'Because it's true, that's what our job is. You fancy him rotten, don't you?' Enid asked her, kicking a fallen pinecone from the path into a hedge. 'You can't help it, can you?'

'What difference does it make?' As she spoke, Cora sensed that if she'd turned around he would still be there by the barbed wire, watching.

'That's how I feel about Les,' Enid said. 'I can't help it either, you see.' She sounded desperately sad. 'What are we going to do?'

'Nothing, in my case. He's a German, so it's pointless, isn't it?' She thought about Idwal: Love thine enemy!

Her mind was on Frank, on the state of him, his swollen face misshapen on one side and his eyes puffed up as if he'd been remodelled badly, pressed out of shape.

He should be safe with his comrades but the SS was a species of its own, superior, which meant that everyone else was inferior. That was the way the world worked, wasn't it? There were the bosses and the workers, the rulers and the downtrodden, the house owners and the servants, the victors and the vanquished. The SS didn't seem to realise that for now at least, they were the vanquished ones.

For a moment she was proud of her job again. *Bomb the hell out of them!*

she thought furiously. *They deserve it!* And she thought of Frank again. 'What's the harm in being nice to someone?'

'Being nice? That's one way of putting it. It's not as if you can do anything about it in there, is it,' Enid said as they reached the stile, 'unless you want to have sex with him through the wire. Like little dogs.'

'Enid! What is *wrong* with you?' They hadn't been brought up to think like that. They'd had had strict values which kept them on the straight and narrow by the shame of being talked about. Shame kept them righteous, not just for their own sake but because of what misbehaviour would do to their parents and their good name.

Cora realised how much Enid had changed in the last few weeks. Working at the factory had corrupted her. She was impressed by the English girls, by their lipstick, their perms, their talk, their freedom. And then there was their daring – at night they went into the dim-out, blue-lit pubs and drank beer, just like men. They were doing the jobs of men, earning more than men, so why not?

'What's wrong with *me*? What's wrong with you, you mean,' Enid retorted. 'Fancying the enemy. Just think, Cora, it might be one of your shells that got him caught, that would be funny, wouldn't it? A shell you wrote your name on. Boom! Bounced him straight in your lap.' She walked on briskly for a few yards and then sat on the stile to let Cora catch up. In an entirely different voice she asked brightly, 'Hey. You know what Les said?'

Cora rolled her eyes. 'No. What did he say?'

'He wants me to leave Temperance and go and live with him.' She looked down at Cora with a faint smile, eyebrows raised, inviting a response.

'That's ridiculous! How can you? You're both married,' Cora said tiredly.

Enid's smile faded. 'I know. It's just a bit of fun. It passes the time, knowing he's around.'

'Yeah,' Cora agreed. She knew the feeling. Time stood still in there. You'd think working as hard as they did would make it pass quickly but every minute was the same as the last one and the next one. She climbed over the stile and jumped down the other side. 'It might be fun but we're not the only ones who notice things, don't forget that,' she said. 'People talk.'

Enid curled her lip. 'Who cares? We might all be dead tomorrow and then there will be nobody left to talk, will there? Help me down, will you.' She held out her hand and Cora steadied her as she jumped.

'True enough, we might be dead, but what if we're not?'

'Hush, you! Anyway, at least he's Welsh, and not German,' Enid said. 'I don't know how you can even look at a Jerry after what happened to Owen.'

Cora held her breath, or her body held it for her. 'My "Jerry" didn't do it though, did he?'

'How do you know? He might have!' Enid was irritable now that Cora wasn't siding with her as she'd hoped. 'And what do you think Jane and Dio would say if they knew you were hanging around the camp? Jane despises them. I've seen her down the fields telling everyone she's shooting rabbits, but you know what she really does? She turns her shotgun towards the huts. Stands there every night, aiming it, with this evil look on her face.'

'Shut up, Enid,' Cora said fiercely.

'Temper!' She gave a one-sided smile. 'I'm only saying. Can't we be friends and stick up for each other? We're in the same boat, we've both got our secrets, haven't we?'

* * *

A couple of nights later, Cora was lying on her bed, looking at the route that Frank had crudely drawn in his cap, tracing her yellow finger slowly through familiar towns.

She knew she cared for him more than she'd wanted to admit. She wanted the best for him, if not for herself. And she came to a decision.

* * *

She asked Gladdie and Megan to help her and they chose a chilly evening when the guards were staying inside keeping warm. In fact, it had drizzled all day that day, and the cold rain spiked their skin and rouged their noses and speckled their coats with damp and blotted out the fields and mountains into a grey smudge.

Despite all this, Frank was waiting for them, a lone figure with a bruised and swollen face standing in the wet clay, holding his spade over his head to keep dry.

They had come prepared. In their pockets they were carrying broken bricks in brown paper bags to aid the cap's momentum.

Frank came up close to the wire and put down his spade.

'Here goes,' Cora said.

Frank watched Cora take a practice swing and move further away.

Megan groaned. 'Not like that! Give it to me.'

Cora handed Megan the cap.

Megan tucked it under her arm and sorted through the pieces of brick they'd brought with them.

'Here's a nice big one for you,' Gladdie said.

'That's too big. We don't want to break their windows, do we? This is about right.'

'Can't we find a long branch and catapult it over to him?'

'Have faith, Cora,' Megan said.

Frank was watching them with interest as Megan retreated down the stubble field, and took a long run up. The cap cleared the first barbed wire fence, but got snagged on the second one.

'Damn!' Megan said, squinting against the rain, 'I was sure—' and just as she said it, the cap and brick dropped by Frank's feet. They laughed with hysteria and relief.

He gave the cap a quick shake, put it on his head, grinned and saluted them.

36

1992

They were all involved in the perilous return of Frank's cap to him.

Telling Elisavet about it the following day when they met on the bridge turned out to be an energising conversation because they each remembered it differently.

Elisavet was sitting on the bridge wall, arms straight, head tilted, her hair plaited over one shoulder.

Cora thought she looked like an orphan from a story book surrounded by three squabbling witches.

'You never told us he'd drawn a map in it, Cora,' Megan said indignantly. 'How did you manage to keep that quiet all these years?'

'I knew about it,' Gladdie said, sounding superior.

'Did you? How?' Cora asked.

'You acted as if it was so important, and you tried to get Arthur, the guard with the bad leg we met that time in the pub, to smuggle it in. So I guessed but I didn't like to say anything.'

Although this sounded highly unlikely, there was no way to prove or disprove it.

Megan continued where she'd left off. 'So, Elisavet, as I was saying, my idea was to carry rubble in our pockets to weigh the cap down, give it a bit of heft to carry it over the wire.'

'Not rubble,' Gladdie argued. 'Bits of brick.'

'Bits of brick is rubble in my view. Anyway, that's not the point. It was ballast,' Megan said. 'I went miles down the stubble field and took a long run up. Dew! Those were the days. I used to love running. I used to run everywhere.'

'That's probably what did your knees in,' Gladdie said. 'Mine are as good as new because I've never run anywhere in my life.'

Megan ignored her. 'It got snagged on a barb and I felt awful for Frank, I'd let him down. But he took a jump at it and dislodged it. It dropped by his feet and he grinned, jammed it on his head and gave us that salute. A British salute,' she added. 'I thought it was lovely of him. He was laughing as well, wasn't he?'

'He was so pleased! And you got it over first time, too, all credit to you.'

'I surprised myself, to be honest. I felt good about it for a long time afterwards. That we'd done the right thing.'

'Yes. So did I. Until—' Cora paused. 'Until the night of the escape.'

'Until the shooting,' Gladdie said.

37

My cap was my ticket to freedom.

I was taking my turn to dig the tunnel.

With the aid of Otto's ingenious breathing system, the tunnellers were able to stay underground up to fifteen minutes at a time. They had made a lot of progress in the past three months, and I was taking my turn that evening.

We dug naked, to keep our clothes clean. Above my head, the men were singing loudly to drown out the noise of scraping. I was singing along with them: Pour in, drink up! It took my mind off my work. Here in the dimly lit tunnel the orange clay was thick and cloying, clogging my lungs, too much like the trenches for my liking. Although it was cold under the ground, I was sweating with the effort of digging, my spine bent as I jabbed away at the earth, muscles aching, my naked body smeared with dirt.

Drink up! And suddenly the singing tailed off just like that.

The breathing tube, made from old tin cans, was hurriedly withdrawn. I heard the squeal of the bed being pushed into place. The guards were doing an inspection.

I crouched, and my shadow hunched next to me in the feeble glow of the stolen bicycle lamp.

Silence, a command, then voices.

I couldn't hear the conversation clearly but I could follow the rise and fall of it. It sounded amiable enough. I guessed the guards were admiring the new pin-up on the wall.

My thoughts went to Cora. She would be passing the camp soon, on her way home. I didn't want to miss seeing her.

The minutes ticked away. Get a move on, I ordered the guards by the power of my mind.

I could hear Otto talking and the guards laughing. They were decent enough, making the best of things. It hadn't seemed a drawback, but one could take these things too far.

I stretched my neck and rubbed the hard muscles at the base of my skull. I was losing track of time. It was getting harder to breathe in the tunnel now. The air was getting stale.

I felt a growing sense of panic. My lungs were labouring and my heart bouncing, dum-dum-dum-dum. The guards were still talking in the room above my head. They'd been there for an age. I wondered what was keeping them, what there was left to talk about.

The bicycle lamp brightened for a moment. But just as suddenly, it flickered and went out.

I crouched blindly in the cold blackness, trying not to panic, and groped for one of the sawn-off bed legs that served as pit props, reminding myself of where I was, that I wasn't in the trenches, although it felt like it.

The sweat chilled and clung, and I felt a rush of dread. Being buried alive was my worst nightmare. I'd dug out pals, too slow and too late, and seen the grimace on their earth-filled mouths, their dead, staring eyes. I shivered. I didn't want to die. I was suddenly filled with such a raw terror that I couldn't breathe.

Yes, you can. Stay calm!

I can't.

You're not in a coffin.

No. Not yet.

I felt around for the digger, it was here somewhere in the dark, lost with me in the cavernous hole of the earth's throat.

I found it and in a panic I began stabbing furiously upwards, gouging through the layer of clay. I punched until the crumbling soil began to rain down and suddenly like a miracle I was looking through a grassy peephole of earth at the black and gold-smudged night sky and the air was fresh.

I sucked it in, filling my lungs with it. Dah-dum-dum-dum, dah-dum-dum-dum. My heart was steadying now and my thoughts were settling into logic. All I had to do was wait for the singing to start up again and for the milk-can breathing tubes to be reconnected to the fan. I would finish my stint, shower the mud off, get dressed as normal.

Nothing bad was going to happen, I knew that now. Not tonight, anyway. I was delirious with relief as I stared up at the sky through the hole, couldn't take my eyes off it.

I wondered, out of curiosity, how far we still had left to go. Using my bare hands, I dug away more earth, scooping it down into the tunnel where it trickled down my torso and piled up on my feet. When the hole was big enough, I pushed my arms through and hoisted myself up, kicking and wriggling, and when I emerged I looked back in amazement. The dimly lit huts were behind the barbed wire. I'd come out in the farmer's field behind the camp. Good old Otto! We'd done it, we'd established a route out of Camp 198.

This was the moment we had worked for and I grinned with sheer elation. For the past months this escape was a matter of honour. Right now though I wasn't too bothered about honour, I was enjoying being solitary again even if it was just for a few minutes. I wanted to enjoy the sensation of being alone in the world, just me, with space all around me, nothing more than that.

I brushed the mud from my naked body as best I could and looked across the black fields towards the gently curving hills. With a growing sense of gratitude I stretched out my arms to the heavens.

I'm alive! And I'm free!

38

1945

He was the first man Cora ever saw naked.

Waiting for him in the usual place at the edge of the woods, looking for him behind the wire with the taste of TNT in her mouth, she was reluctant to leave without seeing him. She knew something was wrong because the singing had stopped. Hut 9 was silent, shapes moving behind the windows.

I'll give him five more minutes.

She glanced at the lookout. Despite the tangle of camouflage netting she saw it was empty, the gun tilted and unmanned. Well, yes, the guards would be in the pub by now, they weren't the most diligent and it was chilly out, still wintery, although the buds on the trees didn't seem to realise it.

The pub, on the other hand, was warm and convivial and the guards could have a moan about women having too much of a good time of it, lording it over them with their jobs and their money and their freedom.

And our yellow faces and green hair, Cora thought bitterly, tucking her hands deep in the pockets of her coat.

She was about to give up on him and go home when she saw through the corner of her eye something pale and amorphous moving in the undergrowth a few yards away from her.

She stood perfectly still, watching. It might be a dog or a badger, it had that snuffling, scuffling look about it. She was trying not to breathe, not to frighten it, curious and happy to be distracted, hoping her presence would be lost in the night.

The pale shape grew out of the ground with quiet grunts, and then she saw it was a man streaked with dirt. And this was the astonishing thing: he was naked.

Two emotions froze her to the spot: joy and fear. Joy, because it was Frank! And fear because he was a German, escaping; the enemy was only a few yards away from her, brought from battle into the heart of their territory, imprisoned by them behind barbed wire, caged like wild animals. And now they'd got free.

He looked lovely, mind, despite the dirt on his skin and hair. He seemed to be made of mother-of-pearl.

Well now, just a minute, she thought. Whose side am I on? She stared at him, holding her breath so he wouldn't see it clouding in the cold night air, giving her away.

First man she'd ever seen naked, not counting Dai the Mac who was simpleminded and flashed everyone. You couldn't take it badly, there was nothing personal about it. But here was a whole naked man, not just a small part of one.

He hadn't seen her. He looked towards the hills and then he flung out his arms as if he wanted to take them in his arms and hug them, and her heart went out to him in his longing.

Hug me too, she thought wistfully. *I could do with a hug.*

He was bending over and kicking around in the grass, hunting for something, turning stones. He picked up a large, flat rock, pale muscles bulging with the effort and causing shadows on his skin, and then he caught sight of Cora.

Cora held her breath. 'Frank, it's me.'

He quickly held the rock against himself for the sake of modesty.

The gesture was so unexpected that Cora laughed. But she was touched by the gesture, that he had tried to spare her feelings, or her eyes. 'Too late for that now,' she said ruefully. Her words carried over to him in the night.

His face was featureless in the dark but she could hear the smile in his voice. 'You waited for me,' he said.

'Yes. I was worried because it's so quiet.'

'The guards are doing an inspection.'

He was beautiful, pale as an angel. She couldn't take her eyes off him, and she didn't want to. She felt the attraction in her stomach, like hunger.

His eyes gleamed, and he was looking at her intently as if she was something interesting he was trying to understand. He was shivering with cold, holding the rock, waiting to see what she would do.

Cora didn't know herself. She took a deep breath. They both knew she should scream at the top of her voice to raise the alarm, obviously, yes. It was her duty to do that. But she'd also given him the cap back, knowing why it meant so much to him and how he would use it.

Just then, *Ein! Zwei! Drei!* the singing started up again from inside Hut 9 in a roar of sound and Frank turned to look, his face brightening as if his friends were calling him home.

Cora smiled. They loved their singing! Dew, they made a good, loud noise of it too, rousing she'd call it, the songs of people having a good time. There was something extraordinarily brave and admirable about singing in prison, in her opinion.

No use screaming now, of course. They'd never hear her.

It was only chance that she'd seen him, after all, that's how she justified it to herself. She could have gone straight home when she saw he wasn't there. If she'd done that she would have been none the wiser. Chance, that was all it was.

Frank looked back at her, trembling from cold and the weight of the rock.

Cora came to a decision, not the right one, but one she could live with. 'You can't just stand here, you'll catch your death,' she said to him.

He stared at her. 'My death?'

'I mean – go back inside.' She scooted her hands at him. 'Quick! Go!'

He looked confused. He dropped the large stone with a thud and kept watching her as he retreated into the hole, wriggling as he lowered himself into the tunnel.

She watched his pale shape dematerialising into the brambles. At the last moment he held himself up awkwardly by his elbows, looking at her through a fringe of black grass.

'Goodbye,' he said. 'Goodbye, Cora.'

She saw his pale hand as he dragged the stone across the opening. Gone!

She felt woken up, quick, lively, jittery, excited, as if she'd had a narrow escape from danger – physical or moral, she wasn't sure which.

Obviously she should report the fact of the tunnel, no question, it went without saying. She knew where the entrance was, too, because the rock marked it. But then she thought of the way he'd stretched out his arms to the hills and she was filled with a sense of her own power and her own freedom, something that the war had given her. There was a difference between what she should do and what she wanted to do.

She waited in the dark as the dew froze on the grass, sparkling in the dim lights of the hut. She stood listening to the singing, and then after quite a few minutes the singing stopped and gave way to rowdy cheers.

He's back, she thought.

39

When Cora got home that night, Dio was waiting for her by the wooden kitchen table, his hands laid flat on the burgundy chenille cloth, the newspaper spread out in front of him.

'You're late,' he said mildly, and it was a question rather than a reproach. He was wearing a white shirt without a collar, and one of his braces had slipped from his shoulder. He looked at her with troubled eyes. 'You're shaking. What's wrong?'

'Nothing,' she said, and lying to him came hard.

He didn't argue. He looked tired. Sitting by the table, Cora felt a flush of guilt. She hadn't been thinking clearly back there in the dark field, because she should have done the right thing and raised the alarm without a second thought. That would have been the proper thing to do.

It wasn't too late – she didn't have to mention the prisoner's naked body. No one ever needed to know how long she'd stared at him before he saw her.

'You're late,' Jane said, carrying the pot of rabbit stew from the stove to the table. 'We were worried. I don't like you walking past that camp,' she said blindly. Her small round glasses had misted over in the steam from her bowl and she polished them with her apron.

Cora looked up. 'I know. But it's quicker than going by road.'

Jane put her glasses back on and studied her daughter closely. She looked pained. 'Still, I don't want the Germans looking at you and seeing what the war's done to you. What are they going to think? It's a victory for them, isn't it, the state of you?'

'Some of the girls powder their hair on purpose, to tint it.'

Jane looked sceptical. 'Yellow hair is one thing. Yours is green. Just look at you.'

Cora paused, looking at her yellow hand holding the spoon halfway to her mouth, hurt by the comment. She'd got used to it. She thought she was lucky to have hands at all, but she didn't say it. They heard the occasional blow ups, and sometimes saw them, but they were forbidden to talk about them outside the factory, so she kept quiet. It made no difference in any case. You saw the proof out in Bridgend, ex-workers missing hands, eyes, fingers, thumbs. They faced danger every day in the factory and having stained skin and tinted hair was the last thing Cora was worried about.

'Temperance is still going on about his escape plan,' Dio said resentfully. 'I don't know why he bothers. Why would they want to escape, anyway?' He pulled his braces back on his shoulders. 'They've got nothing to escape from, have they? They're safe, they're not going to get shot, they don't have to fight, they get fed, they get their laundry done for them, medical treatment, theatre concerts. And all that singing they do, they're on top of the world, dew, they make a good loud noise, you should have heard them this evening! Mind you, it must have taken it out of them because they were quiet for a while afterwards, which was a blessing.'

'But they're not free though, are they?' Cora argued, remembering Frank throwing open his arms to the hills.

'No indeed, and we're not free, either, don't forget,' her father said. 'And we're never going to be in this life. This is only ever our trial run.' He rubbed his hands over his white hair.

In his next life, Cora thought, he would make sure to keep Owen close.

He saw this life as a dress rehearsal for the next one, in which you could get all your mistakes out of the way and learn your lessons once and for all. Cora thought he was right about freedom, though. It was true enough when you looked at it like that.

Jane rested her spoon in her dish and stopped eating her stew because of burping. Talking about the enemy affected her like that, it was bad for the digestion. She waited for it to pass and patted her chest, winding herself like a baby. Which put her in mind of something. 'Did you hear Nia Jones had a little boy? Bright yellow, he is!'

'Never! The whole world is going to—' In lieu of unspeakable words, Dio nodded his head and turned his black-rimmed eyes downwards in the direction of hell, or in the direction of the coal seams, much the same thing.

He checked the time on his pocket watch, got up from the table and switched on the radio. Cora cleared the plates away. It was a habit of theirs to listen to the British fascist Lord Haw-Haw's treacherous nightly broadcast from Germany as part of their routine. Sometimes it was possible to work out where their soldiers had been posted. They found out more from Lord Haw-Haw's broadcasts than they did from the news, tell you the truth. Both sides used propaganda to their advantage, the British to put a good spin on things and the Germans to give the facts. Or vice versa.

It was through listening to him that they discovered that the Germans knew about the existence of Bridgend Royal Ordnance Factory, because over the airwaves he had once promised the pretty girls of Bridgend that the Luftwaffe was coming to bomb them.

And it seemed he was right because one day, a shell did land on P shed, nine people dead including a father and daughter. In the works canteen, Cora gave towards a collection for a wreath, and those who had been there consoled them that it would have been painless because they didn't hear the shell or feel the blast – one moment life was normal and next minute they were floating above the chaos around them.

But they couldn't blame the Germans for that, after all. The shell was fired by gunners at Western Drive, Gabalfa. Friendly fire, they called it, but at the memorial service a few days later, nobody used that most insulting of all terms. The news proved Lord Haw-Haw was wrong though, and gave them one more reason to poke fun at him.

Cora sat down as the broadcast started.

'Germany calling! Germany calling!'

'He's drunk,' Dio said, laying his forearms on the table.

Cora agreed that Lord Haw-Haw's voice was beginning to lose some of its aristocratic superiority.

The tone of his broadcasts had changed since D-Day. He was increasingly slurred, although to be fair the sound on the wireless wasn't always clear, and it was hard to make him out at the best of times.

40

1992

It was a lovely sunny day for the seaside, but heavy going, this walk through the sand dunes. They wanted to show Elisavet the biggest sand dune in Wales, the Big Dipper.

There were Megan's knees to take into consideration but Gladdie and Cora agreed it would be wrong to deprive Elisavet from seeing it just because they weren't as fit as they used to be, and it would be well worth the effort.

But now they were hot and sweating, with aching legs, breath rasping and ankle-deep in sand, they felt differently. Elisavet wouldn't really have missed much.

'I forgot it was just sand and grass,' Megan groaned, shielding her eyes from the sun.

'But it's the biggest sand dune in Wales!' Gladdie said, gripping her trembling thighs.

'First thing I'm going to do is run into the waves and cool off,' Cora said, her heart racing with effort. 'If I live that long.' The three of them stopped where they were, sinking into the warm sand, trying to catch their breath before they carried on. Not Elisavet, though. She strode ahead effortlessly and stood waiting for them on top of the Big Dipper, as cool and patient as ever, her dark hair blowing, her eyes distant. 'Like Florence of Arabia,' Cora said admiringly.

'She's young,' Megan said, 'and we're not. I don't know what's the matter with us lately, acting as if we're in our youth again.'

'Talking about the past, it is,' Cora said. 'I feel exactly the same, and then I look in the mirror and it's a shock to me, to be honest.'

'See, that's where we're different. I never look in the mirror myself,' Megan told her. 'There's no point.'

'Yes,' Gladdie said, 'we can tell that.'

Megan continued, as if she hadn't spoken, 'Because I've got a rough idea what I look like after all these years, and that'll do me. Oh, look, she's coming back.'

Elisavet was bounding down the sand dunes towards them, her bag bouncing between her shoulders, and sank to a halt in front of them. 'You want me to help you?'

Cora wiped the sweat from her forehead. 'No, we're fine,' she said, pink-faced from exertion, 'we're just having a breather.'

'I'm not, you can help me,' Megan said quickly, holding out her hand.

Elisavet grasped it firmly and Megan took a lot of frantic little steps to save her arm from being pulled out of its socket and a few minutes later she was at the top, looking pleased with herself.

'Come on, slowcoaches!'

When they reached the top of the dunes, they saw the sea stretch out in front of them, blue and sparkling, lace-edged with foam. They stumbled down towards this oasis, going down was much easier, and found a spot to leave their things before going for a paddle to refresh themselves.

'Beautiful country,' Elisavet said, standing in the waves. The water splashed and darkened the edge of her skirt as she looked towards the horizon.

'Yes. And it's your country, now,' Gladdie said proudly, getting her feet wet in the shivery cold sea.

'No.' Elisavet turned to face her, her hair veiling her face. 'I belong nowhere,' she said. 'I have no home. I have no language. I am nobody.'

Gladdie was horrified. 'Don't say that!'

'Why not? It's true.'

'You're somebody to us,' Cora said firmly, shying away from the waves. 'And it's early days yet. You'll make friends,' she said, thinking of Gwyn. 'And one day you might go back to Kosovo. Do you think you will?'

'I think about it. But I can't forgive, nor forget.' Elisavet chewed the inside of her cheek, frowning. 'Driving out of town, we were stopped by soldiers with guns. They pulled me out of the driver's seat and dragged me into a truck with a lot of other women. I could see the frightened faces of my family watching, my grandparents, my mother, my cousins, all of them together in this little car.'

'And then what happened?' Gladdie asked.

Elisavet shrugged. 'To them? I don't know.'

The tide hushed and swished, hushed and swished.

Elisavet turned her back to them, and taking the hint, Cora and Megan waded back to shore.

Gladdie stayed behind with Elisavet, her arms folded, knee deep in waves, as if she had to stay there until she came up with an answer.

Cora and Megan sat down heavily by the little island of their bags. Cora had tea in a flask and she poured it into four plastic cups. 'Do we ever leave trauma behind, do you think?'

Megan considered it. 'We're still going back to it years later, if we're anything to go by.'

'Trying to make sense of it, I suppose.' Cora sighed and looked at Elisavet standing firm and straight-backed against the tide. Her heart went out to her. 'I wish we could help.'

'She's talking about it. That's a start,' Megan said. 'We'd better get the paints out, Gladdie's rubbing her hands together,' she added over the surge of the sea.

The tide was coming in, the lace-frilled waves gliding over the damp sand. They hurriedly moved their bags further up the beach and got out their travel paint sets and sketchbooks. It really was a beautiful day.

Sometime later, Cora held her painting out at arm's length. It looked very amateurish and nothing at all like the vast blue sky and the sparkling sea. She leant sideways to look at Elisavet's effort and almost overbalanced but righting herself, she cheered up considerably because Elisavet's looked nothing like anything at all, just a series of circular black blobs in a square. She had a feeling that they represented something important to Elisavet, though.

Gladdie came over to give her opinion with her hands clasped behind her back in her new, headmistressy manner. She stood behind Elisavet making indeterminate noises. Then she stood behind Cora and hummed as if she had something on her mind.

'It's not finished yet,' Cora said quickly, trying to stave off criticism.

'No, I can see that.'

And not a word, Cora noticed, about Elisavet's black blobs.

'You need a focal point,' Gladdie said. 'Like a boat or something.'

'You told us to only paint what we can see.'

'Artistic licence.'

'Make your mind up,' Cora said, and she decided to paint a seagull, abstract like, two huge curves for wings, a curved yellow bill, orange legs, beady eyes. No wonder Gladdie was fixated on birds. They were easier to paint than you'd think.

When she'd finished, Cora got up and emptied her dirty paint water into the foam. She thought about the way Elisavet drew everything monochrome, as if the sun was eclipsed and her sadness had washed the colour from the sea and the drying sand.

41

The candle was flickering in the hearth, the glasses were ready to be filled. Cora uncorked the bottle and showed Elisavet the label. 'It's a Riesling,' she said. 'From the Rhine. It seems appropriate, doesn't it?'

As she poured it, Elisavet picked up the notebook and held it out in front of her as if she was about to swear an oath on it.

The gospel according to Frank, Cora thought.

Elisavet put the notebook on her lap and said thoughtfully, 'Gwyn is like his father, do you think?'

'Oh, definitely, yes,' Cora said, pleased. 'Kind.' Kindness was underrated, in her view. It had slipped down the league of favourable characteristics, below confidence and wit and style. 'Kind is one of those peculiarly British words like "nice" and "mild" that you don't set much store by, but you appreciate it when you see it.'

Elisavet's dark eyes held hers and gave little away, but she nodded.

Cora wasn't used to silences between people, because around here, everyone had an opinion on everything and was keen to share the knowledge. Still, you could communicate in other ways, it didn't always take words, she was beginning to realise that. You just had to recognise the communication for what it was. Elisavet coming here on a regular basis to translate the book of her own volition, that was kindness, she thought.

'So,' Elisavet said, 'we shall start.'

Otto was looking through the window of Hut 9, his hands clasped behind his back as I reached the vertical section of the tunnel where my roommates helped me climb out.

I was not sure what had just happened. My thoughts went back to the curving black hills and the wide, fading sky and the woman, Cora, huddled in her coat, and what she'd said to me. Go back inside.

'How was it down there?'

'Suffocating. I thought I was going to die.'

'The guards were taking great interest in the drawings of the girls,' Steffan said apologetically.

'I thought it would be that. I'm going to get cleaned up.' I grabbed my clothes and hurried to the showers before the guards saw me. Under the feeble flow of water I scraped the clay off my skin, kicking the dirty water to encourage it to flow down the plug hole.

I wiped down the shower stall as best I could, dried off, dressed and went back to the bunk. My roommates were already asleep, and I knelt next to the bed where the tunnel's architect, Otto, lay. 'Listen, we're through,' I told him. 'I wanted you to be the first to know.'

Otto reached for his spectacles and he sat up eagerly, smoothing his moustache. 'Where did it come out?'

'In the farmer's field.'

'Hah!' Otto smiled. 'I knew it.'

'You know what this means? We're going home!'

Next morning I was cleaning my boots, thinking about the escape. The preparations were well underway. We had forged identity papers and would line the tunnel with rags to keep our clothes clean as we made our way out from underground. We were saving portions of our rations to take with us. We had fashioned compasses out of magnetised razor blades and my railway map had been copied onto shirt tails and handkerchiefs.

We had a good chance of making it to freedom. Steffan had seen planes flying low in the distance after take-off and heard them coming in to land, so he knew there were airfields not too far away. All we had to do was make our way to one of these airfields and steal a plane. Get back home.

I thought of finding Cora with the green hair to say goodbye. I would hold her close for a few precious moments, hold her warm, eager face in my hands and thank her for giving me hope for these past weeks, for giving me faith in the goodness of human nature.

Otto moved from the window and cast his shadow over me.

I looked up. It was hard to see the older man's expression. Against the brightness of the day he looked ink black.

'I've been thinking about it. I have changed my mind. I want to come with you when you leave, Frank,' Otto said softly.

'You do?' I said, placing my boots on the floor side by side. We owed Otto everything. It was his engineering expertise that had made the tunnel safe with the use of pit props, it was he who had thought of the practical ventilation system using condensed milk cans, he who had rewired the electricity so we could see what we were doing, and improvised the trolley system for moving the clay. We had to give the man credit for that. Besides, I liked Otto, that was the problem. Without him we would still be planning to pole vault out of there and the tunnel would have caved in weeks ago. He'd made it all possible.

At the same time my spirits sank at the idea of being responsible for him.

Otto wasn't in the best of health, he wasn't fit, he would slow us down, it was easier for one man to hide than two.

The picture I dreamed of, the swift return home, wasn't looking the same at all now. Of course, Otto was a gentleman and he would politely understand but it wasn't the point, it wasn't what I had envisaged. 'What has made you change your mind?' I asked curiously.

'Something bad is going to happen. I can feel it,' Otto said. 'What do you think they'll do to us when it's over?' His eyes were watery. 'I want to go home. I need to see my wife and children again. I don't believe for a moment we are winning the war, no matter how many times they tell us we are.'

'We mustn't lose hope.'

I thought of the mural that Otto had spent some time painting, pine forests and mountains and blue skies. He'd lost himself for hours in the recreation of his homeland and he'd always looked dazed and disappointed to come back to the hut and face the reality of an uncertain future.

'It's over. The Nazis are finished, Frank,' Otto said, polishing his spectacles with his handkerchief. 'It's all coming to an end but they don't realise it. They want to believe, even now, that Hitler is a genius with a vision.'

'And you don't?' I asked, startled.

'He's a delusional madman.'

'Hush, Otto!' I quickly glanced towards the door and waved a warning. 'Be careful what you say. You make me nervous when you talk like that.'

Otto shook his head. 'Don't mind me. I'm getting old. I've seen too much,' he said, sitting heavily on the chair. 'Don't worry, I'm safe. The SS won't kill me until the tunnel's complete and I'd like to see the back of this place. If the British and their allies win this war, we'll be sent to the death camps. Or if we're lucky they'll bomb the camp, get rid of us in one, easy move.'

'Who told you that?'

'Why wouldn't they? It's what we've done to them, isn't it? Tit for tat.'

'Still, as long as it's not Siberia, isn't that so?' I tried to jolly him out of his dark mood. They were coming more frequently these days, the depression of captivity, a sense of hopelessness. I had enjoyed listening to Otto's stories about his capture on the Eastern Front during the last war, and about his long and arduous adventures on the journey home during the Russian Revolution; it was the stuff that heroes were made of. But he'd stopped talking about them lately, which was a shame. Maybe he felt he didn't need to prove himself any longer, that his past spoke for him. And the tunnel was almost finished. It was better in the circumstances to remain as anonymous and invisible as possible and hope for the best.

'Not that bad, no,' Otto said, rallying. 'It's as cold as Siberia though.'

'Here, have a cigarette, cheer yourself up.'

'Cheer myself up?' Otto laughed. 'I'll do my best.'

'That's the spirit,' I said.

42

1945

Cora had a sense of things coming to a head when Temperance came round one evening and popped his head around the door.

Cora was scraping carrots in the sink, preparing the dinner.

'Hullo! I'm looking for Enid, I am,' he said. 'Didn't she come home with you?'

'No. Now she's in dets we don't see her so much.'

'Ah.' Temperance rubbed his jaw in agitation. 'Is Dio in?'

'Sorry, they've gone to chapel for a vestry meeting.'

'Convenient for her, isn't it, changing section,' he said with an edge to his voice. He unbuttoned the starched collar from his shirt and stretched his liberated neck. He looked utterly miserable. 'She's usually home to cook the meal.'

Yes, it was convenient for Enid, Cora thought, he was right about that. 'I'm getting the dinner started,' she said, turning to him. 'You can join us if you like.'

'You're all right, she'll be back soon, I expect,' he said. 'I don't believe she's capable of deceit.' He looked at Cora, the question bright in his eyes. 'I don't want to believe it, anyhow.'

She swallowed her dread. The inevitable was happening. It had been building up to the point of no return – no hiding Enid's confidence, her lies, her excitement – because in Les she had found the glamour that had been missing from her life. As she said, what was the point of behaving properly, Cora thought, peeling the carrots with great concentration, when we could be dead tomorrow?

'No, flirting, that's all it is,' Temperance said, going off on his own trail of thought. 'Enid always likes to flirt because it means she gets her own way. There's nothing in it, not really, everyone knows that. Dio and Idwal warned me before I married her: spoilt she is, too pretty for you, but it was water off a duck's back. I trust her, Cora.'

Cora thought of the way that Les looked at Enid, and the way Enid looked back at Les, sharing a secret, speaking to each other with their eyes as if the rest of the world had grown invisible around them. Well, it hadn't.

'There's going to be nothing left of that carrot if you keep on like that,' Temperance advised. He rolled his collar and tucked it in his pocket. 'I'm going to look for her.'

Alarmed, Cora dropped the knife into the sink with a clatter. 'Where?'

'The factory.' He opened the door and along with the rush of cold air came the roar of singing from the camp and the discordant percussion of spoons on plates amplified momentarily. 'Listen to that,' Temperance said to her morosely. 'They've started a band, now.'

It was an assault on the ears and the sleepless nights weren't doing any of them any good. She didn't know how the prisoners survived, singing marching songs all night like that. And then in the daytime there was no peace either, with the announcements of Allied victories blaring out through the amplifiers. It was like living in a railway station.

She had a knot of anxiety in her stomach and she put the carrots into cold water and quickly rinsed her hands. Her anxiety was turning into anger because Enid really should have got home by now, no matter what. Even if there were – the word 'shenanigans' popped into Cora's head – taking place, surely she was sensible enough to at least act normally for everyone's sake.

Unless...

Unless Enid really was going to leave him for Les.

In a sudden flurry of panic, Cora grabbed her coat and hat and started running past the camp and along the road. It was a frosty night and the path was slippery underfoot. She caught up with Temperance on the main road and they hurried together towards the factory, their rapid footsteps echoing in the night.

An Austin 10 was parked at the side of the road, its windows steamed up, shielding the occupants from view.

Like a madman, Temperance dashed across to it and pulled open the passenger door, bellowing: 'How could you, Enid!' Reaching in and grabbing her arm, his own wife's bare arm, and Enid fighting back furiously, hitting in a flurry of limbs, matching his anger with grunts of effort, hot noise in the darkness.

'Let me go!' she screamed.

Les got out of the car, buttoning his trousers and dancing in agitation around the fighting pair. 'No harm done,' he was repeating, 'no harm done!'

'Get home now!' Temperance ordered Enid hoarsely.

'No! Leave me alone! Go away! I'll come when I'm ready!' Enid shouted in his face. As Temperance let go of her she shrugged away from him, pulling her cardigan together and sobbing with anger. She ran around the car and turned to Les for comfort.

Les patted Enid's shoulder as gingerly as if she were a hot coal.

Temperance was bent double under the weight of his agony, making small sounds of desperation, *ah me, ah me.*

Cora couldn't bear to see him so distressed. 'Come on. Let's go back,' she said to him.

'Aye,' he agreed.

Cora took his arm as if he was an old man, and as they walked, she matched her steps to his. Her mind was jangling with the awfulness of it. She had no words to comfort him. Not for a second had she thought Enid would be in that car. She'd thought Temperance had lost his mind until the scuffling and the fury.

They were halfway home when he stopped unexpectedly. In the distance, Island Farm Camp's relentless merrymaking continued.

'What am I going to do, Cora?' he asked her.

She had no idea. It seemed as if their marriage must be irrevocably broken and there was no going back, but despite that, she said vaguely, 'It will be all right, I expect.'

'Will it?' he asked her, and just then they heard the staccato clip-clop of stilettos coming up behind them and turned to see Enid's slender figure hurrying towards them.

They waited for her and when she reached them she waved them away and said, 'Don't! I can't talk about it just now.'

The three of them carried on walking in silence, their wild thoughts raging in their heads.

But she was at least going home with him, Cora told herself, and that was the main thing.

* * *

When Cora got back to the house, it looked strange, as if they'd been away a long time. She remembered the carrots cut up in the pan of water. Instead of going home, Temperance and Enid followed her inside into the No Man's Land of Jane's kitchen.

Enid sat at the table with her coat on, her elbows on the table, her hands on her cheeks, her face puffy from crying. Tendrils of auburn hair had come unpinned. She wasn't wearing her hat. It was probably still in Les's car.

Temperance leaned over her. 'Why, Enid?' he asked her dully, shaking his head to settle his feelings into place.

'I don't know why.' She bit her lower lip, seeing the pain in his face. 'I don't know why,' she repeated. 'Everything's different, isn't it? Everything except for you. You've stayed the same.'

Temperance looked back at her helplessly, because he couldn't avoid being who he was.

'I don't know how to change, Enid,' he told her. 'I don't know who you want me to change into. I can never be him. I can never be Les.'

'No,' she agreed sadly.

His gaze roamed the kitchen as if it was a lost kingdom, and then, dazed, he settled his attention on her again. 'I suppose he sweet-talked you into it, did he?'

She was silent for a moment. 'Not really. I can't blame him for my faults. I thought it would be—' Her face screwed up as if she was in pain. 'Can you understand?' she pleaded, looking up at him.

Temperance scratched his forehead. 'And if I try to, then what? You'll carry on working there, seeing him every day?'

'If I promise...' Enid began, and then she tailed off. She had no faith in her own intentions. 'But I can't, you see?'

Cora heard her parents' voices and she'd never been more relieved to see them than when they walked through the back door. They were in a good mood and were completely taken aback to see Temperance at their table clutching his head, and Enid in tears.

'What happened to the dinner?' Jane asked, looking at the carrots in the pan in dismay. 'What's going on?'

'Enid's upset,' Temperance said. 'It's Les, it is, Les Pugh. Do you know him?'

'Of course I do,' Jane said, 'he goes to Salem chapel. Good singing voice. Tenor. His wife's nice, too,' she added, glaring at Enid.

'Excuse me.' Cora kissed her mother's cheek and went upstairs because she couldn't bear the tension any more. She didn't want to hear the words that got them nowhere. She wished they'd go home. She was exhausted from the night's upset, and she lay on her bed and tried unsuccessfully to imagine their marriage going back to normal again.

She tried to imagine what the alternative to normal looked like – she imagined Enid going to live with Les. The war would finish, the factory would close, they would patch up their lives as best they could, grow old.

'Please help Temperance cope with it,' she prayed into the darkness with her eyes wide open.

Downstairs, she heard the door open and then beneath her window, Temperance talking to Enid in the dark.

The energetic, patriotic singing blared from the camp and muffled again as they slammed the door shut.

43

The following morning it was foggy out, and as she walked to work, Cora had the sensation that her familiar world had disappeared and she was totally and frighteningly alone.

During the night it had occurred to her that Les might want nothing to do with Enid now. *No harm done!* She put her clothes in the locker and changed into her clean overalls, slid her feet into rubber-soled shoes and tucked her hair into a turban.

Enid came in, looking for her. She had blue smudges under her eyes and a fragile look about her, as if she hadn't slept at all. 'I'm sorry about last night, Cora.' She chewed the inside of her cheek. 'Temperance shouldn't have dragged you into it.'

'It wasn't like that – he came looking for you, that's all. It was cruel of you, you know, letting him find you like that.'

'Crueller still not to be honest, don't you think?'

'What do you mean?'

Enid sighed. 'Why won't you understand? I've got a chance to have a different sort of life with Les.'

It hurt Cora to hear her say that. 'You still ought to act decently towards Temperance,' she said. 'Can't you try to make it work?'

'Cora, what difference does it make to you what I do?' she asked, her voice breaking. 'You'll fall in love and get married and I'll still be stuck here with him, the rest of my life stretching in front of me, and spend it putting my domestic training skills to good use. I can't do it. I know now what I've been missing. Excuse me. I need to talk to Les before the shift starts.'

Cora joined the queue to be checked for anything metallic that might cause a spark – hair grips, jewellery, something she might have overlooked.

She was deemed clean, and as she went into the filling shop she saw Enid looking at the cards by the clocking-in machine. Cora glanced at the time. If he was coming, he would have been in by now.

Enid looked at the time, too. 'Have you heard from Les?' she called over to Winifred, the overlooker.

'He's not in.' Winifred smirked. 'Worn him out, have you, Enid?'

'I don't know what you mean.'

'Please yourself,' Winifred said, amused.

Enid went back to dets and Cora stood at her bench and started filling the shells. It was going to work out for the best, she realised with relief, because Les had made his decision, by the looks of it, and he was doing the decent thing by putting a stop to the affair. After all, Les hadn't been looking for trouble, he'd been looking for fun. True, it was cowardly of him not to turn up and tell Enid to her face, but that wasn't the point, was it?

'Cora?'

Winifred was standing over her, jolting her out of her thoughts.

'Enid's falling behind and she's in a state. I want you to take over and she can work here, just until you catch up.'

Cora hated dets. 'Why me? Please, can't someone else do it?'

'You work fast,' Winifred said. 'Don't look like that, it's just for now, Cora, until she pulls herself together. That Les! She's not the first to fall for him and I daresay she won't be the last. Come on.'

Cora left her workbench reluctantly and followed Winifred.

Enid was sitting at her bench in the dets section, her head bowed as if it was too heavy for her neck. Her lips were moving as she counted out the detonators. *One two three four five.*

Her job was to put them in the box, counting them into twenties so that they were ready to go into the bombs.

She put the box in front of her and glanced up quickly, as though she sensed him, or as if she still expected to see him at any moment. *One two three four five*, she mouthed.

'Wait here until she finishes that box,' Winifred told Cora, 'and then you take over.'

'All right.'

Cora saw that Enid's hands were shaking. Poor Enid, she thought.

One two three – Enid picked up the detonators in her trembling hands.

Suddenly there was a huge dazzling flash.

Cora felt a scorching burn of light and heat, as if the sun had fallen in. The factory walls bleached white and in the brightness of the blast all the women workers were reduced to black shapes, and Enid was flying, weightless, into endless night.

44

Cora was sent to the nurses' room to recover from the shock. The nurse gave her two cigarettes to calm her nerves, and made her a cup of strong tea. After a short break she took her to sit with Enid until her husband came.

Enid came back to consciousness in the factory surgery.

She let out a high-pitched whine of pain and she raised her right hand to her face where the shards of metal were bristling her skin.

'Hold her still, can't you,' the doctor said.

'Is it a blackout?' Enid asked fretfully. 'Don't touch my face! Wait till the lights come on again.'

'No, love, it's not a blackout.'

'Put the light on,' she croaked. 'It's hard to see.'

Cora stood in the doorway with her fists clenched under her throat, tears for Enid rolling down her burning cheeks.

'Don't you worry about us,' the doctor said. 'We're managing fine.'

'Les? Is that you?'

'Sorry, love.'

'Where's Les? My heart hurts,' she said with difficulty before being swallowed up by the night again.

* * *

In the pellets section, Gladdie and Megan heard the blow-up. Stifling their screams in case the vibrations caused a chain reaction, the machines rumbled on, the radio blared out and the smell of chemicals and dirty smoke drifted in the air and hung on the ceiling as the first-aiders ran to help.

'I knew it was Enid as soon as I heard the blow-up,' Gladdie said to Cora while they waited in the surgery after their shift ended. They were waiting for Temperance to come. 'The funny thing is, I don't remember feeling any emotion, do you? Just a numb sense of shock, knowing that it was going to happen one day, that it was bound to end like this, violently and badly. This happened because this happened, like a bomb dropping.'

'Me too,' Cora agreed superstitiously. But she thought it was because they'd found Enid in Les's car.

Gladdie turned to look at her strangely, blinking. 'Poor Enid. I dread to think how Temperance is going to take it.' Above the top of the bandage, Enid's red hair had burnt to a dry frizz. The lower part of her face was red raw, smoothed over with white ointment. The bandage was covering her eyes like a blindfold. Her hands were bandaged too.

When Temperance came in he stared at her, dumb with the horror of what had happened to her. 'Oh, Enid,' he said.

When he spoke to her she struggled to sit up. 'Temperance,' she said, slurring her words. 'You still love me, don't you? Take this dressing off so I can see you.'

'Leave it on for now, love,' he said.

'But it's too dark. I hate the dark,' she said pitifully.

Temperance looked for some part of her to touch, to comfort her. He cupped his hand under her elbow.

'You still love me, don't you?' she asked him again, speaking with difficulty, and before he could answer she said, 'I'm sorry.'

'You mustn't worry about anything,' Temperance said firmly. 'Just get better, that's the main thing.'

'Ask them to uncover my eyes, will you?'

'Yes, I'll ask.'

Enid was quiet for a moment and then she relaxed and slipped into sleep. They tiptoed out of the ward, afraid to wake her.

Cora lifted her burning face to the balm of the cold wind.

'Poor old girl,' Temperance said, keeping his head low against the icy wind. 'My lovely girl.'

And he started to cry.

45

It was an awful time. The rumours spread around the town like currency. All those who worked in their section knew that Enid and Les had eyes for each other and it was like a judgement on them, or on Enid, at least. No one spoke about these rumours in front of Temperance, though, not even as a joke.

But a few days later a letter was published in the *South Wales Echo* under the pseudonym Disgusted Husband. The writer was condemning the way men working at the factory preyed on the women incessantly until they gave in, put their morals aside and let them have their way.

When Cora read it she knew that Temperance was the Disgusted Husband. Incessantly was his favourite word. She'd passed the newspaper over to her mother to read. 'Look at this.'

Jane studied the letter and raised her eyebrows at Cora, obviously thinking the same thing. 'It could be anyone,' she said, trying to be fair, putting the paper down and sipping her tea, 'but it's Temperance, it is, no doubt about it. A man doesn't like to think his wife is to blame.'

'Makes a change,' Cora said, 'to have a husband blaming the men. It's usually the other way around.'

* * *

Cora was staring at the picture of Temperance's grandfather in his front room and coming to the conclusion she was going to give the anti-escape meetings up as a bad job because they had turned nasty now.

With Enid still in hospital, Temperance directed his raging fury towards the Germans. 'If the bloody Nazis hadn't started the war, there would have been no need for munitions and Enid would have stayed respectable and she'd never have gone to work in a factory and met Les. I would rather she had divorced me than see her like this,' he said.

Dio patted his friend on the shoulder. 'I know. But these things happen.'

There was such understanding in his voice that Temperance looked at him in surprise. 'Has Jane ever—?'

Cora glanced at her father – she almost laughed at the ludicrousness of the idea.

'Jane? Good grief! No.' Dio tried to be rational about it. 'Be fair, man, she's a different kettle of fish,' he said.

Temperance sucked his cheeks in. 'True enough,' he conceded. 'I worry she'll see Les again.'

'She's not going to see him or anyone else, is she, that's the whole point,' Dio said soberly with a flash of dark humour.

Cora frowned at her father, and wondered if he'd gone too far with his plain speaking.

The tragedy was getting to all of them. Temperance had lost a great deal of his inherent optimism and belief in fair play since finding Enid in the car with Les. Now that he wasn't energised by love, he was fuelled with anger instead.

It turned his weakness into strength.

'When the escape happens, I'll be ready,' he said. 'I swear on my mother's grave I will get my revenge.'

46

1992

'And after that, she was okay, Enid?' Elisavet asked Gladdie, listening to this story on Old Bridge.

'Not really, no,' Gladdie said. 'Enid lost her eyes.'

'Lost them?'

'They stitched them shut over empty sockets while she waited for glass eyes, and once she realised that she was blind, she couldn't bear it. She couldn't bear ugliness, not in herself or in others. She stayed in bed and wouldn't let us visit. Life was over and she couldn't imagine a future for herself. She didn't believe that Temperance could love her as she was. She'd always enjoyed being admired, but she couldn't stand him pitying her. She hated that.'

'But then she went to St Dunstan's,' Megan said. 'Finish the story properly, Gladdie.'

'Yes, she went to St Dunstan's.'

Elisavet frowned. 'It is a church?'

'Not a church, no. It was a place for servicemen blinded during the Great War. They expanded it to include people serving on the Home Front. Enid had the opportunity to go there because she was a munitions worker, see, so she qualified. Temperance talked her into going and she went for his sake, really, so that he could have a break from her and her misery. She changed a lot after the accident.'

'Dew, saved her life, it did, didn't it, Cora?' Gladdie said, remembering.

'It's true,' Cora agreed. 'It saved her life. It was full of people like her, people who understood what she was going through and who knew it wasn't the end of things, that the world was still full of joy and hope. She mixed with people of all ages, too, young and old, it was a real community and it was a cheerful and happy place. It was a training and rehabilitation centre, and the people who trained them were blind themselves, so there were no excuses, they knew everything that was possible, that you could achieve great things in life. Enid loved that. She learned shorthand typing when the burns healed and she was good at it, she recovered flexibility in her fingers – well, she'd been nimble fingered to start with from handing the dets. When she came home from Church Stretton two years later she got a job as a shorthand typist in an office, and she stayed there until she retired.'

Elisavet leaned back against the bridge wall and stared at the blue sky, watching the clouds slide across it like foam. Her hair blew free in the breeze. 'It was an interesting place?'

'Yes. She said that the St Dunstaners switched the light back on in her existence.'

'And this Les she loved? What happened to him?'

'He carried on as usual, didn't he, Cora?'

'Yes. Good-looking man, he was, fair play. It was the white jacket and the white hat that did it, made him look continental. All the Budgies fancied him.'

'Not all,' Megan said.

'No, not all,' Cora agreed with a smile.

'And her marriage?'

'We saw a different side to Temperance. He was very angry, and because he didn't know what to do with it he redirected his anger to the Germans in the camp. Wouldn't let it drop. He had a rifle he used for shooting foxes, spent a lot of time cleaning and oiling it.'

'But that's not the point of the story,' Megan said quickly. 'The point is, they lived to celebrate their golden wedding anniversary. That's fifty years! There we are! As we say in all good fairy stories, they lived happily ever after.'

Elisavet looked doubtful but said nothing.

Cora didn't blame her. Although they'd always thought of it as a story with a happy ending, it had a touch of the Brothers Grimm about it.

* * *

That evening when Elisavet came round, Frank's journal entry seemed to reflect the tone of the day. Happy outcomes, Cora thought, didn't erase the pain that one felt before reaching them.

In the days before the escape, I was the most tired I'd ever been. We were on limited rations now, putting food aside for the escape, enough to keep us going until we reached safety.

I was always hungry and sleep was a longed-for escape. Sleep, and Cora, with her sharply angled eyebrow, the sweet smile, her grey eyes. The rest of her I guessed at.

It was impossible, of course, to think we had a future together but at lights out I lay with my arm across my chest as if it was her arm. I wondered what lay ahead for me when the war was over. I just wanted normal things, a job, a wife, children, and they were nice thoughts, happy thoughts. I tried to hold onto them but the undercurrent of uneasiness that was preventing me from sleeping also prevented me from being too hopeful. It was better to expect the worst and have it fulfilled than hope for the best and be disappointed.

The last thing I thought before I fell asleep was that I would like a wife with green hair and a yellow face. It didn't seem too much to ask.

At six o'clock the following morning I climbed down from my bunk to go to join the queue for the washroom.

Otto was in a deep sleep and hadn't even stirred.

'Time to get up, old man,' I said. I put my hand on his shoulder and gave him a shake. I felt the unnatural coldness of Otto's skin through his vest. The colour had gone out of him. My spirits plunged. I knew what it meant. For a moment I stood there without moving, feeling the creep of despair and sorrow.

Otto hadn't been in the best of health. He was a good man, a man of morals and integrity. Without his knowledge and ingenuity, the tunnel would have been a far more uncomfortable and dangerous experience, if it had ever been started at all. Otto had been so close to going home.

His funeral was held a few days later on an overcast day.

Cora fetched her scrapbook to show Elisavet the yellowing newspaper cutting she'd pasted in it. 'It's not much of an obituary,' she said. 'I remember feeling that at the time.'

Island Farm Camp Death

Mr Ivor Davies reported that the whole camp was allowed to parade in the marketplace for the funeral of Otto Fiegel, an Army construction expert, and that they goose-stepped through the town giving Heil Hitler salutes.

'Their arrogant behaviour and their contempt of the present guards,' he said, 'made us all believe that their treatment was far too lax. But we were told that the reason for the special privileges accorded to them was that they were entitled to special treatment under international convention.'

47

Gwyn called on Cora one evening and it was obvious he had something on his mind. He crouched down to look at her paintings propped up in the hall.

'For Gladdie's exhibition,' she explained.

'Nice.'

He stayed looking at them for longer than he needed to and in the meantime she began to wonder whether he wanted to talk about him and Elisavet. For a moment her mind span in that direction. They might be good for each other, both of them intelligent and interesting. Elisavet would be her daughter-in-law. Cora was determined not to be a demanding mother-in-law, keeping her son for herself, no indeed not, and if he wanted to go to a war zone, well. Whatever he decided to do, she would be happy for him, happy for them both.

'We've named the date,' Gwyn said. 'August the 10th. Frank's birthday.'

'That was quick!' Cora patted her heart.

'Not really. I've known Fiona for three years now and it's time.'

'Fiona?' Cora couldn't keep the astonishment out of her voice and when he looked at her sharply, it was that look people gave when you'd said something crazy and they suspected you were losing your mind. She recovered herself. 'A summer wedding!' she said. 'I shall wear a hat!'

'Good, she was hoping you would, she wants it traditional. She's put up with a lot from us, but she's stuck around and I'd be crazy to let her go.' He smiled. 'She's going to talk to you about it, flowers and things, but I wanted to break the news to you first. Lottie is going to be maid of honour.'

'Lottie is?' Surprise upon surprise!

'It's funny, once we decided to get married, everything changed. They are completely different with each other. We're going to be a family. It makes it permanent, doesn't it? She knows that Fiona's not just – someone who's going to be here now and one day will walk out of our lives. She's here to stay.' He plucked his lower lip and smiled wistfully at her. 'I know how you felt about Regina. You loved her like a daughter. But I'm ready now...'

'Yes, I'm ready too,' Cora said firmly.

He looked surprised, and relieved. And then he nodded, as if she'd behaved in exactly the way he'd hoped she would.

They smiled at each other, his big wide smile mirroring her own.

'By the way, just warning you, they're going to invite you on a wedding dress hunt with Fiona's mother, making a day of it. I'm not supposed to tell you, so act surprised.'

'How exciting! I will!' She reached up and cupped his gentle face in her hands. She looked into his eyes. 'You're a lovely son,' she said warmly.

There was going to be a wedding!

No need to ask if he was sure – she had never seen him happier.

48

11 MARCH 1945

In the early hours of the morning a pistol shot jerked Cora awake from a deep sleep. She sat up in bed, the noise ricocheting through her dream.

She could hear shouting, men's voices, and she got out of bed and opened the window.

A man was screaming in the icy darkness and the sound carried over the open fields and into the night. She flinched at the pain in it. It was followed by the roar of commotion. Steady, she told herself. It's not an escape. The alarm isn't sounding. If it was an escape, there would be an alarm.

And then the alarm did sound, wailing mournfully through the night as if she had provoked it, and she could hear movement from the bedroom next door and Dio's agitated voice. She dressed quickly and met him on the landing, his troubled sooty eyes puffy with sleep.

'They're out,' he said, his voice tight, and he went back into the bedroom to pull his trousers on over his pyjamas.

Jane was putting on extra clothes against the cold. 'This is it,' she said through gritted teeth, buttoning up her cardigan.

'Don't go.'

Jane laughed, and her face was flushed and animated. 'Don't be stupid, girl! It's what we've been waiting for! Eye for eye, tooth for tooth.'

'It won't bring Owen back, will it?'

Jane gave a hungry grin. 'A life for a life.'

She wasn't listening, Cora knew that. Their thoughts were running along different lines. She ran downstairs to the kitchen and pulled her coat on over her nightdress. Jane was picking up the shotgun propped against the dresser and emptying cartridges into her chapel coat pocket.

Cold with dread, thinking of the shot, the scream, Cora sat on the doorstep pulling on her wellingtons. Out of two thousand prisoners, there was no reason why it should be Frank, she told herself sensibly.

She hurried down the lane and into the night with her torch, flashing the small circle of light onto black shapes merging against the silver fields. Bedlam. Men were shouting, dogs barking. Guards standing on the roofs of the huts directing flashlights at the fields, and shapes converged in beams of light, the gleam of gun barrels, the howl of the hunt. In the camp the prisoners were banging their spoons against their metal plates. It was a frenzy of chaos, and in the din, Temperance was yelling: 'Spread out, men!'

Cora saw Idwal standing alone on the path, shoulders hunched, watching it all from a distance. She shone her torch on him. 'What's happening?' she asked. 'I heard a gunshot.'

'The guards shot one of them,' he said.

'Dead?'

'No, no. Thankfully. Go home, Cora. Go home,' he repeated, turning to face her. 'You shouldn't be here. There are killers on the loose.'

'Not all Germans are killers,' she said, thinking of Frank.

'I'm not talking about the Germans, am I,' Idwal said. 'Our lot, I mean. Bloodlust, that's what it is.'

The search party was spreading out across the fields, men shouting, dogs barking, flashlights playing, and her mother screaming victory amongst them.

Cora flashed her torch across the scene.

She heard her mother's voice, pitched high with adrenaline: 'Murderers!' and Temperance shouting in his football hooligan's voice: 'Spread out! Don't let the devils get away!'

'How many have got out, do you think?' she asked Idwal.

'The first ones left before midnight, according to May,' Idwal said. 'They'll be well away by now. These are the stragglers, the opportunists. Poor blighters.'

She felt a surge of relief. Frank would be long gone. For him the important thing was to get as far away as possible, as quickly as possible. 'Thanks, Idwal.'

She switched her torch off and turned to go home, keeping close to the entangled hedgerows at the edge of the field, away from the barking dogs and the roaring crowd. So that's that, she thought hollowly. It was over. Frank had gone. She was glad for his sake that he'd gone. At the same time, the thought of not seeing him again broke her heart.

Behind the knotted branches, a thin streak of a flashlight lit her up.

She heard a dog bark and Shep was by her side, panting, his tongue lolling. She bent and rested her hand for a moment on the dog's head. The loud report of a shotgun reverberated across the field.

Frank, she thought in panic, and in the time it took to think his name she felt a blow, a sharp sting of shot like a swarm of bees in her scalp. She crouched in shock, hugging herself. 'Don't shoot me!' she screamed, as if the shock waves of the plea would hold her mother back.

Her fingers were sticky with blood, the pellets embedded as little bumps. The blood was hot as it rolled down her neck.

There was a babble of voices, and the loudest was her father's.

'No-no-no-no-no!' Dio was yelling as he ran, as if it wasn't too late to stop what had happened.

Cora's head burned with pain, and her knees buckled. Dark shapes were running towards her, guns down, but her father reached her first and fell on his knees beside her.

'Oh, my girl.'

She hurt, and her head pulsed with hot and fiery agony. The night had gone quiet, and the noises from the camp ceased. She heard her name passed around, spoken softly.

Dio put his arms around her and lifted her up and he pressed her forehead against his rough tweed overcoat. 'My dear girl,' he said with abject pity, his voice so low that that she couldn't hear the words, only feel them vibrating through his chest, as if he'd only now remembered she was his child.

The house was still and strange when Dio carried her in. He took a teacloth out of the kitchen drawer and put the kettle on and filled a bowl with water, murmuring to himself all the while with his back to her. 'And forgive us our trespasses,' he whispered urgently, pausing on the words as though it was a strange language only he could understand, 'as we forgive those who tres-pass against us.'

As he dabbed her hair, Cora saw that he was crying.

'Don't worry, I'm all right,' she said, sad to be causing him pain and scared for his pride's sake to wipe his coal-black tears.

He poured the hot water into the kitchen sink and helped her out of her coat, shiny with blood. 'Come here.'

Cora bent over the sink and stared into the water, watching the swirls of pink as he poured gushing jugfuls over her head.

The towel was rough as he wrapped it around her head. 'Cup of tea?' he asked gently.

'Yes, please.' Cora touched the towel. 'What will happen to me?'

'The pellets will work their way out in time. Better than having them cut out, in my view.'

'Oh.' She stared at the tea shimmering in the cup and looked up at him, her heart aching for Frank. 'I'm scared.'

Dio fell back on old comforts. '"Let not your heart be troubled, neither let it be afraid." I don't know. It's something to hold onto, Cora,' he said desper-ately, like a man swimming to a leaking life raft.

* * *

Cora was lying in bed awake. The noises from the fields behind the camp had died down.

She was praying to move beyond the pain in her head and the bigger pain in her heart, to a time when Frank would be like Gladdie's GI, Charles: a name which brought a momentary sense of happiness and regret and nothing more.

Cora heard raised voices and she got out of bed and stood listening as Dio let his anger loose.

'You shot your own daughter! You bloody fool!'

Cora wanted to hear her mother's reply. Her head felt huge and hot.

'Not on purpose as you very well know!' Jane snapped back at him, unre-pentant. 'I thought I'd got one of *them*,' she added, and the disappointment was thick in her voice.

That very evening the anti-escape committee met at Temperance's house for the final time, just to tie things up, like.

Temperance put Cora in his own chair.

Her father had bandaged her head and it was like a white flag reminder to them all that the escape hadn't gone the way they'd envisaged it. There was no getting away from that.

It had the heaviness of shame about it, as well as failure. Despite their plans and their meetings, they had behaved like a wild rabble of barbarians. Guilt shimmered in the cold room.

Not only that, there was the awkwardness of Jane turning up to join them, tight-lipped and defiant. She sat on the lowly tapestry footstool and no one could look at her, not even Dio.

They glanced at each other over her head and didn't condemn her or sympathise, but no one understood it really, how Jane could have shot at a shape in the dark when it could have been any one of them.

Temperance cleared his throat and read from his final notes. 'The tally so far is sixteen German prisoners arrested locally and twelve further afield. Two only got as far as Llanharan, they must've walked in a circle, and one got caught trying to find the port in Port Talbot. Not to worry, though. They'll round them all up eventually.'

There was an awkward atmosphere in the chilly front room.

And then Jane spoke up. 'I want it noted that after all these months of talk, I was the only one with guts enough to shoot them,' she said.

They all turned to look at her as one, like cats.

Jane jutted her chin, as though in her mind she had shot a German with undimmed justification and it was Cora's fault that she hadn't.

'But you didn't, Jane,' Idwal spoke out, stating the obvious on behalf of them all. 'You shot your own daughter!'

It crushed Cora. She said quickly, trying to catch her breath and dampen down the explosion, 'It doesn't matter, it could have been worse, a miss is as good as a mile.'

Silence. No one pointed out that actually Jane hadn't missed, but they were all thinking it.

Cora felt saliva sweeten her mouth. She was going to be sick with sheer misery. She swallowed hard and jumped to her feet. 'I'll be back in a minute,' she said. 'I left—' She was in too much of a hurry to invent the lie any further. 'Sorry,' she said, covering her mouth.

Out in the quiet street she put her hands on her knees and doubled over. She spat the sourness into the gutter. The blood rushed to her head and she straightened, feeling the scabs throb.

Never a word of apology from her mother, she thought bitterly, and it was hard to face that she meant so little to her. She took a few deep breaths, pulled herself together and went back into Temperance's house.

Her mother was talking, justifying herself. 'I did it for Owen,' she said, flushed. 'You might have forgotten what they did to him but I haven't and I never will.'

Dio gave a twitch of the head like a horse ridding a fly.

'Hey, come on, Jane,' he said, 'we haven't forgotten him, not for a moment.' He frowned at the outrageous unfairness of her words because each of them carried a small lump of grief for Owen that they only felt in the dread of a restless night.

'Well, that's that, anyway. It's over. With the best of intentions we went out to fight the Germans in our own land,' Temperance said. He pinched the bridge of his nose, and blinked. 'I can't see that any good came from it, mind. Any other business before I call our final meeting to a close?'

There being no other business they got to their feet and left for home, heads bent, glad to be out of there in the silent and uneasy manner of the guilty.

49

1992

'Your mother shot you?' Elisavet said, frowning over her coffee cup.

Cora set the flask down on the bridge wall. 'She did.'

'Still got the bumps, haven't you?' Gladdie said, stirring a saccharine in with her pencil.

'Still got the bumps,' Cora agreed cheerfully.

'And all those Germans escaped through the tunnel?'

'That's right. Half of them got out after roll-call. They'd gone before anyone noticed.'

Elisavet stared at them and shook her head slowly in a disbelieving sort of way.

Cora didn't blame her. It was a bad few days, that's what she remembered. Awful. She couldn't see forward to a time after that time. She was trapped, with no hope of any kind of happiness, just work and sleep and despair.

'Dew, the excitement,' Gladdie said, remembering it differently, 'you've never seen anything like it! People went out hunting for the Germans in the wood and in the sand dunes and there were reporters everywhere, all eager to hear our stories, asking us who'd been shot and what we'd seen, and Alva Liddell on the news, do you remember him, Megan? Alva Liddell giving updates every evening on how many prisoners had been caught and how many were still at large, working out the tally.'

* * *

The next time Elisavet came round, Cora called her upstairs. She was on her hands and knees in the spare room, dragging a box out of the cupboard. 'I'm not sure why I've kept them for all this time,' she said to Elisavet. 'On the other hand, when I imagine throwing them away, I think: keep them, Cora, because what difference will another year make! They might come in handy one of these days! And I was right,' she ended modestly, smiling up at Elisavet.

The newspapers were broadsheets, old and yellowing, and they had a peculiar, acrid smell to them.

'Let me,' Elisavet said, picking the box up effortlessly.

'Let's put them on the bed. You'll enjoy this,' she promised. 'The German Great Escape was very much the hot topic of the day, as you can imagine. Like a soap opera, it was, we couldn't get enough of it. And all the time I was hoping for news of Frank but the truth was, I wanted him to get away successfully and make it home somehow, all in one piece. Here. Help yourself.'

They sat either end of the bed with the box between them and started to read.

Monday, March 12th
News Chronicle
70 Nazi Prisoners Escape
Home Guards and planes in search

Seventy German prisoners of war escaped from a camp at Bridgend (Glam.) in the early hours yesterday.

At night thirty-six were still at large: thirty-four had been recaptured during the day at various places in the neighbourhood. There was some shooting and one prisoner and a woman civilian were slightly wounded.

Four stole a car and got into Gloucestershire where planes were used in the search.

Hundreds of the home guard living in Bridgend, which lies about midway between Cardiff and Swansea, at once volunteered to help in the search.

Warning in churches

Regular soldiers, police, civil defence workers and farmers were also out. At chapels and churches in the district, morning service was interrupted to read police warnings.

* * *

Tuesday, March 13th
Daily Worker
NAZIS DUG A 45-FT TUNNEL
Twenty-Seven Still at Large

The German prisoners of war who escaped from the camp at Bridgend, Glamorganshire, on Sunday, had planned their escape with elaborate care for many weeks.

They burrowed a tunnel 45 feet long and one and a half feet in diameter from inside a hut, under barbed wire, into a field. It was just large enough for a man to squeeze through. The horizontal portion was so large that men could walk about without stooping.

Tons of earth must have been removed. They carried it outside in haversacks and empty food tins when they went on parade and scattered it in small pieces.

Twenty-seven of the seventy who escaped were still at large last night.

* * *

Tuesday, March 13th
Daily Mirror
ATS girl grabbed fleeing Nazi

As soldiers, home guards, police, land girls, farm labourers and even schoolchildren searched the Welsh hills throughout daylight yesterday for the remainder of the seventy Nazi prisoners who escaped from their camp near Bridgend, Glamorgan, people in the district were hailing a brave ATS girl whose courage ended the escape bid of two of the men almost before it had begun. The girl saw the men skulking across a field not far from the camp.

Without hesitation she grabbed hold of one and held him.

The other man with him surrendered and the girl in khaki handed them both over to the authorities.

A Welsh housewife out shopping yesterday set the pursuers on the track of three other prisoners.

She heard the sound of twigs snapping alongside the road on the outskirts of Bryntirion in Bridgend and saw three men, obviously Germans in uniform, in a field.

'One of the men was on the side of the wall nearest me. He saw me looking towards him, jumped back over the wall and all three ducked out of sight.

'I wasn't unduly alarmed but I thought it wisest, being a woman, not to tackle them on my own.' A cordon was immediately thrown around the area.

The men who escaped include rough, young, fanatical Nazis, including paratroopers and SS men, who have been causing trouble for many weeks. Residents have been complaining of their shouting and singing at all hours. Twenty prisoners were still at large at noon yesterday.

Many of the prisoners were thought to have found cover in the Welsh hills or sparsely populated parts of the valleys only a few miles from the camp.

Good cover too is available on the sand dunes and rocks and caves of the wild Glamorganshire coast 6 miles from Bridgend.

Dispatch riders patrolled all roads in Glamorgan and border counties, while soldiers in extended formation covered the countryside.

All aerodromes are guarded by soldiers with tommy guns.

Four men caught by the police were trying to escape in a car they had stolen.

* * *

Wednesday, March 14th
Daily Voice
GIRL'S HUNCH TRAPS NAZIS

Five found in copse where she played hide-and-seek

A hunch of a twenty-two-year-old girl led to the recapture yesterday of five more of the seventy German prisoners who, earlier this week, escaped from a camp near Bridgend.

Later tonight two more prisoners were picked up by special constables within 200 yards of Kenfig Hill police station, while three more were found by war reserve police near a Pencoed factory.

All so far captured have had good supplies tucked away in their knap-sacks – German black bread and bully beef hoarded from their Red Cross parcels, as well as bits of food saved from meals at the camp before breakout.

None was armed and none had discarded his uniform. The patches torn off their camp clothes have been found on hedges and in ditches near the camp.

Army trained Alsatian dogs have been brought in to help in the search.

Soldiers and airmen men in the manhunt are armed with tommy guns or rifles, and arms have also been issued to members of the old home guard.

The Welsh committee of the Communist Party has protested at this laxity. 'The Welsh people,' Mr Idris Cox, secretary of the committee, told me, 'are alarmed at the thought of Nazis roaming at large in their midst.

'We demand stricter control in such camps and the suppression of Nazi influence in them.'

Home Guards refused petrol

The people here are also indignant at the slowness with which they allege the military authorities at Western command have tackled the job.

Local home guard officer told me that if they had had the necessary petrol, it would have been possible to throw a cordon of at least two thou-sand ex-home guards around the area within six hours.

Application was made to the Western command for the necessary petrol with the support of the local police.

But the application was refused and as a result valuable time has been lost.

Officers and men now engaged in the search are of the opinion that the escape plot was very well planned. With the main object of ensuring the getaway of a small group of not more than half a dozen picked Nazi officers, it is believed that the rest were to serve as a cover for the selected few and draw the scent away from this group.

* * *

Sunday, March 18th

THE SUNDAY EXPRESS LONDON

Note to guard told of Nazi escape plan

First warning that mass escape was planned from the German war prisoners' camp at Bridgend, Glamorgan, came in a note, apparently written by an anti-Nazi, and thrown through the barbed wire fence surrounding the compound.

The note was picked up by a sentry. Orders were given that guards should be doubled. Sentries stood with rifles at the ready. Flares were placed at intervals round the wire which surrounds the camp. No signs of movement could be seen, but while the sentries stood in readiness, seventy Germans crawled through a tunnel that had been dug from inside the hut to a point outside the wire and disappeared silently into the darkness. All but three of the escaped prisoners have now been recaptured. Most of them were caught within a few miles of the camp, but a few were caught as far away as Southampton and Birmingham.

Camp split up

Investigation has shown that many inmates of the camp were aware of what was to happen, and as a measure of precaution the prisoners are to be split up and sent to different camps. The first party of thirty left yesterday.

Preparations for the escape had been in progress for some months.

Few sentries

British troops who guard the camp bitterly resent Press criticism accusing them of laxity.

British at the camp are fewer than 150 and the guard company is only about ninety strong.

There are some 2,300 – 1,700 officers, mostly Luftwaffe, SS and para-troops, and 600 other ranks.

Ten sentries guard nearly a mile of wire – approximately 176 yards to each man – and the men feel this is too few at night.

'Interesting stories,' Elisavet said as she was reading the copy of the *Sunday Express*. She folded it in half. 'Look at this, Cora! It says a note was thrown through the wire fence and picked up by a guard. But why?' she demanded. 'It makes no sense to throw it out of the camp. The prisoner could just hand it discreetly to the guard: here, take. More sensible, don't you think?'

Cora laughed, because there was a sparkle in Elisavet's eyes that she hadn't noticed before. 'Absolutely,' she said.

For a moment they looked at each other.

Elisavet tilted her head. 'You know what I think? I think the note was from Frank to you.'

'Well, that is sharp of you! The guard caught him throwing it. I felt guilty because it was obvious the guard would report it and the tunnel would be found. But it wasn't. It was bittersweet, the night the alarm sounded. The note was Frank's goodbye.'

50

1945

One week after the escape, Cora and Gladdie were heading home from the late shift. The rain had turned the street to gloss. Gladdie tucked her arm in Cora's as the moonlight was breaking through the clouds.

'You'll be all right, Cora,' Gladdie said. 'You'll get over him.'

'Yes, I know.'

Cora caught a movement by the hydrangeas at the front of her house, a shadow sliding against the wall, and she saw the way the shadow's cap sat on his shadow head.

Her heart soared in disbelief and then crashed in alarm. 'Good night then, Gladdie,' she said, keeping her voice steady. 'See you in the morning.'

'Good night, Cora. Sleep tight.'

The side of the house threw its darkness over her and she bumped right into Frank. 'It's you! Hello!' Solid, he was, and real, and wet. Trying to see each other in the dark, she was astonished he was here. It was a miracle, was all she could think. She ran her fingers over his face to see if he was real.

'Cora,' he said softly, resting his hands on her shoulders.

He was so cold.

He pressed his face against hers, and feeling the damp chill of him, she was thinking wildly about their options, where she could hide him, tugging him towards the coal shed. Not the coal shed! Because Dio might want to fetch a couple more lumps for the fire.

The greenhouse, then, at the bottom of the garden. She led him down there and the night smelled of springtime; damp and mossy. She nudged the brick from the door and took him into the dark fragrance of peat and tomato leaves, her heart thumping. She upturned a pail for him to sit on and knelt in front of him, patched up by moonlight.

'Are you all right?' she whispered, her voice hoarse with fear and excitement. 'What are you doing here? I thought you were long gone. Why did you come back?'

'Cora,' he whispered back, and took her hand and pressed it against his face, rough with stubble. 'I had to see you.'

'I'm glad you did.' *And I'm so frightened*, she thought.

She could feel his hard cheekbones under her fingertips and the muscle clenched in his jaw. She put her arms around him, to warm him. He was very thin.

'What are we going to do?' she asked him desperately. She was responsible for him now, this man, this German, this enemy, who had escaped to freedom and now come back to her.

Suddenly she thought of Idwal and his sandwich board that day outside the station. Here was a test for him!

Idwal would give him something to eat, to fulfil the promise he'd made to God, and Megan would be nice to him, because Megan was always nice. 'Listen, Frank, I'm going to take you to see friends of mine. The girl with the yellow hair?'

His eyes held hers in the dark.

They walked back furtively along the garden path from the greenhouse and Cora's heart had taken on a racing, cantering beat that throbbed through her head. She froze in fear as the back door opened, leaking a wedge of dim light. Jane looked out and saw her. 'Oh! There you are! You're late! Where have you been?' She paused as she saw Frank. 'And who's this?' she asked sharply.

'Frank,' the German said and offered his hand to her.

Jane shook it and tried to see him in the dark. 'Dew, look at the state of you!' she said, opening the door wider. Just then she saw him properly for the first time and saw his greatcoat, and realised what it meant, and she let out a wail of furious anguish.

'Hush, Mam, please,' Cora pleaded, shielding Frank from her, 'we're just going.'

'No, madam!' Jane snapped. 'You're not going anywhere. Get in the house. Now!'

Frank glanced at Cora and took his cap off his head, holding himself soldier straight and his muscles quivered with the effort.

As soon as he stepped inside the kitchen he saw the shotgun leaning on the dresser, barrels pointing to the ceiling. He looked nervously from the gun to Jane.

'Don't move, boy,' she said, picking up the shotgun. 'Let me have a good look at you.'

'Mam, please—'

Her mother lowered the gun as the kettle started whistling and her father came in to take it off the boil, startled to see the three of them standing by the door, and even more startled as he understood what he was seeing: a German, a gun, and Jane.

But that wasn't all that he saw.

Cora was looking at him, pleading for him to understand and he saw a young man come to the end of his hope.

Her father's gaze lingered on Frank for a moment and he pulled out a chair and said in his normal, everyday voice, 'What's your name?'

He swallowed. 'Frank.'

'Come here, lad.'

Her father ran his hand thoughtfully over his white hair. 'There's nothing to be done, Cora. We'll have to hand him over, you know, I'm sorry about that. But there's no need to rush it, is there? Let him get warm first.' He said to Frank, 'Sit down and have something to eat.'

Frank did as he was told, and sat down.

Her mother stared at her father for a moment, narrow-eyed, and left the kitchen, taking the shotgun with her. She closed the door behind her.

He turned his quizzical, black-rimmed gaze on Cora. As her father, he put together the hope he could see in her face with the rumours he'd heard about her. 'I'd been told about you waving at someone behind the fence. A guard, was it?'

Cora flushed. 'Not a guard, no.'

'They play football, don't they, guards against prisoners. There's a lot of tackling, so I've heard. More like rugby, tell you the truth.' He looked at Frank, and then he looked at Cora again. 'I've never had to worry about you,' he said. 'At least, not in the deep, unsettling way I worried about Owen.' His gaze softened. 'There's stew in the pan,' he said. 'We've been keeping it hot for when you got home. There's enough for two.'

Cora filled the bowl and put it in front of Frank and fetched him a spoon. She paused as he raised his grateful, tired eyes to meet hers. He had a lovely, open, fresh face, she thought, a face of bland perfection even now, as if he had transcended the tragedy of his situation.

He ate politely and quickly, mindful he was a guest, closing his eyes now and then as if he was savouring a dream.

As he was eating, Dio went upstairs, leaving the two of them alone. Cora could hear him moving about overhead. She wondered nervously where her mother had gone.

She didn't have to wonder for long because moments later, to her dismay, Jane came back into the kitchen, holding Owen's photograph in her hands. Her chair squealed on the tiled floor and she sat down at the table next to Frank.

Cora's heart sank.

'See this boy?' Jane said loudly to Frank. 'He's my son. Killed by one of your torpedoes.' She took off her spectacles and studied the photograph intently. Her hard face softened with longing for Owen. She turned to Frank. 'Do you understand what I'm saying?'

Frank looked at the photograph and then nodded at Jane, wordless.

'Aye,' she said quietly to herself. Her eyes filled with tears. After a few moments she turned to the enemy, face to face, her eyes seeking his. Looking at him, her face was full of the tragedy of war and the agony of love. 'And if he had lived long enough to be called up to fight,' she said, 'I would have hoped with all my heart that some German mother might treat him kindly.'

Dio came back downstairs, glanced into the kitchen and saw that Jane was holding Owen's photograph in her hand and that Frank's bowl was empty.

'Finished? Come with me, lad,' he said, jerking his head.

Frank stood up uncertainly, glanced at Cora and followed Dio into the front room.

Cora cleared the table, hearing them talking but she couldn't make out the words.

When they returned to the kitchen, Frank was wearing her father's suit and Dio was carrying the visitor's damp clothes in his arms.

Cora made to take them from him. 'I'll put them by the fire to dry.'

'No, you're all right, I'll do it,' Dio said. 'You two go for a stroll. The rain's stopped but take my umbrella, just in case. You've got a lot to catch up on, I expect.'

That night, Frank and Cora walked along Island Farm Avenue to the woods under the sheltering canopy of the umbrella. They could see the camp in the distance. Guards with Alsatian dogs patrolled the perimeter and Frank stared at the dimly lit huts from the shelter of the trees.

'I wish you didn't have to go back in there,' she said.

'Yes.' Frank closed the umbrella and hooked it on a branch. He put his arms around her tightly, knotting his fingers over her shoulder blades, holding her close to him.

She breathed in the mysterious, familiar scent of him, like coming home after a long journey apart. Sliding her hands under his borrowed jacket, sharing her solid warmth with him, heartbeat to heartbeat.

She could feel the thud of his heart in her own heart like an echo and she rested her head in the warm, soft crook of his neck, feeling the blood beat in his veins. The weight of terror and trepidation had slipped from her without her realising it, her longing for him taking its place. She sighed with bliss, at the same time knowing how awfully brief this time would be.

Frank's arms loosened around her and he took a box of matches out of his pocket and lit one. The flame flared and reflected in his grey eyes and she saw in them an intense belief in a future together. The match burned out and as if he knew what she was thinking, he took her face in his hands and held back her green hair from her face.

'It will be all right,' he promised.

She nodded, believing him with all her heart. 'We'll make it all right.'

He kissed her forehead, her eyelids, her mouth. There was a lot to say but the important things were the here and now, being close, the rightness of it, the relief of being together after the long and impossible journey.

Drips of rain from leaves ticked the minutes away and they swayed in each other's arms.

Reluctantly they knew their brief time together was over. They left the woods and walked home and Frank put on his old clothes again and her father took his suit back.

It was the worst feeling in the world. He was their guest, and then they had to hand him over. 'It won't be long now,' Dio said to Frank apropos of nothing as they walked through the rain-whipped empty streets to the police station. Cora was silenced by the agony of the distance between them. It was true, she thought, it didn't take long. The distance had never felt shorter. They seemed to be flying there, every second taking them closer to the moment of separation and Cora had a sick feeling deep inside her, praying for time to slow down.

At the station, Dio explained to the duty sergeant at the desk that Frank had returned willingly of his own volition.

The sergeant thought about it and looked towards the window where the branches were fighting against the wind. He turned to Frank. 'Aye, I don't blame you. It's cold out there.' He picked up his pen. 'Your pals will be glad to see you back, I expect.'

Frank raised his head for the first time and asked curiously, 'Did any of them make it?'

The sergeant glanced at Dio and then at Frank again. He rubbed his jaw. 'Well, son,' he said, 'it's early days.'

Cora didn't want to take her eyes off Frank, the straight line of his dark eyebrows, the pouches under his eyes, the shadow of his unshaven cheeks, his solemn mouth that had kissed hers. She was memorising him so that she could keep him in her mind always and her heart was breaking.

They said goodbye and left him there. The silent going home was slow and miserable, like walking in mud.

'Sorry,' Jane said abruptly when they turned into the street, without saying what she was sorry about, or who to, and neither of them asked.

51

1992

'I don't know, it's hard to explain how our attitudes changed,' Gladdie said to Elisavet, wiping her paint-streaked hands on her apron. 'It wasn't just Dio and Jane. Despite the newspaper headlines about Nazis on the rampage and all that, we knew what really went on. The truth of that time was whispered along ration queues and in the pubs, not out of shame but with pride. We all knew that there was kindness shown, in many different ways. It was a hard winter, see, and we knew what it was like for them trying to live off the land. We felt for them. We imagined them out there, cold and hungry, trying to get home.'

'Idwal left food for them on our windowsill, in case they came by,' Megan said. 'It was gone by the morning.'

'Nancy Thomas made cups of tea for two young men while they waited for the police to come.'

'Elizabeth Davies from the farm found an exhausted prisoner at her door as she was baking,' Cora added. 'He'd followed the smell of her cakes. She was so pleased that he'd found it irresistible that she invited him in for tea, but he couldn't accept because he said he had two friends outside. Civilised, see? So she invited them in too. Germans in her kitchen! Who'd have thought! She made them a meal while her son cycled to the camp to tell them to come and collect them.'

The three friends laughed at the memories.

'There was a rumour that three got back to Germany, so I heard,' Gladdie said. 'Unofficial, like.'

Megan agreed it was rumour. She'd heard it, too.

Cora thought of Frank and the ball of dried clay on the mantelpiece. 'It would be nice, wouldn't it, to know that after all those weeks of digging, three of them made it home.'

52

The escape meant the end of Island Farm Camp 198.

The majority of prisoners were quickly separated and transferred to other POW camps. The huts on the perimeter were out of bounds, and the garden, too, and a new influx of guards and dogs patrolled the barbed wire with rigorous enthusiasm.

The remaining hundred or so of us prisoners were moved to accommodation in the centre of the camp, well away from the fence. It was the worst outcome for me, because I had no more opportunity to see Cora.

I kept hold of the sensation of her palm on my cheek, my mouth on her hair. I could see her in my mind's eye but more importantly I felt the essence of her, her smell, her smile, her warmth. I longed for her painfully and hopelessly.

A new camp commander, Major Topham, was put in charge of the diminished prison. In the following weeks, the war rushed to a close. On 12 April the news was broadcast that Roosevelt was dead. On 28 April, Mussolini was killed by partisans. And on 30 April, Hitler shot himself.

We received the news with silence. It was over. We gave up the dream that the mighty power of the Third Reich would make the world a better place. A new German Empire hadn't proved to be a good thing after all and after months of trying to work out the direction of the war, the guesswork was over. Through the news we learned of the devastating destruction of German cities and the awful death toll.

Hitler, our glorious leader, had made a mess of it. He'd bailed out like a coward and had willingly abandoned us to the disaster he'd created, leaving us like orphans to fend for ourselves.

A month or so later, we were invited to listen to a lecture on British democracy, and then, by way of a bribe, we were told that this would be followed by a documentary.

'Be cautious,' Kurt said to me. 'They're brainwashing us, of course.'

But when each day was the same as the last and the same as the next, any deviation from the norm was very welcome.

Not only that, although it was described as an invitation, attendance was not optional.

We filed into the cinema and I sat on an uncomfortably hard chair, arms folded, telling myself to try to be open-minded about it.

I listened to the speaker, knowing that I wouldn't be able to work out the truth until I returned home and found it out for myself but I was beginning to wonder if the truth was impossible to find.

They are brainwashing us, I reminded myself.

I sat forward intently, my arms resting on my knees, listening to what the British officer had to say about democracy and the parliamentary system. I wasn't finding it easy. It was surely easier for citizens to be told what to think and do, because if they were left to their own opinions, what if they made the wrong choice?

But I found it interesting that the lecturer emphasised the importance of open discussion. He also pointed out the difference between patriotic Germans and Nazis.

I had always believed they were one and the same, but I began thinking of the brutality of the SS and their arrogance, their pride, their use of violence as the mood took them.

Of course, I reasoned, trying to be fair about it, the Nazis wouldn't have to be brutal if people just behaved themselves, so it was a reasonable response, wasn't it? I wondered if my own beating had been a reasonable response.

The British officer was concluding his talk. 'I have faith in our ability to start afresh after this, to rebuild, and to begin to understand each other's *feelings a little better,' he said. 'Or at least,' he added with a faint smile, 'head in that general direction.'*

I thought about the officer's lecture, wondering gloomily if there was room in my own head for this different point of view. Putting my fingers to my lips to whistle so as to add to the noise, my opinions were confused and drifting, and then the lights were dimmed and a cine camera flickered into life onto the screen in front of them, blotches of black and white.

A film!

We cheered heartily at this new piece of entertainment.

For a moment, seeing the barbed wire, I thought it was a film of Island Farm Camp. 'We're going to be famous,' I said to Kurt, nudging him, and he joined in with the bout of foot stamping which thundered through the room.

But when we saw the internees of the death camp we fell silent. The screen was filled with shuffling skeletons with dull eyes, too near to death for hope. Hairless men and women, suffering, and mountains of naked bodies in the background.

My chest tightened. I couldn't breathe.

It was hard to watch, and because it was hard to watch I didn't want to believe it. I started doubting it as I'd doubted so much in the last few weeks. And then I wanted it to stop.

On the flickering film we watched the SS forcing concentration camp victims to dig their own grave. Then bang, bang, bang, pistols firing, they toppled into it one by one.

'It's a lie, isn't it,' I asked Kurt, flinching in horror. 'I don't believe it for one moment.'

Kurt didn't take his eyes off the screen and he didn't turn his head. 'Don't you?' he asked tiredly.

Did I?

If it were true it didn't bear thinking about and yet I desperately wanted to understand the truth of it. I thought of my church at home, and the one single teaching that I remembered from that time when I was a boy and the world still seemed reliable and regular: God Is Love.

It had been wonderful to know that. I'd believed it with all my heart, which was easy because I was loved. I lived comfortably with my mother, father, little sister and God, safe and loving in our midst.

But on the screen was a relentless world of nightmare brutality, bodies being thrown naked, children, adults, babies piled up in a heap in a tangle of limbs and the impassive Nazi guards watching it unmoved. 'Nobody is seeing the horror,' I said to Kurt desperately, tugging his arm.

By the time the film rattled to an end the jeers had stopped and the room was filled with a heavy silence, broken by Kurt.

'You're wrong about that. The whole world is seeing it, Frank,' he said.

For the first time since my imprisonment, I felt the urge to go and talk to the German military padre, to see what he thought.

I liked the little chapel that they'd set up, with its homemade wooden altar, hand-drawn pictures of saints and the good-looking Virgin Mary with her fair hair rolled back from her face in a modern style that I found very relatable. It had been turned into an SS gym at one point, and now it was a chapel again.

The candles flickered their gentle glow over the padre who was praying on his knees when I got there.

I shut my eyes and tried to pray myself, looking deep into the bleakness of my thoughts. I wondered if I'd lost my faith, not so much in God as in man.

I waited patiently while the padre finished his prayer.

The priest straightened up very carefully, as if he was in pain, and turned to me with a strained smile. He looked tired. 'How can I help you?'

I could see white hairs threaded through the priest's dark hair. 'I'm not sure,' I said uncertainly. 'I don't know what to think any more. I just came here to talk things over with you, really. It seems the right place.'

The desperate look in the padre's eyes made me feel as if both of us were sliding slowly down a steep hill with nothing to stop us except the bottom of a crevasse. 'I was hoping you would tell me something reassuring.'

'I'll do my best. What is it you want to be reassured about?'

I told him about the lecture on free discussion and tolerant thinking, and about the film they'd shown us of the death and the suffering. 'I want to be able to recognise the truth when I see it.'

'They say the first casualty of war is truth,' the padre said with a broken smile.

I nodded with nervous impatience. 'Yes, but that's not much help to me, is it?' I didn't know if I was brave or crazy for believing in democracy. How could you tell? 'Is tolerant thinking the answer?'

The padre looked down at his hands, and he closed his eyes. He was silent for some moments. Then he said, 'Look where the alternative has got us.'

It was a depressing thought. I looked at the Virgin Mary, who in the candlelight seemed to be suffering with us. 'Padre – will I ever see my family again?'

'I'm not a fortune teller. That way of thinking didn't work out very well for Hitler, did it,' he replied ruefully. 'But one day you will have a family of your own, no doubt. A wife, children, and you will find in them the qualities you thought were lost.'

It wasn't the answer I wanted and I covered my face with my hands for a moment. My thoughts flickered on Cora, and her father's worn suit. I looked up. 'But in the meantime – will it help me to pray about it, do you think?' I asked hopefully.

The padre gave an unexpected laugh. 'It always helps!' he said.

Some time later, I was instructed to go and see Major Topham.

I saluted and waited patiently for my new orders.

The commander flicked through forms, shuffled his papers and finally looked up at me.

'You're probably wondering why we are keeping you here. We are shortly to have an influx of generals staying while awaiting war trials in Nuremberg. We need you and men like you, decent and fair men, to ensure their stay here is as comfortable as possible in the circumstances.' Major Topham gave a faint smile. 'You know what the top brass is like – helpless as children. They're used to being looked after. In the meantime you can enrol on an English course, if that is something that would interest you? It's tough on you still being kept here now that the war is over, but as soon as the order comes for you to be repatriated, we will see you get home safely, you have my word.'

'Jawohl,' I said smartly, wondering whether home still existed. 'Thank you, sir.'

With the arrival of the German generals, Island Farm Camp now became Special Camp X1.

I was very busy during that time. My job was to make sure that the generals understood the charges against them, and in the meantime to see to it that they were kept in relative comfort, considering the circumstances. They trusted and respected me, and gave me their military medals for safe-keeping, and in return I respected them. I particularly liked General von Rundstedt and found him good company, especially when he was in a cheery mood. On occasion, he would do a very amusing imitation of Hitler at his most frantic and furious. And he shared our frustration at being kept there despite the war being over.

A new influx of prisoners was brought in from other camps to repair the bomb damage and rebuild the infrastructure in the town. Shortly after they arrived, there was a knock at the door of the office. The messenger told me apologetically that there was a man here in the camp asking to see me personally. No one else would do.

'All right. Send him in,' I replied.

'I'd heard you were here,' a familiar voice said. To my utter astonishment it was my dear father, stooped and round-shouldered, greeting me with his warm and gentle smile.

We caught up over cups of Camp coffee. Six years had passed since we'd last seen each other. The news from home was as grim as I had expected. Although I had guessed that there could only be one reason for my mother not to reply to my letters, I'd always hoped that she and my sister were alive. But here was my father sitting in front of me, solid and comforting, and we talked about putting our lives together again, about rebuilding for the future as best we could.

Now that I knew I had no home to go back to, I told my father about the girl with green hair.

'Don't get too hopeful,' my father warned me sympathetically, polishing his glasses as if in the hope of seeing the situation more clearly. 'I don't expect you'll have a very warm welcome, you know.'

However, at Christmas, the local people handed in gifts for us, small things which meant a great deal to us at the time. And in return we gave them wooden toys that we'd made for the children in the town. Another rule broken, for the sake of good.

And I could see that was how the healing of nations would start; through kindness and a person-to-person peace.

53

Gladdie decided the Old Bridge was the subject of the day, as it were, seeing as it resonated with Elisavet too.

'Like its twin in Prizren,' she added, to show Elisavet she'd remembered, so they were sketching it from a bench on the Tondu Road end.

Elisavet was, in Cora's opinion, going rogue and filling in the sheet of paper with graphite. The pencil marks took on a metallic sheen in the sunlight. Every so often she would stop to sharpen the pencil.

Gladdie patrolled past the three of them, making noises over their shoulders that were meant to be encouraging but somehow reeked of critical disappointment.

'Worried about your exhibition?' Cora asked above the engine-loud roar of the river.

'Our exhibition,' Gladdie corrected her.

'Ours?' Megan said irritably, fastening her hair into bunches to keep it out of the paint. 'Don't blame us now. This is your vanity project and you forced us into it under the false pretences of showing Elisavet the sights. To be honest, we could have done that in a day.'

Elisavet looked up from her pencilling and twisted her hair around her hand. She looked holy and innocent. 'It's therapy, no?' she asked seriously. 'With a little psychology thrown in?'

The way she said it reminded Cora of her mother's 'sorry'. You could read it any way you liked. She flushed as if they'd been caught out. 'It's boring listening to old stories,' she said apologetically. She looked at her own painting of the bridge, not abstract this time, because a bridge was basically stones and arches so it should have been easier to draw, and it was also a metaphor, if Gladdie asked.

'I have a story,' Elisavet said. 'The story of how I got here.'

'Oh, good!' They sat up straight and looked at her expectantly, like obedient children.

'You remember I told you I was in the back of a truck with many women,' she said flatly. 'After maybe an hour, the truck stopped moving and some soldiers in battle fatigues climbed in with torches to look at us. We guessed, no, we *knew* why they were here. Not this one, not this one, yes, this one. You know? The light shining in our faces so bright it hurt, and the girls are crying. *Not me, not me,* I hoped, but at the same time I thought, *why not me?* And one of the soldiers, he pulled me to my feet, took me outside the truck. My fiancé! It was crazy! He had come to find me. He took me on his motorbike to the United Nations safe area and from there I went to a refugee agency. And after a few weeks more, to here.'

Gladdie broke the silence that followed.

'That's a story,' she said. 'And then your fiancé—'

Elisavet shrugged. 'I'm the enemy now.'

She was right, but although they remembered perfectly well what the fiancé had written in a letter, he had also helped her get away.

Elisavet ran her fingers over her mouth. 'Also,' she said, 'I have something else to tell you. The International Red Cross is finding my family. I have hope at last.'

'Oh, that's good,' Cora said with relief. She would send them a donation, she decided. Gwyn would know where to send it.

'Always hope for the best. My father took credit for the war ending,' Megan said to Elisavet, 'because of the promise he made to God.'

'You are strange people,' Elisavet replied after a long pause. 'This is a national characteristic?'

'Probably,' Megan agreed.

Elisavet went back to her artwork. In the middle of the page she had drawn a small circle the size of a sequin, and was shading carefully around it.

It was strange to be called strange by a stranger, in Cora's opinion. She was squinting critically at the scene in front of her. 'There's something wrong with my bridge,' she said, sitting back to look at her own effort.

Gladdie put her pad down and came rushing over. 'Mmmm. You need perspective, Cora,' she said. 'It looks as if it's levitating. The thing is, it's not about painting what you know is there, but how you see it.'

'You've been reading a book, haven't you,' Cora accused her. In her head the painting had been perfect, but somewhere between her brains and hand there was a serious flaw in translation.

'It's called teaching, Cora.'

'I need yellow,' Elisavet announced.

'Cadmium yellow or yellow ochre?'

'The brightest one. And a fine paintbrush.'

Megan swished her brush in the water and pinched it dry. 'Here you are.'

Don't ask why it seemed a momentous occasion, but the three of them watched Elisavet put a dab of yellow on her china plate paint palette and transfer the yellow blob to the circle with the paintbrush. 'There! Finished!' she said, sitting back.

It could pass for something modern and cutting-edge if you were feeling generous.

'Lovely,' Cora said.

'The light at the end of the tunnel,' Megan said dryly.

Elisavet wiped the fine paintbrush with a tissue and gave it back to her. 'And now I must go. I'm meeting someone for a drink.'

'Anyone we know?' Cora asked.

Over the din of the water Elisavet seemed not to have heard. She put her bag over her shoulder and gave a little wave as she headed for the bridge.

'She's having us on,' Megan said cheerfully, looking at the Elisavet's picture again. 'Humouring us with artistic irony.'

'Look, she's worn this pencil down to a stub,' Gladdie added in dismay. 'It's not as if they grow on trees.'

Cora squinted at the picture. 'It might be the torch that her fiancé shone at her.'

'I was just going to say that,' Gladdie objected. 'Listen, we should give our pictures titles. We'll have to, for the exhibition catalogue, in case people want to buy them.'

Megan snorted. 'Gladdie! Nobody's going to want to buy them! You and your artist's eye! If you had any kind of an eye for art, you'd abandon the idea of an exhibition right now.'

Cora was still looking at the drawing. 'He looked for her, he found her, and then he made sure she was safe. Despite what he told her, that sounds very much like love to me.'

54

It was the day of Cora's surprise birthday present to visit Island Farm Camp on its Open Day.

They were waiting for the taxi because the entrance to the camp was on the main road.

Elisavet and Gladdie were in the hall and Gladdie was giving her advice on how to draw a feather convincingly, using wild hand gestures.

Megan was leaning against Cora's kitchen table, reading the sheets of paper again. 'Uneven ground, it says here. Dew, and me with my knees.' She put the instructions down and buttoned her cardigan right up to the neck in preparation. 'I'm still going, mind, Gwyn. Tell me, is there anything *to* see? It's not just buildings, is it?'

Gwyn pushed his sunglasses on his forehead. 'There's the tunnel for starters.'

Cora laughed, only half believing him. 'Never! Is the tunnel still there?'

'You know what the Germans are like: *Vorsprung Durch Technik*,' Gwyn said, straight faced.

Cora laughed. *The tunnel*, she thought with a shiver of excitement.

Lottie looked at her quickly.

There was something wrong with Lottie today, or at least something different about her. She was preoccupied, that was the best way to put it.

Cora decided she would ask her what was wrong, if she got the chance.

She had never been one for asking questions, and she'd never worked out whether that was a good thing or not. She meant it to be tact, but it could just as easily come across as a lack of interest, which was a troubling thought.

Lottie smiled at her. 'You never talk to me about those days, do you? About the war, and about you and Frank. You ought to, seeing as I'm his granddaughter.'

Cora was surprised she cared. She didn't answer straight away – she'd done nothing but talk about them recently. After a pause she admitted, 'No. I suppose it's because we live in the present, don't we, and that's more than enough to be thinking about. Why? Do you want me to talk about them?'

'Yes, I would. Elisavet has told me a bit about – you know. What you've been telling her. What it was like for you. You should write it down.'

Cora suddenly remembered that about five years ago Gwyn and Lottie had given her the gift of a black, leather-bound, gilt-edged notebook to write her life story in. She had been a little offended by this gift, truth be told, because a story had to have an ending and she was pretty certain she was nowhere near the end of hers at that point, and time had proved her right.

The doorbell rang and Gwyn went out to talk to the taxi driver, looking handsome and wondering behind his sunglasses if they were ready yet.

Lottie took Cora's arm, and they wandered out into the garden arm in arm as if there was more to be said. In the shade of the apple tree the magpies were inspecting the lawn, as if they'd lost contact lenses.

'Love's weird, isn't it,' Lottie said. 'You have to be brave to love someone. Fiona's brave now that she knows Dad loves her. They're happy now.' She glanced at Cora. 'I want to know how you worked it out. With Grandpa, I mean.'

Cora didn't really understand the question. 'What do you want to know, exactly? Tell me, and I'll do my best to answer you.'

Lottie turned to face her. 'How did you recognise love?'

Cora blinked in surprise. 'What a question!' she said.

Lottie looked towards the house. 'We'd better go. Dad's waiting,' she said.

'Yes.' Cora felt she'd let her down. 'Tell you what, let me ponder on the matter, will you? And you're right, I should write it all down, and I will, for you. I'll write it in that lovely notebook you gave me, now that I've got something to write about.' I'll put it in the tin box with Frank's notebook, she thought.

'Will you? Thanks! No rush.' Suddenly Lottie's mood brightened. 'Come on then, get ready for your trip into the past.' She dotted a kiss on Cora's cheek, and laughed. 'Who knows, it might jog your memories, mightn't it?'

55

The taxi drew up at the entrance to the camp on the A48. Elisavet and Lottie jumped out, and Gwyn held the car doors open. Cora and Gladdie decanted themselves while Gwyn and Lottie offered Megan supportive hands to pull her onto her feet.

'Wait till I get my knees straight,' Megan said, exiting the taxi in a crouch, bunching her yellow dress around her thighs out of modesty. Once inside the boundary fence the five of them walked or hobbled in single file along the shady, musty, tree-lined path, with the sun flickering through the branches, teasing them with warmth.

All of a sudden, the exciting, alarming noise of German marching music startled them, and they jumped, and looked at each other wide-eyed. Cleverly, to enhance the camp's experience, the past blared out of speakers hidden in the undergrowth and Cora swung her arms, tempted to march along to it. It had a good, enlivening tempo that got the blood going.

'Dew, it takes you back, doesn't it!' Gladdie puffed from behind her, her thoughts going down the same route and her face flushed as pink as her hair. 'All that singing used to drive my father into a rage, you know, Lottie. He thought singing was the privilege of the Welsh, and in his mind they'd stolen our own best characteristic from us. When they sang long into the night he thought that was deliberate, too, to keep us awake. It tortured him. He took it personally, didn't he, Cora?'

'I know,' Cora said. 'I remember.'

Megan turned to Lottie. 'My father, Idwal, was a miner and a preacher. He lost his mind during the first years of the war with good reason, and found it again later. Some said it was the other way round, that he was in his right mind to begin with and then he lost it for the rest of his days. It depended on the viewpoint, of course.'

Lottie laughed.

'I preferred the singing to the commotion the Germans made,' Cora said, 'banging pots and pans in protest and shouting Heil Hitler at the tops of their voices. As if their lives depended on it!'

The path through the woods led to the camp, which was surrounded by a wire fence.

The entrance gate was manned by an unsmiling sentry guard in khaki uniform who took their tickets and handed them over to a soldier who saluted them and escorted them across to the hut. It felt seriously thorough and alarmingly authentic. The present-day Hut 9 had its own NAAFI, and two women from the Re-Enactment Society, with aprons around their uniforms, were selling cakes and coffee through a hatch.

'Wartime Favourites from Original Recipes', announced a sign.

'There's thorough,' Megan said to them, raising her eyebrows. 'But it's a mistake. From what I remember, even in wartime those recipes were a disappointment.'

Cora held onto Gwyn's strong linen-clad arm to go inside the hut, any excuse to be close to her son. He had lovely arms and he was a good hugger. His arms were made for hugging and his mouth was made for smiling.

It had atmosphere, that hut; she felt it as soon she walked in through the door. She took a deep breath. It smelled of dry plaster warmed by sunlight. The whitewash was flaking off the walls. So this was where Frank lived!

The long corridor was shady, opening onto a series of small rooms.

Gladdie was humming 'Deep in the Heart of Texas' softly because Charles had lived here too, the GI she'd been scared to love.

There was no guide, and so they wandered along the corridor looking into rooms as the fancy took them. They were furnished just as they would have been during the war, a stove, drying laundry hanging from a clothes maid, two wooden chairs by the table, a desk.

Cora imagined the prisoners living here, locked up together far away from their homes, waiting for the time to pass.

She caught a glimpse of an old brown wireless through an open door. Her parents had had one just like it. It was like stepping into the past. 'Look, remember that, Gwyn?' she asked him.

'No, can't say I do.'

She let Gwyn's arm go and turned to beckon Gladdie. 'Come and see this!'

But further inside the room, three black-and-grey-uniformed SS officers were sitting at a table, and they looked up at them from their card game, sharp and large as life.

'Sorry,' she said, backing into Gladdie, her heart jolting.

Well, that was ridiculous when she knew very well they were historians and nothing more than that.

Gwyn popped his head in to look at the room after her, to see what had disturbed her. 'Oh, hullo,' he said to them amiably.

'They look smart though, don't they?' Gladdie said, smoothing back her pink hair. 'Better than our lot.'

'You sound just like Enid.'

What Cora really wanted to see was the escape tunnel in Frank's room. It had always fascinated her, the fact that he and other ordinary men with very little in the way of equipment could, over months, dig their way deep underground through orange Welsh clay to freedom.

Elisavet was walking along the corridor from the other direction, looking thoughtful, dark hair shrouding her shoulders. *Like someone out of a fairy story*, Cora thought.

'It's crazy,' Lottie said, coming out of a small kitchen. 'I don't get it. They brought prisoners all the way from Europe just to lock them up here?'

'Well – it was to save them from killing our chaps,' Cora said reasonably.

'Yeah, I know, but – who decides who is the enemy? I mean, who has a right to say that?'

'Churchill did,' Megan said, turning to look at her doubtfully. 'You've heard of Winston Churchill, haven't you?'

'Yes, of course I have,' Lottie said. 'I'm talking about morally. Who decides who the good guys are? How are you supposed to know?'

Elisavet caught Cora's eye and raised her eyebrows.

'We all think we're the good guys,' Cora said. 'That's the problem.' She pressed her palms against the cool wall to feel the past against her skin; the dust of the past powdered them.

She could sense the emotions in the walls: anger, discipline, boredom, homesickness. Old places held memories in their fabric and she could feel the draught Frank made as he walked briskly up and down these corridors in his uniform. She understood now why the place had the reputation of being haunted even though no one had died here.

Well, hang on, that wasn't entirely accurate, was it? One man had died here, she knew that, because Frank had told her about him. Couldn't remember his name, but it would come to her. Otto. That was it.

She was keen to see the escape tunnel under the bunk where Frank slept but the entrance to the tunnel had been boarded over. The room was basic, furnished with a couple of wooden straw-seated chairs. A grey uniform was hanging on the foot of the bed, a cap was perched on a bed post. The beds were neatly made, grey woollen blankets lacy with moth holes tucked under a thin mattress. She stroked the blanket gently as if she was trying not to disturb him. She had the urge to lie on it.

'Cora!' Elisavet said with a sudden, thrilling laugh.

Cora looked at her in delight. Elisavet was happy! It was as joyful and as unexpected as a baby's first smile. And she was the cause of it, even if she couldn't for the life of her think why. 'I was looking at the moth holes.'

'Not moths, the painting,' Elisavet said, pointing. 'Look!'

'Lor!' On the wall at the foot of the bunks was a life-sized drawing of a pin-up girl with her hands behind her head, round breasts, a lavish amount of pubic hair, and one eyebrow raised quizzically.

That eyebrow. That was the giveaway.

Well, not just that. In neat, black, Gothic lettering, as if the suggestive eyebrow wasn't enough to identify her by, was her name. *Cora*.

'Bloody hell, Cora!' Gladdie said, coming up behind her. She clapped her hand on Cora's shoulder. 'It's you, girl. Look at you! Shameless, you are!'

Cora felt her mind jumping into a different dimension. She was twenty again, in love, and guilty for all sorts of reasons. 'Come on, let's get out, quick,' she said, trying to push them out of the room. 'Don't let Lottie see it.'

'See what?' Lottie asked from the doorway.

Too late.

Lottie put her hands on her grandmother's shoulders and looked at the drawing over her head. Her mood changed to anger and she turned to them with a mixture of fury and indignation. 'Why would *anyone* draw me like that? That is – that's harassment. Seriously, trust me, I didn't know anything about it – I don't even—'

'Calm down, Lottie, it's not you, it's Cora,' Megan said, pulling up one of the wooden chairs to get a better look and so that her wild grey hair wouldn't block their view, because she was thoughtful like that. 'Got her name on it, see?'

'Oh! Wow.' Lottie quickly fanned her flushed face with her hand. She wasn't quite so appalled now. 'Wow. Yeah. Yikes! How embarrassing for you.'

'I'm not embarrassed,' Cora said. 'As a matter of fact, I'm rather proud.'

Although it couldn't be described as an entirely accurate representation of her, it was too stylised for that and her breasts were round as apples but nevertheless the artist had caught something of her and although Cora felt she should be as indignant as Lottie, she also thought with a thrilling, secret smile: that's what I looked like to him all those years ago. It's how Frank imagined me.

Frank had never mentioned this mural of her, not in all their time together, but he had told her about the artistic sketches of girls they'd distracted the guards with as they dug their tunnel and she'd found it funny. She still did. And for all her faults, she wasn't a hypocrite.

The distraction had worked, too. In her own small way, she'd helped him to escape. The thought amused her.

They looked at the drawing, and it was hard to know why it was so compelling. Apart from the arched eyebrow that promised all manner of earthly delight, it had an innocence about it, the rounded breasts, the neat navel, the pubic hair.

'Doesn't it bother you knowing that they were looking at you that way?' Lottie asked.

'During the war it wasn't the worst of things.' Cora tried to remember what she'd said to Gladdie not that long ago about them being good times, and Gladdie reminding her about Owen. The thing was, whatever happened, you just had to keep moving forward.

'Anyway, the Germans have got fewer hangups about nakedness than we have,' Cora added. 'Everyone knows that. They invented nudity.'

'Maybe they could paint a swimsuit on you,' Lottie suggested.

'Or give you a Brazilian,' Gladdie said with a smirk.

'To be fair,' Megan added generously, 'you've always had a good figure, Cora. She has, hasn't she, Glad?'

Gladdie turned to look at Cora. 'Aye. Fair play.'

Cora grinned. 'I know.' That was the best thing about growing old, the experiences of the past layered themselves on her protectively, insulating her like a good coat.

'There's a sort of periscope outside where we can look down into the tunnel,' Gwyn said in his loud, carrying voice as he came to find them.

The women turned to look at him.

'Let's go and have a look at the tunnel, shall we, Gwyn?'

They filed back out into the sweet open air. The afternoon sky was a deeper blue now, grass soft underfoot and littered with daisies, the dark, sweet smell of hawthorn, and a handful of uniformed soldiers, British and German, saluting, mingling, chatting. Cora scrutinised their faces, looking for Frank, and finding him safe in her heart.

Behind the hut a corporal was standing next to the large periscope dug into the grass. 'Have you come for the tunnel?' he asked.

'Yes.'

'Here we go.' He lifted the lid and through the hatch they could see down in. 'See? This is as close as you can get to it, health and safety. For some reason they don't think the public can be trusted to crawl into dark, muddy spaces.'

'Not very trusting of them, is it? Here we go,' Cora repeated. Shrugging away helping hands, she got onto her hands and knees and put her head inside the hatch. She breathed in deeply so that she could smell the clay, see the redness of it, imagine Frank digging naked, and escaping to freedom, and after that, coming back home to find her.

'Your white frock is suffering something awful,' Gladdie observed. 'Oh dear, you've got grass stains on it now as well. Mind your mother doesn't see.'

Cora laughed, knowing that her two friends felt the same as she did about being here – that time didn't really move on at all, that it was static, a vast hangar you could move around in and stand in different spots, experiencing different ages the same way you'd lived them, and the space kept expanding miraculously the older you lived. 'Help me up.' She got to her feet again, brushing herself down, marvelling. 'Heck of a job, digging their way through that,' she said.

'Aye,' the corporal agreed. 'It's not easy, digging through clay, as I know from gardening. It's a devil. Hold your hand out.'

Cora held her hand out and the corporal handed her a ball of orange clay from the windowsill of the hut. She thought of Frank's lump of clay, and realised what it meant to him, it was his souvenir of effort, toil, sweat and dreams.

'Feel it! Heavy, isn't it? Imagine how much clay they had to move,' the man said, looking into the hole. 'But they did it though, and fair play to them, I say. You know what I think? They must have started the construction as soon as they got here. Animal instinct, isn't it? To want to go home.'

Cora agreed that it was. She handed him the clay back and walked across to the green, sun-warmed railings separating the camp from the field beyond it and put her face against them. The barbed wire had long gone and out there was the grass shimmering in the breeze, leaves fluttering in the trees, open countryside and blue sky, with the fading blue Glamorgan hills beyond.

For a moment she put herself in Frank's shoes, a captive in enemy territory, looking out at the land he was not part of and waiting for something to happen: mail from home, news of the progress of the war, German cigarettes, a glimpse of the four of them – Cora, Gladdie, Meg and Enid – as they passed the camp on their way to and from work.

'What are you looking at?' Elisavet had come to stand next to her and Cora caught the scent of her perfume, light and floral.

'Freedom,' she said without turning. 'That's what they saw through the wire, wasn't it?'

'Freedom,' Elisavet echoed softly.

Lottie came to join them, leaning on Cora with an easy familiarity and looping her arm around her shoulder. 'Enjoying your birthday present?' she asked.

'I am!' Cora suddenly remembered the question that Lottie had asked her. 'How do you recognise love, that's what you asked me, wasn't it?'

'Yes. But *please* don't tell me you just do.'

Cora thought about it. 'It's the truth, though. You know when you love, or don't love, and you know when you're loved or not loved. If you don't recognise it, it's because it's not there.'

Elisavet looked at her sharply. 'Oh!' she said, her lips parted in under-standing, her dark hair whipping around her face in the breeze.

56

I remained in Island Farm Camp for two more years after the war ended, knowing that my turn for repatriation would eventually come. But now when I thought of home, I thought of Cora's house, Jane putting the kettle on and white-haired Dio getting his suit out for me to wear so that I could feel normal again.

'Let's get married,' I said to Cora one evening, and Cora said, 'Yes, let's,' just like that.

Despite our engagement, I thought it might be impossible considering all the rules I'd lived under for the last seven years.

But Cora was more confident and she applied to the Home Office for permission for me to live in Britain permanently, and it was granted.

In Island Farm Camp XI, on the morning of 31 January 1948, I was in my room looking in my shaving mirror and straightening my tie. I wetted my comb and ran it through my hair, then took a deep breath and turned to Kurt. 'How do I look?'

Kurt grinned. 'Exactly as a proud bridegroom should look. Lucky you,' he added enviously, punching my arm, 'you'll have Cora to warm you in bed tonight.'

'Yes.' I grinned, imagining it.

'How does it feel to be marrying a former enemy?' Kurt asked slyly.

I turned the question around in my head, and shrugged. 'I was never her enemy, nor she mine,' I replied, because I knew it to be the truth. I had thought a good deal about the deaths of my mother and sister, and of Cora's brother, and I believed that they above all would approve of our love. 'Right. I'm ready. Let's go.'

'Wait a minute, we've got something for you.' Kurt beckoned towards the door and suddenly the room was full of pals and they passed a home-made wedding card from hand to hand.

'Signed by von Rundstedt himself,' Kurt said cheerfully, handing it to me with a flourish.

It was addressed to Mr and Mrs Frank Muller, 5 Island Farm Avenue, Bridgend.

The message inside read:

On the day of your wedding our very best wishes for a long life full of happiness and good companionship.

31 January 1948
Signed: Kurt Smuts
Adam von Trott
Gunter Schneider
Gustav Sandig
Wolfgang Tirpitz
General-Feldmarschall Gerd von Rundstedt

I was very pleased. Tonight, as her husband, I would show Cora the card from the camp, wishing us a long life full of happiness and good companionship, signed by my friends.

When we reached the parish church, a little group of well-wishers had gathered by the lychgate. Kurt and I shyly nodded our greetings and went inside, into the cool and holy dark.

I saw Jane, Gladdie, Megan, Idwal, Temperance and Enid sitting in the congregation, flowers in their lapels, turning to us and smiling.

Moments later Cora came down the aisle on her father's arm. She was carrying a bouquet of purple hyacinths and her expression was serious.

As she stood next to me I breathed in the scent of her bouquet. 'Cora,' I said, worried that she was having doubts.

When she looked up at me at last, her face cleared. Her grey eyes met

mine and she smiled joyfully, as if she'd been scared to look. I smiled too
and I couldn't stop smiling. Back then, when we'd first met, Cora had given
me hope for the future. Now I was giving her hope for the future and it felt
right to make my home with her here in my new Heimat. My homeland.

Elisavet closed the notebook and looked up at Cora. 'The story finishes here.'

'You've brought him back to me,' Cora said, smiling through tears. 'It's been a lovely time for me. Thank you. I've enjoyed our evenings together.'

'And me, too.' Elisavet stretched and then she finished her wine. 'Love makes things possible,' she said, her gaze lingering for a moment on Cora, on the candle, on the clay. 'Good night.'

57

Elisavet came to visit Cora unexpectedly the following evening just as the sun was setting. She was outlined in gold.

'I would like to talk with you,' she explained on the doorstep.

'Oh, yes, of course, by all means. Come on in. Glass of wine?' Cora asked hopefully. 'Or tea?'

'Wine. Thank you.'

Cora took a bottle from the fridge, and because she hated suspense, she asked, 'What's it about?'

'I'm going home to Kosovo,' Elisavet said.

'Oh!' Cora paused in the pouring. It felt like a dreadful failing on their part. 'Why?'

'My parents miss me.' She gave Cora a quick glance. 'My fiancé, too, they tell me.'

Cora nodded. She understood. *We'll* miss you, she thought but she didn't say it, there was no point in making Elisavet feel responsible for that. 'When are you leaving?' she asked, taking the glasses through to the sitting room. She put them down and switched the TV off.

Elisavet sat on the edge of the sofa, holding the base of the glass in the palm of her hand. She hesitated before answering. 'Soon,' she said.

'Soon? I hope you're not going to miss Gladdie's exhibition.' Cora gave a rueful laugh. 'Dew! That's not why you're going, is it? Can Megan and I come with you?' She had nightmares about it. Their accumulated art efforts looked exactly what they were: amateurish.

Elisavet pressed her lips together in a smile.

Cora took a sip of wine. 'What's made you decide?'

'I haven't been able to leave my misery behind,' Elisavet said.

'Ah. No. Unfortunately, misery clings.'

'For you, too?' Elisavet's dark eyes held hers accusingly. 'You made it seem easy.'

'Did I?' Cora flushed. 'I'm sorry. It wasn't.' She swirled the wine around in her glass. They'd reduced the past to an anecdote, their part in the Germans' Great Escape. There was a happy ending in their long, companionable marriage. Frank joined the choir, and the joy of singing gave him a tingling feeling of belonging that never failed to move her. He got a job in construction and then joined the fire service. They had Gwyn, and Frank became a thorough Welshman, proud of it too.

To be fair, as an anecdote it was good, heartwarming even, if you left the pain of it out. 'It's hindsight, it is, Elisavet,' she said apologetically. 'We didn't know it would be all right. It was agony at times.' The unendurable sadness of war was that you did endure it, you carried on living.

'We didn't survive for any noble reasons. It wasn't out of faith in the future, nothing like that. The truth is, I can't say I had any.' Cora's gaze rested on the mended ornament on the mantelpiece, the broken boy with his sock around his ankle. 'But the thrill of being with Frank in the greenhouse and my mother's hatred cracked open in front of us, and walking out under an umbrella, him in my father's suit, they were the highpoints of my life, where life jumped forward out of the mud onto something solid and good.' She pressed her fingers against her mouth. 'But in between that, there were times when there was nothing to look forward to, except for sleep. I would dread waking up. I wished I was dead during that time, just to put a stop on it.'

She looked up at Elisavet's tight face with the sudden clarity of agonising brightness, and for the first time she felt Elisavet's pain as if it were her own pain, as if Elisavet's dear heart were her heart.

She'd gone about it the wrong way, trying to make it better through words. She held out her arms.

Elisavet's eyes blazed pink with tears, and Cora's too, and Cora held her and held onto the awful jerk of grief that shook through Elisavet's body into hers.

They stayed like that for a while, holding onto each other, and when their embrace loosened a little, Elisavet said one muffled word: 'Home.'

58

Elisavet didn't show up to clean at Megan's on Tuesday afternoon.

Megan popped round to Cora's, see if she knew anything, and then they went to Gladdie's. Over a cup of tea in Gladdie's cluttered kitchen they agreed it seemed unlikely she had forgotten it was Megan's cleaning day because she was normally very reliable. They decided they would wait a bit longer to hear from her. She wouldn't leave without saying goodbye, they felt.

But when evening came without any word, they reconvened and decided to go to the hostel in Queen's Lane to check on her, see she was all right.

The skinny bare-chested man answered the door, blocking their way as if he was afraid they would rush him. 'She's gone back home,' he said. 'Packed her bags and left for the airport. You haven't missed her by much.'

They retreated down the mossy path past the rusty bike frame, feeling dazed.

'Gone! Without so much as a by your leave!' Gladdie said, outraged. 'Well!'

They walked slowly home from the hostel in the warm summer night under a sky pricked with stars.

They stopped on the Old Bridge, that ancient route for travellers seeking peace. Megan pointed at the stars, and Gladdie argued in her teacherly way that some of them were planets.

Megan said so what, stars was more poetic because nothing rhymed with planets.

'Gannets,' Gladdie said.

Megan snorted. 'I suppose a gannet will be the subject of your next painting, will it? Wearing some kind of footwear? Flip-flops?'

In Island Farm Avenue they stopped under the streetlamp in front of Megan's house.

'I don't know if we helped her at all, do you,' Megan said thoughtfully, 'and I've no idea what she thought of us. I suppose to her we were just three old ladies going on about the past.'

'Old? We're not old, we're middle aged,' Gladdie argued. 'But we did our best to make her feel at home. And in return she made our homes all clean and new.'

'She made our lives all clean and new, too,' Cora said thoughtfully. 'It's been a good life, hasn't it, looking back.'

After saying good night, she went down her path and let herself in through the front door. A large envelope was lying on the door mat with her name written on it in neat black letters.

She guessed it was from Elisavet. She took it into the kitchen and made a cup of tea before opening it. A thank you card, she supposed. She thought fondly of anyone who sent a thank you card, it was the sign of a good upbringing in her opinion. She opened it eagerly, preparing herself to be delighted. Inside was a terse, one-line message:

From Jelisaveta.

Cora closed it and looked at the picture on the front. It was brightly painted, unusual for Elisavet. It was a scene of the Old Bridge in perspective – *won't Gladdie be pleased!* And the three of them were standing on the cobbles, sunlit, Megan with her grey hair in bunches and Gladdie, all pink and lopsided, and Cora with her hand on her hip, one eyebrow arched, an old version of her young self.

On the bottom of the picture was written:

MY GRANDMOTHERS.

Well! There was an accolade. Better than a thank you, Cora thought.

She smiled to herself and propped it up on the table.

'Fair play,' she said.

* * *

MORE FROM NORMA CURTIS

The next utterly heartbreaking, emotional read from Norma Curtis is available to order now here:

https://mybook.to/NewNormaCurtisBackAd

AUTHOR'S NOTE

This story is fiction, but it's based on truth. Twenty-five thousand, two hundred and fifty-two German prisoners of war stayed on in the UK after World War II, some because they had no homes to go back to, others because after seven years away they had forged new friendships and this country now felt like home. There was a great deal of kindness shown on both sides, and I think that's amazing.

The German Great Escape from Bridgend was the biggest mass breakout of the war and happily, some of Island Farm Camp is still there to visit, thanks to Brett Exton and the Hut 9 Preservation Group.

The escape tunnel the prisoners dug with ingenuity, hard work and dreams of freedom is just as they left it, and the seductive painting of Cora which distracted the guards remains on the wall to this day.

ABOUT THE AUTHOR

Norma Curtis is an award-winning author and former chairman of the Romantic Novelists' Association. Born and brought up in North Wales, she now lives in London.

Download your exclusive bonus content from Norma Curtis here:

Visit Norma's website: www.normacurtisauthor.com

Follow Norma on social media here:

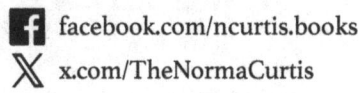

facebook.com/ncurtis.books

x.com/TheNormaCurtis

Letters from
the past

Discover page-turning
historical novels from
your favourite authors
and be transported
back in time

Join our book club
Facebook group

https://bit.ly/SixpenceGroup

Sign up to our
newsletter

https://bit.ly/LettersFrom
PastNews

Boldwood

Boldwood Books is an award-winning fiction
publishing company seeking out the best
stories from around the world.

Find out more at www.boldwoodbooks.com

Join our reader community for brilliant books,
competitions and offers!

Follow us
@BoldwoodBooks
@TheBoldBookClub

Sign up to our weekly
deals newsletter

https://bit.ly/BoldwoodBNewsletter